MISS B...

# THE
# LORD
# OF
# COLD
# COMPTON

KAREN BAUGH MENUHIN
& ZOE MARKHAM

Copyright © 2024 by Karen Baugh Menuhin

Published by Little Cat Publishing, Ltd.

All rights reserved. No part of this book may be reproduced or used in any manner without written permission of the copyright owner except for the use of quotations in a book review.

NO AI TRAINING: Without in any way limiting the author's [and publisher's] exclusive rights under copyright, any use of this publication to "train" generative artificial intelligence (AI) technologies to generate text is expressly prohibited. The author reserves all rights to license uses of this work for generative AI training and development of machine learning language models.

Cover image from Shutterstock

This is a work of fiction. Names, places and incidents either are the product of the author's imagination or are used fictitiously. Any resemblance to actual persons, living or dead, events, or locales is entirely coincidental.

ISBN 979-8-3382990-8-1

*For Gail,*
*with thanks for all the walks and wisdom.*
*From Zoe.*

# CHAPTER 1

*Cotswolds: September 1923*

'Best buttered scones, strawberry jam and clotted cream,' Maggie Trounce announced, setting the plates down with aplomb.

Bright sunshine streamed through the large bow window of Lily's Tea Rooms onto their table, casting a glow over the plates as if they were a gift from above. Which, Miss Busby felt after her long walk from Bloxford, they rather were!

'Thank you, Maggie,' she said, her blue eyes bright. 'This looks delicious.'

'We've got a new chef.' Maggie beamed down at them. 'He does it lovely!'

'And how is he with tea?' Enid Montgomery looked up and arched a brow.

'The tea's my department, and I'm just getting it for you now,' Maggie replied, having grown immune to Enid's impatience.

Miss Busby had taken to enjoying an eleven o'clock treat at the tea rooms every Saturday with her friend from Spring Meadows Retirement Home. They would catch up on the week's news and Enid would enjoy a little light sparring with the staff. It was a treat for them both.

Miss Busby smiled to herself as she took up her napkin. At a little over seventy years, she was short and slim; although her natural curiosity and bright, inquisitive eyes often brought the term "Bird-like" to mind, she had lost none of the appetite of her youth. Not least when she'd enjoyed a good walk to spur it on beforehand.

Dressed in lilac with a matching cardigan, her silvery grey hair pulled up into a neat bun, she sported stout walking shoes and was considering a stroll around Little Minton Lake after their treat. It was a beautiful day, and with the shadow of autumn just around the corner she felt compelled to make the most of it.

She was about to suggest the idea to Enid when Maggie arrived with the tea, her face flushed with excitement.

'I've just seen the newspaper,' she said, setting down the pot and dispensing cups on the gingham tablecloth with practised ease. 'The delivery boy was late again. Have you heard?'

Enid, dressed colourfully as always in a yellow silk blouse and navy skirt, narrowed her eyes. 'That the delivery boy was late? Hardly news. Yours is always late on a Saturday, isn't he, Isabelle?' The sunlight picked out the last few streaks of auburn in her thick, white hair, and her steel-grey eyes shone with mischief.

Miss Busby nodded. 'He's late most days.'

'Now, you know that's not what I meant, Mrs Montgomery,' Maggie chided. 'I meant, have you heard the *news*?'

Enid sighed. 'How can we answer without knowing to which particular *news* you are referring?'

'You haven't, then, or you'd know.' Maggie grinned. 'Shall I pour?'

'Please,' Miss Busby said.

Enid waved an impatient hand and commanded, 'Enlighten us.'

'It's that awful Lady Compton,' Maggie said, filling both cups and setting the pot back on the table.

'Who?' Miss Busby asked, brow furrowing at the unfamiliar name.

Enid set down her fork and looked up with interest. 'Lady Sylvia Compton, of Cold Compton Manor?' She looked to Maggie for a nod of confirmation, and received it. 'An unpleasant woman,' Enid went on, spreading cream thickly onto the scone. 'Presides over the village of Cold Compton like a despot from the Middle Ages. Mr Waterhouse's old valet used to play cricket with a chap from the village,' she added in explanation. 'What has she done now? Forbidden people from opening their windows on a Thursday, or whistling on a Tuesday?'

'What?' Miss Busby asked, now thoroughly confused.

Enid took a sip of tea before replying, 'The woman passed a draconian decree several years ago forbidding anyone in the village from hanging their washing out on any day other than Monday. An edict so ridiculous that it even made the local newspapers.'

Maggie nodded knowingly. 'And she's done worse.'

'Lord Compton died years ago,' Enid explained for Miss Busby's benefit. 'And left her running the estate until their son, Theodore, was of an age–'

'Hah!' Maggie exclaimed. 'Except she never did let the young lord do anything!'

'Thank you, Maggie, I was coming to that,' Enid said tartly. 'When her husband died, power went to her head and she ran the estate like a tyrant. By the time young Theodore reached twenty-one, any sense and decency the woman may have once had was utterly displaced. She absolutely refused to let him take over.'

'I don't know as there was much sense or decency there to begin with,' Maggie added, glancing around to make sure she wouldn't be overheard. 'And those decrees she made just got worse.'

Miss Busby's eyes rounded. It wasn't like Maggie to speak ill of anyone. 'Goodness,' she said. 'But surely people don't actually comply with such diktats in this day and age?'

'They have to,' Maggie said earnestly. 'Lady Compton could have them thrown out of their homes if they don't.'

Miss Busby looked to Enid, who was now dropping jam onto the thick cream. 'All true,' she said.

'My Derek's nephew knows a man who used to be a tenant of one of Cold Compton's farms,' Maggie went on. 'She caught him making ready to till the top field with a tractor he'd borrowed from the next village over and that was that.'

Enid tutted.

Miss Busby still felt she was missing something. 'What was what?' she asked.

'Her ladyship don't hold with modern methods,' Maggie explained. 'She won't have machinery on the farms. Had him take the tractor right back and him and his whole family were put out of their home by nightfall.'

'Good Lord!' Miss Busby exclaimed.

Maggie nodded. 'Ruled with a rod of iron, that one. Even if her rules made no sense.'

'Isabelle, your tea will go cold,' Enid chided. 'And what nonsensical rules has the woman enacted now, Maggie?' she asked.

'Oh, it's not about that this time. She's only gone and got herself murdered!'

Miss Busby dropped her teaspoon, just as the bell over the tea room door clanged.

'Oh! Here's Mrs Fanshawe,' Maggie said cheerfully.

Miss Busby turned in surprise – she hadn't been expecting to see Adeline until tomorrow.

'Isabelle! Why weren't you at home?' Adeline boomed as she approached purposefully.

Tall and of comfortable proportions, Adeline was striking in a flowing red and gold dress, which clashed somewhat with her rather flushed cheeks. She fanned them with a folded newspaper as she took her seat with a nod to Maggie.

'Another plate of scones, is it?'

'Just coffee, please,' Adeline said, glancing down at her waistline with a sigh. Then added, 'with cream and sugar.'

'Right you are then.' Maggie gave the newspaper a knowing look. 'I expect you'll have lots to talk about,' she called over her shoulder as she left.

'Ah, so you've heard.' Adeline nodded. 'I telephoned as soon as I saw the paper, but you weren't home.'

'I left early with Barnaby. The weather is so lovely we walked the old trail through the fields to make the most of it.'

Adeline glanced under the table, but there was no sign of the little Jack Russell terrier.

'He's at the police station with Sergeant Miller,' Miss Busby added.

'In custody is he?' Adeline asked wryly. 'What has he done?'

'Nothing!' Miss Busby smiled. 'They have mice. The station cat's getting on and isn't interested, so I offered Barnaby's services.'

'Excellent thinking. Good to have Miller onside before we start.'

'Start what?' Miss Busby asked.

'Our investigation, of course.' Adeline set the newspaper on the table as if it ought to be perfectly obvious.

'Isabelle I do wish you'd finish your scone,' Enid

reminded her. Having finished hers, she pushed the plate aside and pulled the newspaper towards her.

'Yes, but –' Miss Busby tried.

'When you didn't answer your phone,' Adeline went on, 'I drove straight to Lavender Cottage.'

'But you knew she wasn't there,' Enid pointed out without looking up from the article.

'Yes, but I thought she'd be back by the time I arrived.' Adeline sounded pained.

'But she wasn't.' Enid's eyes were shining with mischief again.

Miss Busby sighed and turned her attention to her delicious treat, feeling she was now in need of it.

'Clearly.' Adeline sniffed. 'And when Barnaby didn't bark the place down I supposed you'd taken him for a walk. I drove around the green, and you weren't there either. Then I remembered your newfound fondness for elevenses in Little Minton, and here you are.'

'Bravo! You are not the only sleuth at the table, Isabelle,' Enid declared.

'Sleuthing, is it? I thought as much!' Maggie called merrily, arriving with the coffee. 'I'll leave you to it, dears. Sing out if you need anything.'

'Thank you, Maggie,' Miss Busby said as the cheerful waitress bustled off.

Adeline tapped a finger imperiously on the newspaper and declared, 'Some cad has murdered a lady in cold blood. We must find him!'

Miss Busby took a slow breath, and gathered her

strength. '*We* must do nothing of the sort, Adeline. It's for the authorities to find whoever's responsible, and bring them to justice.'

Adeline's eyebrows shot up. 'I hope you don't mean Inspector McKay, because—'

Miss Busby leaned forward. 'Adeline, were you acquainted with Lady Compton?'

'Well, no—'

'Or anyone else in Cold Compton?'

'No, but—'

'Then I'm afraid, although it is tragic, it is really nothing to do with us.'

Adeline deflated, her usual bluster evaporated, and a quiet sense of sadness fell over her. 'But Isabelle, I rather thought… It's been so long since we *did* anything together…' She trailed off, sounding lost. Miss Busby was reminded of her young pupils when they invented a new schoolyard game but were unable to convince their friends to play.

'We do lots of things together,' she said kindly. 'We're meeting for choir practice before church tomorrow morning, for one.'

Adeline waved a hand dismissively. 'I mean proper things, Isabelle. Exciting things.'

'There's nothing exciting about death,' Miss Busby said quietly.

'No. Of course not,' Adeline concurred. 'But there *is* something exciting in bringing murderers to justice. And that's something you're rather good at,' she pressed.

Miss Busby found her heart lightening a little at the compliment, but remained resolute. 'As is Inspector McKay. I'm sure he will see justice done.'

'He tends to do a lot better with your help, Isabelle,' Adeline pointed out.

'Well, perhaps,' Miss Busby conceded, 'but he's improving. 'I'm quite sure he doesn't need us any longer.'

'What makes you think it was a man?' Enid looked up from the paper.

Adeline turned to her in surprise, as if she'd forgotten she was there.

'You said "some cad" murdered her,' Enid reminded her.

'Well, yes.' Adeline shrugged. 'Lady Compton was killed with a shotgun, I can't imagine a woman using such a weapon.'

'Why not?' Enid asked. 'It's as simple for a lady's finger to pull a trigger as a man's. It's foolish to assume–'

'It really is for the authorities to decide either way,' Miss Busby cut in firmly.

'It states in the article,' Adeline pointed at the newspaper still in Enid's hands, 'that Lady Compton was a staunch supporter of good causes in foreign parts.' She rallied with fresh determination. 'And I believe a good, charitable soul should not go unavenged.'

'The term "charitable" could hardly be applied to Lady Compton by anyone who knew her,' Enid objected, and pushed the newspaper towards Miss Busby. 'No one is saying you ought to investigate, Isabelle, but there's no harm in reading the article. If a murderer is loose in the vicinity, we should all arm ourselves with the facts, at the very least.'

'Yes, and what if the inspector *does* come to you for help this time?' Adeline added, brightening.

'That's hardly likely,' Miss Busby replied, thinking back to his attitude towards her after their previous encounters. 'But if he does, I'm afraid he'll be disappointed.' She cast an eye over the article nonetheless.

'She was shot in her garden,' Adeline said, regaining some of her earlier vigour. 'Sometime yesterday afternoon.'

'And the son found her body in the evening,' Miss Busby mused, reading on. 'Lord Theodore Compton. He was their only child.'

'The young lord will inherit now after all…' Enid mused, adding, 'doesn't it seem strange she should lie dead in her own garden until the evening?'

'He must be our primary suspect!' Adeline pronounced. 'Frustrated young man, unable to shrug off the shackles of an overbearing mother, and surely no stranger to a shotgun–'

'And wouldn't someone have heard the shot?' Miss Busby interjected. 'And found the body sooner?'

'Cold Compton is a small village far deeper into the countryside than Bloxford,' Enid explained. 'Shots will ring out frequently, no one would have batted an eyelid.'

Miss Busby nodded, although wasn't entirely convinced. A loud shot near houses would surely not have gone unremarked. 'If he were the killer, I doubt the young lord would have admitted to finding the body, Adeline.' Then, after a moment's thought, she added, 'he'd have left it for someone else to discover.'

Adeline floundered, then exclaimed, 'Aha! That would explain the delay! He left her to be found, but as the afternoon wore into evening, and with no observer, he panicked and faked the discovery himself!'

'It's possible.' Enid poured the last of the tea into her cup and considered. 'But Lady Compton had run the estate into the ground, according to rumour.'

'Is that a rumour from Mr Waterhouse's old valet?' Miss Busby asked.

Enid nodded. 'Although I should think it's common knowledge. You've only to drive through the village to see the deprivation. I can't imagine it's a particularly inviting inheritance. Certainly not one worth killing for.'

Miss Busby closed the newspaper and pushed it back towards Adeline.

'The police are questioning suspects,' she said. 'It states they already have several. I wonder who wrote this article? It's awfully detailed.' She glanced to the end but didn't recognise the name, Daisy Fellows. Sir Richard Lannister owned the *Oxford News*. Daisy must be another junior reporter keen to rise through the ranks like Richard's daughter, Lucy, she supposed. 'They really do seem perfectly on top of things.'

Enid looked to Miss Busby, brows raised. 'You surprise me, Isabelle,' she said. 'Your natural curiosity would usually be picking over details like Barnaby at a bone.'

'I have had quite enough of bones for the time being,' she replied quietly, thinking back to her last investigation earlier that spring.

'Ah,' Enid said, nodding as understanding dawned. 'Well, if anything, I'm surprised it's taken this long for someone to bump Lady Compton off,' she continued. 'I doubt we'd find anyone in the village who won't simply shrug and say *"good riddance".*'

'Well, *really.*' Adeline picked up the paper with a huff. 'Murder is murder, regardless.'

'How old is the young lord, Enid?' Miss Busby asked.

Enid thought a moment. 'He must be around twenty-four now. A man, I suppose, although still a babe in arms to my mind. They do take such a long while to mature, boys.'

'And would he say "good riddance", too, do you think?' Miss Busby asked. 'Losing your mother is the most awful pain at any age. However domineering she may have been, she *was* still his mother,' she added softly.

Adeline looked up eagerly, but Enid cut her off. 'What we need is something less maudlin than death to divert us. I find I can't stop thinking about Mary, you know,' she said gently, placing a hand on Miss Busby's arm. 'So I do understand.'

Silence fell across the table. Mary Fellows - Miss Busby's former neighbour and the original owner of Barnaby, the little Jack Russell who now made his home with her at Lavender Cottage, had finally succumbed to her angina in June, and her wit and kindness were greatly missed.

from the station before leaving, and she smiled as she remembered young Bobby Miller looking so proud of the new Sergeant's stripes on his sleeve as he'd handed the little dog over.

'*He din't catch any, Miss,*' he'd said, ruffling the terrier's ears. '*But he scared a few of 'em off I reckon.*'

'*Perhaps I ought to have brought Pud instead,*' she'd said. Mice and shrews were common in the hedgerows and country gardens, and Pudding, her ginger tom, tended to do a better job with them than Barnaby. Whilst the dog would chase and tease and play, the cat would pick his moment, strike fast, and enjoy an extra meal. Cats were so much more practical about things.

'Ah, the van's gone,' Adeline announced as they turned into the lane, drawing Miss Busby from her thoughts.

'Perhaps they were just having some furniture delivered, rather than moving in as such,' Miss Busby mused, dismounting and letting Barnaby out.

'I don't think so,' Adeline said, as they both registered the loud music drifting across the still air.

Miss Busby's heart sank. 'Jazz,' she muttered.

'You said you quite enjoyed it at Sir Richard's party,' Adeline reminded her.

'To dance to, yes. That was rather fun. But it's not necessarily something I want to hear on a Saturday afternoon in my back garden.'

'Oh, I don't know,' Adeline said, looking over towards the cottage. 'It might be nice to have someone liven the place up a bit. Shall we knock?'

'I suppose we ought to,' she said, bracing herself. Miss Busby prided herself on being a quiet and respectful neighbour, and was unsure how to feel about loud music.

'Now, come on, Isabelle. It's just a bit of jazz on a summer's afternoon. Probably a moving-in celebration. And Enid will expect us to have ferreted out full details of the new occupants by tomorrow. We mustn't disappoint!'

'No, I suppose we mustn't. It's a shame Enid didn't come with us, so she could see for herself,' she said, making for Mary's old cottage.

'It would be hard for her, I suspect, given how she's still missing Mary.'

'Oh. Yes, of course. Silly of me not to realise.' Miss Busby opened the front gate.

'And I think she's rather more fond of her Mr Waterhouse than she lets on,' Adeline remarked. 'When I offered to drive her home, she was adamant about meeting him in the marketplace so they could take the bus back together.'

Mr Waterhouse was another elderly Spring Meadows resident. He'd admired Enid from afar before finally catching her eye at the spring dance held for Richard Lannister's birthday.

'They do seem to have grown rather close,' Miss Busby agreed, 'although whenever I mention it, Enid is insistent it's a matter of companionship rather than romance.'

'A little *too* insistent, perhaps?' Adeline suggested with an arch look.

Miss Busby laughed and raised her hand to knock just as the front door to the cottage flew open. A tall young woman with a blonde bob and voluptuous figure clad in a fashionably short dress, glared out at them.

'Is that motorcar yours?' she asked, in cut-glass tones. 'You'll have to move it. My garden furniture is arriving any moment.'

Adeline instantly bristled and drew herself up to full height. Miss Busby rested a gentle hand of restraint on her arm, lest matters got off to an even worse start.

'Good morning,' she said. 'My name is Miss Isabelle Busby. I am your next-door-neighbour-but-one.'

'Oh. Hello.' The young woman glanced down at her, seeming surprised, before extending an elegant hand adorned with several rather expensive-looking rings. Miss Busby's eyes flicked to her other hand as they shook, and noted no wedding or engagement ring present. 'I'm Rowena.'

Miss Busby waited, lest a surname be forthcoming. It wasn't.

'And this is Mrs Fanshawe,' she added, gesturing to Adeline.

'Hello.' Rowena nodded cursorily. 'Are you a neighbour too?'

'No. I am not.' Adeline sniffed.

'And Barnaby is around here somewhere,' Miss Busby added quickly. She glanced around, but the little terrier was nowhere to be seen.

'Is he your son?' Rowena asked, looking marginally more interested in the conversation.

'Her dog,' Adeline supplied.

'Yes, he's rather sweet,' Miss Busby explained. 'He used to live here in your cottage, with the former–'

'I'm allergic to dogs,' Rowena interrupted, leaning out to look impatiently down the lane. 'You really must move your vehicle. I think I can hear the van now.'

'Really?' Adeline shot back. 'I can barely hear a thing over that music.'

Rowena blinked down at her.

'And a "please" would certainly not go amiss,' Adeline continued. 'I don't know where you are from, young lady, but around here we implement good manners.'

Miss Busby sighed and closed her eyes for a moment. When she opened them, Rowena was looking at Adeline with a strange mixture of amusement and what looked like grudging respect.

'I'm a local,' she said. 'Henley, to be precise, although I've been in Scotland for the last few years. Perhaps I developed some rather barbaric habits whilst I was there.' She arched a perfectly shaped eyebrow, and drew her lips into a smile that didn't reach her eyes. 'You really must move your vehicle, *please*.'

Adeline appeared torn for a moment. Miss Busby knew she'd both detest the faux sweetness whilst simultaneously being hard-pressed to resist a shared view of the Scots as barbaric. In the end, she *harrumphed* loudly before turning on her heel and marching off towards the Rolls.

'Thanks awfully!' Rowena called after her, her tone verging on the sarcastic.

'Well,' Miss Busby said into the awkward silence that followed. 'I ought to find Barnaby and take him inside if there's a van on the way. It's nice to meet you, Miss…?'

'Just Rowena. Goodbye, Miss…Busybody, was it?' She tilted her head to one side, eyes alight with what could have been mischief, or malice. It was hard to tell.

'Bus-by,' Miss Busby replied, slowly and deliberately, trying to get the measure of the young woman.

'Busby, yes!' Rowena laughed. 'Memory like a sieve, I'm afraid.'

Miss Busby gave a tight smile and turned to leave before she was tempted to say something unladylike.

Rowena called lightly after her, 'Pop over tomorrow night. I'm having drinks at 8. Bring friends, if you'd like. The more the merrier.'

Miss Busby turned and nodded her head in polite acknowledgement as the over revved growl of the Rolls being manoeuvred into a new spot cut off any reply.

'Barnaby, that's quite enough,' Miss Busby commanded several minutes later, as she carried a jug of lemonade and two glasses out to the garden. The little dog was running in circles, barking wildly while several men shouted noisily to each other as they arranged Rowena's furniture two gardens over.

Adeline sat in the shade of the mulberry tree, fuming so intently she'd forgotten to chastise him.

Producing a hard biscuit from her cardigan pocket, Miss Busby made him sit quietly a moment before giving him the treat and watching him settle under her outdoor table.

'At least the music has stopped,' she said, pouring lemonade into their glasses.

'The cheek of it,' Adeline hissed. 'If she weren't your neighbour, I would gladly have–'

'As would I,' Miss Busby agreed in principle. 'Still, it was nice of her to ask us for drinks,' she added, trying to look on the positive side.

'Nice? Isabelle, *really*. Drinks at 8pm? Who on earth starts an event that late in the countryside? She won't expect you to actually go, of course.'

'Won't she?' Miss Busby smiled as she took a sip of the cool, deliciously tart drink. 'She'll be in for a surprise, then.'

'You're going?'

'I may.'

'I wonder who else will,' Adeline began and turned the conversation to local gossip of various comings and goings.

The hubbub died down, and the pair relaxed once more into the usual quiet of Lavender Cottage's pretty garden. The persistent warmth of the late summer kept the beds awash with colour and fragrance even as autumn crept in. Each day that Miss Busby was able to sit outside and enjoy the simple beauty of her peaceful sanctuary felt like a gift.

They enjoyed the sun, each other's company, and the potted sandwiches Miss Busby had ducked inside to make. They talked companionably of Mary Fellows and how she would have loved one more afternoon in her pretty garden, and James, Adeline's late husband, who would have adored motoring around the countryside in the Rolls he'd worked so hard for. Randolf wasn't mentioned, although he wasn't forgotten, nor ever would be, as long as Miss Busby still had breath in her.

'How is Sir Richard faring now?' Adeline asked, polishing off the last sandwich. 'You don't seem to see half as much of him since he moved closer. Isn't that odd?'

'Yes,' Miss Busby sighed. 'It's all been rather unfortunate.'

Miss Busby had befriended Lucy Lannister, the young reporter, on her first case of murder. Her father, Sir Richard Lannister, had fast become a dear friend, and recently purchased Enid's old house, The Grange, on the outskirts of Little Minton. After finally handing over the running of the paper to Lucy and her brother, Anthony, Sir Richard had intended to enjoy a quiet retirement in the countryside closer to Miss Busby. Ill health, however, had chosen a cruel time to strike; rheumatoid arthritis had worsened to the point he could barely walk and was in constant pain.

'Is he no better?' Adeline pressed.

'He's worse, if anything. Endlessly back and forth to London for tests and some experimental treatment or other, and the travel exhausts him. He says if it were up to him, he'd let nature take its course, but Lucy is adamant they explore every possible avenue.'

'Well, he has a good few years left, I'm sure, and if the doctors in London can make them more comfortable, then well done Lucy, I say. And James would have said the same.'

Miss Busby smiled. James had been an excellent surgeon, with an outstanding reputation. 'Yes, I'm sure he would. But the treatment leaves him with the most awful headaches and dizzy spells. And it's happened so quickly. I can't help but wonder if the move was too much for him…'

'Nonsense. It was what he wanted. And none of us can predict the future, after all. We must simply pray that he recovers.' Adeline rose to her feet, preparing to leave. 'Which we shall, in church after choir practice tomorrow. I shall pick you up at nine.'

'Lovely, thank you.' She smiled. 'I'll see you out.'

Having cleared away the plates and glasses, Miss Busby picked a few late roses from the garden, filled a small vase and placed it on the mantel over the unlit fireplace. Clean and tidy as always, the cosy living room was cheered by the blooms, the pinks and reds reflected in the colours of the chintz cushions and floral wallpaper.

Selecting the latest library book from the set of shelves in the corner, she had just settled into her favourite armchair when a tentative knock sounded at the front door. Tired from her earlier long walk, she contemplated not answering, but Barnaby's eager yaps and the wide open windows indicated her presence.

The distracted figure on the step when she opened the door looked even more fatigued than she felt.

'Hattie, what a pleasant surprise,' Miss Busby said, pleased to see the stout community nurse. Hattie Delaney had become a firm friend over the years. 'Is everything alright?' she added, noting the creases around her eyes and down-turned lips.

'Isabelle, I'm sorry to disturb you, but I don't know who else to turn to.'

Miss Busby ushered her inside, concern eroding her fatigue in an instant. Nurse Hattie Delaney was usually the most cheerful person she knew. 'Whatever is it?' she asked, feeling a flutter of fear in her chest as she gestured to the sofa and took a seat beside her old friend. 'Shall I fetch a tot of brandy?'

'No, thank you, Isabelle. I still have rounds to make later this afternoon. But I've been worrying myself silly since the news came out.'

'News?'

'About the death of Lady Compton. It was in the paper this morning.'

Miss Busby was surprised to find she'd forgotten all about it. The pantechnicon and encounter with Rowena had indeed given her something less maudlin to focus on.

'Yes, of course, I did read about it. Were you acquainted with Lady Compton?' she asked.

'In a manner of speaking.' The nurse twisted her hands in her lap nervously. Miss Busby's concern intensified. Usually forthright and stalwart, particularly in a crisis, she had never seen Hattie Delaney look so uncomfortable.

'I…discovered something about Lady Compton, many years ago,' she continued. 'It was a personal matter, and I have never mentioned it before to anyone. But now, well, I find myself in something of a quandary.'

'I'm sure we shall find the answer together.' Miss Busby adopted a businesslike tone. She had heard the nurse do the very same in times of trouble, and resolved to emulate her at her strongest.

Hattie took a breath, and nodded before continuing, 'Lady Compton was an awful woman, and feared most dreadfully in the village, but something happened that convinced me she'd perpetrated a terrible deception.'

Miss Busby felt a tingle along the back of her neck. 'Regarding a medical matter?' she pressed gently.

'Yes. A very personal medical matter. And whilst there's no particular reason I shouldn't tell the police, it still feels like a betrayal. I know that sounds foolish, but I really can't think what is the right thing to do,' she confessed.

Miss Busby considered her words for a moment.

'I assume you're worried this *deception* may have had a bearing on her death?'

Hattie nodded glumly.

'But surely divulging the deception can't hurt her, now she's no longer with us?'

'No… but it could very much hurt someone who doesn't deserve it.'

'Really?' she ventured carefully.

'Yes.' Hattie nodded once more. 'The young Lord Compton,' she replied with a sigh, eyes downcast.

'I see.' Miss Busby thought for a moment. 'And could continuing to hide this long-held deception also hurt him, do you think?'

She looked up, surprised. 'I hadn't thought of it like that.'

'Perhaps consider it now,' Miss Busby encouraged, 'while I make some tea. A strong cup with plenty of sugar might help.'

She left the nurse to think whilst she set the kettle to boil and prepare the tea tray on the small kitchen table. Pudding jumped up onto the windowsill outside and chirruped through the glass. Opening the door to let him in, she left it ajar to let the steam from the kettle find its own escape.

The ginger tom wound himself around her legs, looking up expectantly. He had his own china bowl left for him on the quarry tiled floor. Barnaby had tried stealing from it once; the cat had batted him round the ears and he'd never tried it again.

'Peckish, are we?' Miss Busby bent to stroke his soft fur, before going to the pantry to find some scraps of ham to put in his bowl. Barnaby instantly appeared as if summoned by magic, and as he'd had such a good walk that morning she offered him the same treat. He ate his helping far quicker than Pud, then trotted out to the garden to find a suitable patch of sun for a quiet snooze.

By the time she took the tea through, Hattie was sitting straighter and looking more like her usual self.

'Isabelle, you are a Godsend,' she pronounced.

'Nonsense.' Miss Busby placed the tray on the low table and stirred the pot before sitting down. 'But if my thinking aloud helps you, then I'm very glad of it.'

'It did help me, and it may help others, too. I'm not entirely sure of it all, Isabelle, but if there's even a chance he killed Lady Compton, who's to say he wouldn't kill again if the fancy took him?'

Miss Busby tilted her head to one side, trying to unravel the convoluted sentence as she poured the tea.

'I'm afraid you've rather lost me.'

'Well, they don't always stop at one, do they?' Hattie went on. 'If he gets away with it once, he might kill again.'

'I should imagine that's always a possibility. But I'm sure someone would only kill if they believe they had cause,' Miss Busby mused. 'But who is this *he*, Hattie?'

Hattie took a sip of the hot tea, followed by a deep breath. 'Theo's father,' she answered.

'Lord Compton?' Miss Busby's eyes widened in surprise. 'Enid said he died years ago.'

'Lord Compton died ten years ago, yes. But I believe Theodore's true father is alive and well.'

# CHAPTER 3

Miss Busby returned to the kitchen in search of something to accompany the tea, her mind whirling. The process of fetching plates from the cupboard and slicing the fruit cake she had made earlier gave her time to think before responding.

'Have I shocked you?' Hattie asked when she returned to the sitting room.

'Not at all.' Miss Busby prided herself on being rather worldly. 'That sort of thing has been going on since time immemorial.'

She proffered a floral plate with a wedge of cake and a silver fork perched on the side. 'I thought you might like a slice. There's rather a lot of brandy in it.'

The rich smell of the fruit, along with delicious hints of cinnamon and alcohol, provoked a smile. 'That would be lovely, thank you. I haven't eaten all day.'

Miss Busby had suspected as much, and was glad to see her friend accept.

'It's remarkable how much better I feel just for telling someone,' Hattie continued between bites.

'*Bear one another's burdens, and so fulfil the law of Christ,*' Miss Busby quoted. 'Galatians, if I recall. I know I always feel better when I talk to someone about whatever's worrying me.'

'Perhaps I ought to attend church more often,' Hattie mused.

'It's the choir that's drawn me into attending regularly again,' Miss Busby explained, having recently become the newest member of Little Minton's choral society. 'Everyone is so friendly, and there's such joy in singing.'

'Not for me. I can't hold a note.'

'Oh, that doesn't stop some of them.' She set her own plate on her knees and wielded the fork. 'I believe Theodore Compton is twenty-four now?'

Hattie nodded. 'He'll be twenty-five next month.'

'And how long have you known this secret?'

'All his life, give or take. There's no proof, naturally. And I would never have mentioned it – but since the rumours began...'

'Rumours?'

'There's a lady in Cold Compton,' Hattie explained. 'Miss Majorie Townsend, a former schoolteacher like yourself, Isabelle. Fiendishly intelligent, but awkward as they come. I met her a long time ago. Their old district nurse had just left to retire. The new nurse was supposed to have taken over from the old, but she caught measles and couldn't come till she was better, so I agreed to stand in for a couple of weeks.'

'And is that how you met Lady Compton?'

'It is.' Hattie took a sip of tea. 'Such a strange twist of fate that I was in the village at the time. If their new nurse hadn't been delayed, the secret would have been hers to keep rather than mine.'

'*Dreadful is the mysterious power of fate,*' Miss Busby mused.

'In this instance, yes. Shakespeare?'

'Sophocles.'

'Ah. I do wish I had more time to read. Well, Majorie was a rare delight when we met. Argued endlessly with the doctor and refused to do anything she was told unless it was all thoroughly explained to her first.'

'Didn't you find that rather frustrating?'

'Not at all. Everyone deserves to understand their care. It was just a matter of having the patience to sit and talk. We got on so well we've kept in touch over the years. I still visit every few months to see how she is.'

Miss Busby nodded, and hoped Hattie Delaney would still be nursing if she ever needed help.

'Well, Marjorie Townsend keeps her ear to the ground, and when I saw her last month, she mentioned a man had been seen around the estate, and that he bore a striking resemblance to the young master.'

Miss Busby straightened in her chair, her eyes glinting with curiosity.

'How old is this man?'

'Oh, middle-aged, or a little older.'

'So unlikely to have been perhaps a by-blow of the late lord's.'

'No, I shouldn't think so, he didn't seem the sort. Anyway, it brought it all back to me. The day I was attending patients in the village almost twenty-five years ago.'

'Do you feel able to tell me what happened?' Miss Busby asked, pouring fresh tea for them both.

Hattie considered for a moment. 'I oughtn't break a patient's right of confidentiality. I certainly didn't tell Marjorie, although she gave the impression she knew, or had guessed.' She set down her cup and took a breath. 'On the day in question, a stable boy from Cold Compton Manor was sent to fetch me away from the patient I was seeing, a young farmer's wife. The boy was clear that I was to go at once. Well, I feared some sort of tragic accident and went immediately. When we arrived, I was hurried straight to Lady Compton's room by a young maid. Her ladyship was sitting up in bed looking perfectly well, so I was a bit flummoxed why it was such a rush. She was very high handed and told me she'd returned from her family estate, Granville Park in Berkshire, the previous evening. Then explained that she'd decided to spend the later stages of her pregnancy there and have the birth and confinement under the supervision of her own family's doctor and midwife.'

'Would that sort of thing have been usual at the time?' Miss Busby asked.

'It wasn't *un*usual, not for the toffs anyway,' Hattie replied. 'And she implied the local midwife wasn't up to her standards, which I didn't think fair - babies are babies, after all, and they all come out more or less the same way. Then she said Lord Compton would manage matters of the estate better without the disruption of the birth.'

'Really?' Miss Busby raised a brow. 'Was he so cold-hearted?'

'No, not at all. He was a decent sort by all accounts, and she was inclined to play the martyr. He was older than her, but browbeaten from all accounts.'

Miss Busby nodded. 'And why did she want to see you?'

'She demanded I examine the baby, which didn't make sense as her midwife would have done it before she left Berkshire.'

'I expect, as a new mother, she was simply overly concerned?' Miss Busby attempted to play devil's advocate.

'If she'd been a younger woman, I would have agreed with you. But Lady Compton was already over forty by that point. Older mothers tend to have a little more common sense.'

'Although if it was her first child…'

Hattie nodded. 'I know, it could have been a simple lack of experience and overzealous concern. Anyway, I checked the babe thoroughly, and he was in perfect health. Beautiful head of blond hair, and lovely eyes, sky blue they were. And a cheerful little soul who didn't so much as grizzle the whole time I was there. I couldn't find a single reason for concern and told Lady Compton as much. I enquired after her own health, in turn. Giving birth at that age isn't without risk, although I thought she looked remarkably well and showed no sign of any physical discomfort.'

'And did the baby resemble her?' Miss Busby asked.

'She was blonde-haired and blue-eyed, so there was nothing to indicate the little tot wasn't hers, but…oh, I don't know,' she sighed.

'But you suspected something, nonetheless?' Miss Busby said.

'It wasn't suspicion as such, it was really a feeling that things were rather…' She paused, reaching for her tea cup again as she searched for the right word. 'Artificial. As if she were play-acting. I asked how old the baby was, judging him to be around six weeks, and she told me he was only ten days. I asked how she was coping with breastfeeding, and she said she'd had a local wet nurse back in Berkshire, but she was now going to start him on the bottle. The young maid was to take over feeding duties.'

'Again, I imagine that's hardly uncommon among the upper classes.'

'Perhaps, but her breasts weren't even swollen, nor her tummy – as far as I could see, there was no sign at all that she had recently given birth. Added to the fact that she'd chosen to spend the birth and confinement away from her husband and home…well, I left feeling unconvinced about everything she'd told me.'

Miss Busby nodded. 'And she never called on you again?'

'She did not. I saw the rest of my patients that afternoon and then the new district nurse arrived the following day.

If it hadn't been for my fondness for Marjorie, I doubt I'd have ever returned.'

'And when Marjorie told you of the mysterious gentleman visiting the estate…'

'It brought the matter to mind for the first time in decades, yes. I thought perhaps she was testing me, to see what I may suspect, but I pretended to know nothing. And then I saw the headline in the newspaper this morning.'

Miss Busby placed her plate on the tea tray before leaning back once more against the chintz cushions.

'The issue of foul play changes everything. I believe you should tell the police, Hattie.'

The nurse gazed into the unlit hearth. 'That was my first thought too, but think of the consequences. Young Theodore could lose everything if word gets out.'

'Perhaps, but you're not responsible for the machinations of the gentry,' Miss Busby reminded her. 'And if the man who has been spotted about the village really is his father, I'm sure the truth will come out soon enough of its own accord.'

'Then perhaps it doesn't need help from me?' Hattie suggested, rather hopefully.

Miss Busby considered for a moment before answering. Her gaze followed the nurse's into the fireplace, set with kindling and paper twists ready for the next cold evening.

'I think your conscience needs help, more than the truth,' she concluded. 'The matter is obviously upsetting you, Hattie. You looked quite unwell when you first arrived.'

'I do feel much better after talking to you. And I can't help thinking that if you were to work your magic, like you did with Vernon Potter and Gabriel Travis…'

'Vernon Potter's murder was rather closer to home,' she said. 'And Adeline's friendship with Ezekiel Melnyk was the reason we became embroiled in the Travis case. I don't have any "magic", Hattie, I just try to help my friends, and our community, wherever I can. I've never been to Cold Compton, and I don't know anyone who lives there. I'm afraid it wouldn't feel right if I were to become involved.'

'But we're friends, aren't we?' Hattie pressed, leaning across to take Miss Busby's hand.

'Of course we are. And if it were a dear friend of yours in distress, I'd do everything in my power to help. But given the circumstances, I think it's far better you talk to Inspector McKay. I'm sure he'd be happy to talk to you in confidence. I know he's a little gruff, but he has far more resources at his disposal. I could telephone him, if you'd like me to?'

Pudding stalked into the room, his tail swishing, as Hattie considered Miss Busby's words.

'Perhaps you're right,' she conceded. 'It was so long ago, and I never had any connection to Lady Compton. She certainly wasn't the type you'd warm to.'

Pudding sprang into her lap, and she laughed as he sniffed disdainfully at her skirt. 'That's Duncan you can smell,' she told him, scratching him under the chin. 'You wouldn't like him. He's not as gentlemanly as Barnaby.'

Miss Busby rose to her feet and collected the tea tray.

'Let me help,' Hattie insisted.

'No, you stay there with Pud. He would enjoy a cuddle. I'll just take these through, then I'll telephone the inspector.'

With Pudding's contented engine-like purr resounding through the sitting room, Miss Busby stood at a small table beside the coat stand in the hall, candlestick receiver to her ear, as she was connected.

'Oxford Police Station,' a brisk voice announced.

'Good afternoon. May I speak to Inspector McKay? It's Miss Busby. Please tell him it's with regard to Lady Compton.'

'Hold the line, Miss.' There was a scuffling noise, then distant muttering, then only the crackling of the line.

'Mabel?' Miss Busby enquired politely.

'I'm going now, Miss,' the young operator said, rather sulkily. Miss Busby had had occasion in the past to remind her to disconnect, no matter how intriguing the ensuing conversation may sound.

'McKay.' The one-word greeting, wrapped in its Scottish brogue, made her smile. She could picture his brow furrowed beneath his fiery red hair, lips thin as he no doubt prepared himself to admonish her. 'Please tell me you have not already become involved in the murder at Cold Compton, Miss Busby?'

She smiled, before assuring him, 'I have not. In fact,

I have been resolute in staying out of the whole nasty business, Inspector. But I have a friend here who has something rather bothering her–'

'Ah. Now let me guess,' he interrupted in turn. 'That would be Mrs Fanshawe, no doubt.'

'No. May I continue, or would you like to try again?'

'Please continue,' he said with a sigh of irritation.

'District Nurse Harriet Delaney would like to speak to you about Lady Compton regarding a rather delicate matter.'

She heard a rustling in the background; the inspector pulling his notebook from his jacket pocket, no doubt.

'And where might I find Nurse Delaney?' he asked.

'She lives in Bloxford, in Oak End Cottage, just off the bridleway. She's here with me now if you would like to talk to her.'

'I should think it's a conversation best had in person,' he replied. 'I will be in Bloxford tomorrow evening on a personal matter. Perhaps you could ask her if I may call before my…erm…engagement?'

Miss Busby's mind switched gears. What could the inspector possibly be doing in Bloxford? Unless…

*No*, she thought. *Surely not.*

'What sort of time?' she asked.

'It would be in the evening, if that's convenient. Around seven forty five?'

Miss Busby fell silent for a moment. Then, 'Let me just check.' She placed her hand over the receiver and considered. Bloxford was a small village, and the inspector had never, to her knowledge, visited it for any reason other than to come to Lavender Cottage. Now a young lady had moved in, a lady who had lived in Scotland for the last few years, and who was having drinks tomorrow night. Around eight.

One shouldn't jump to conclusions, she reminded herself. And then she thought, *But that's precisely what Hattie's doing regarding the young Lord Theodore Compton and the mystery stranger. And so had she... Had she truly thought through the effect on the young man? Such a revelation would have profound consequences.* She'd been keen to lift the worry from her friend's shoulders, but now realised she should have given the matter deeper consideration before acting. Mind whirring, she decided to prevaricate; besides, she was rather curious about the inspector's intentions...

Miss Busby uncovered the handset and asked, 'How is Lucy, Inspector?'

'I– pardon?'

'Lucy. How is she? I haven't seen her in a while.'

The young reporter and the inspector had become close since Sir Richard's birthday party. Lucy was the happiest Miss Busby had seen her, despite the stress of her father's illness.

'Oh. Fine, as far as I know,' McKay replied. 'But I understood you were checking something with the nurse?'

'Will Lucy be in Bloxford tomorrow evening too? I should very much like to see her,' Miss Busby pressed.

'Ah, no.' He cleared his throat. 'Just me. And I'll be on quite a tight schedule.'

'I see. Seven forty five is a little late to call on Nurse Delaney,' she said. 'I'll suggest she contact you at her earliest convenience. Good day, Inspector.' She replaced the handset before he could reply.

She looked down at the telephone with a sigh of consternation, before going through to the sitting room and telling Nurse Delaney there had been a change of plan.

'Is everything alright?' she asked.

'Yes. I'm just reconsidering the situation,' Miss Busby muttered.

Hattie looked confused.

'Now the news has had a chance to settle, I wonder if we might leave mentioning anything to the authorities until Monday?'

'Yes, of course, but whatever changed your mind?'

'Well…' Miss Busby cleared her throat. 'I think we ought to present any concern couched in a rather more solid basis than suspicion and rumour, neither of which, as the inspector's gruff tones have reminded me, he has any fondness for. We oughtn't jump to conclusions, however pressing the evidence. The consequences could be devastating for Theodore Compton. I'm sorry, Hattie, I should have thought more carefully.'

'Don't be silly.' Hattie waved the notion aside, before gently sliding the sleeping cat from her lap to the cushion beside her and rising to her feet. 'We will do whatever you think best. You know the inspector better than most, after all. And besides, I did drop a bit of a bombshell on you, particularly on such a lovely afternoon!'

Miss Busby laughed. 'I wonder,' she added, 'might you be free tomorrow after church? To discuss it with Adeline and Enid? We were together this morning when we heard about the murder.'

'Yes, I should think so. Oh!' A slow smile spread across her round face, her customary cheer making a welcome return. 'Will you be working your magic after all?'

Miss Busby's lips twitched into a smile. 'I prefer to think of it more as discussion and…extrapolation, if you don't mind sharing your suspicions? We'll emphasise discretion, of course.'

'In that case, I don't mind at all.' Barnaby came over to see what was happening, and the nurse bent to stroke his head before making for the door. 'I knew you'd help, Isabelle, thank you,' she added, her voice rich with sincerity.

Miss Busby glanced at the telephone in the hall as she closed the door behind her, wondering if she had done the right thing.

'Time will tell, Barnaby,' she mused.

He trotted agreeably behind her as she returned to her armchair and picked up her book.

# CHAPTER 4

Sunlight broke through the woodland surrounding Little Minton Lake, bright rays sparking off the rippling surface like diamonds dancing on the water. Miss Busby smiled at the notion; there was a richness in the natural beauty that sat perfectly with the image. She and Barnaby were halfway around the broad expanse of water, now some distance from where Nurse Hattie Delaney was sharing her concerns with Enid and Adeline on the bench beside the cinder path.

She passed purple loosestrife crowding the water's edge, tall and bright and buzzing with industrious bees, causing Barnaby to eye them warily before giving them a wide berth. Damselflies darted between yellow flag irises, while dragonflies hovered on iridescent wings above lily pads the size of saucers.

'All God's wonders,' Miss Busby murmured to the little dog, who cocked a brown and white ear in her direction. Choir practice earlier that morning had been a cheery, exuberant affair. The following service was rather more sombre – hymns aside – but inspirational in its solemn devotion. She began humming *All Things Bright and Beautiful* and extended her stride to complete the full circle and return to her friends.

Enid stood to make room for her on the bench. 'I can't sit for long,' she said, using her stick for support. 'It plays havoc with my hip.'

Miss Busby gave a sympathetic nod as she sat down beside Hattie. They'd collected the nurse in Little Minton after church. She was smartly attired in her navy uniform, ready to attend patients at Spring Meadows after lunch.

'Now that you've both heard the story, what do you make of this mystery man?' Miss Busby asked.

'He sounds highly suspicious to me,' Adeline declared from the other side of Hattie. Her dress was a riot of colour; hues of pink and blue on a black background – every bit as dramatic and commanding as the woman herself. 'We must uncover the truth. Ask questions. Take action!'

'Lord Theodore is no longer Adeline's primary suspect,' Enid commented wryly. 'And I should think informing the police would be action enough,' she cautioned. The oldest of the group, she felt the cold more keenly than the others, and wore a long woollen cardigan over a russet skirt and blouse, enlivened by a necklace of large amber beads. 'I thought you preferred not to become involved, Isabelle?'

'I do,' Miss Busby admitted. 'But this mystery man presents rather a dilemma.'

'Hattie has explained why you don't think it a good idea to go directly to the authorities yet, Isabelle,' Adeline said. 'And I believe you are perfectly correct. Inspector McKay won't listen to mere suspicion. We should do a little digging first.'

'Do you think it a bad idea, Enid?' Miss Busby asked, looking to her older friend as the voice of reason.

'Well, I shouldn't think it could hurt,' she replied thoughtfully. 'This man could be completely innocent, of course, and heaven knows what we may bring down upon him, and the young lord, if we tell the police without good cause.'

'And we don't even know if he *is* the boy's father,' Hattie added.

'For the sake of debate, let us assume he is,' Enid suggested.

'And that if he is up to no good, then we shall find out,' Adeline was quick to add.

'I've been thinking,' Hattie said. 'It's been a couple of months since Marjorie mentioned him. If he'd been seeking to do harm, I'm sure he wouldn't have waited this long.'

Adeline sniffed. 'Rather a coincidence, regardless. He could have been watching the place before making his move.'

'To what end?' Enid asked.

'He will be after the fortune, of course!' Adeline exclaimed.

'I shouldn't think there *is* one, given the apparent

mismanagement of the place,' Enid countered. 'Besides, what there is will go directly to the boy.'

'Where it will surely be easier for this man to get his hands on it. And it's all *relative*,' Adeline pointed out. 'If the man was destitute enough to sell a child, then any fortune, however small, would appeal.'

'Adeline, we have no idea if he sold the child. We should be careful not to rush to extreme conclusions,' Miss Busby cautioned, attempting to rein her in before she could build up speed. 'We have no idea of the circumstances surrounding the boy's birth.'

'Do we possess *any* facts about the man?' Enid pressed, striking a nettle gamely with her stick.

'No,' Hattie replied glumly.

'Not even a name?' Enid asked.

Hattie shook her head.

'Well, he must live close to Cold Compton,' Miss Busby said, 'if he's been seen around.'

'Not necessarily. He could have taken the train from just about anywhere.' Hattie's earlier gloom appeared in danger of returning.

'The train is expensive,' Enid pointed out. 'And it's a long walk to Cold Compton. I think it more likely he's staying locally.'

'But then why wait until now?' Hattie repeated. 'It doesn't make sense.'

'What does it matter where he lives?' Adeline objected. 'The man is obviously a cad, regardless. Either selling his…his…' she fought for a word. 'His *services*, or the child itself. The very sort to murder someone in cold blood where even the sniff of financial gain may be in the offing.'

Miss Busby blinked in surprise. 'Are you suggesting *he's* the father and Lady Compton the mother?'

'I'm simply considering all avenues, however indelicate.' Adeline huffed, her cheeks turning pink. 'I had heard Lord Compton was older than his wife. And she was no spring chicken.'

It certainly wasn't an avenue Miss Busby had envisioned. 'It's rather inventive, but in the same vein, this mystery man could have been duped for all we know. Hattie's observations at the time do suggest Lady Compton wasn't the mother, though.'

'Well, who *is* the mother, then?'

'Are you changing your mind about it being a man who pulled the trigger?' Enid asked, a smile spreading on her face.

'Whichever side of the moral scale the mystery man falls upon,' Miss Busby jumped in before Adeline could respond, 'how could he have found Theodore? Surely Lady Compton's primary concern, if taking such drastic measures, would have been to ensure neither parent could find the child and disrupt her family after the fact.'

Hattie nodded. 'I thought the same. She would have done everything possible to cover her tracks. Theodore would lose all rights to the estate if any doubts were cast.'

'She didn't want him to *have* the estate, though. She's been running it herself,' Adeline pointed out, bouncing back with aplomb. 'Why did she continue running it after he came of age? No, I see it now,' she hurried on, fresh on the trail of a new thought. 'She purchased the child, one way or another, and the father tracked her down to demand money with menaces. Lady Compton may have acquiesced initially, and kept Theodore out of estate matters to hide the payments, but it wouldn't surprise me if the bounder's demands grew ever more unreasonable, which would explain the delay in him taking action.'

Miss Busby frowned. It all sounded rather convoluted.

Enid was caustic. 'It's no good simply throwing dramatic statements about. This is just idle conjecture.'

Adeline huffed and folded her arms across her ample chest.

'If you're correct, why did she acquire the child to begin with, and why did the true parents give him up?' Miss Busby tried to steer them back to the heart of the matter.

'Precisely,' Enid declared. 'What motivated them all?'

'Well, as a woman already past forty,' Hattie said, 'the most likely explanation is that Lady Compton realised there was little hope of a natural heir, and so "procured" one.'

'As countless others in her situation have done over the years,' Enid added.

'Yes, I've heard such things happen,' Hattie continued.

'If Lady Compton followed the most common example of others in her situation, she would have travelled some distance from home to avoid suspicion, and sought either a new mother with too many children of her own to care for, or a child newly born out of wedlock.'

'What about a workhouse?' Adeline suggested, having recovered; she was always as quick to forgive and forget as she was to huff and sulk. 'They tend to be overrun with the latter.'

Hattie shook her head. 'No. A paper trail would have been created, in much the same way as if she'd adopted a child. Lady Compton would have taken an unofficial route, with no questions asked and no record made.'

'Rendering it a needle in a haystack if the birth mother is to be sought. And yet somehow,' Miss Busby mused, 'the father apparently has been able to find the boy.'

'Well, it would be easier that way around,' Enid remarked. 'There are a finite number of Ladies of the Manor in need of an heir, in contrast to countless young women in want of support.'

'He would need to be intelligent, and determined,' Hattie suggested, 'to have tracked Theodore down. Perhaps he truly mourned for his lost baby. It might have been his life's work to find him.'

'Or he may simply be desperate and cunning.' Adeline was not to be deterred. 'Either way, we shan't find out by sitting here and guessing. I shall drive us to Cold Compton and we will find Miss Marjorie Townsend,' she declared, rising to her feet. 'There is no time like the present! Isabelle, do we need to call at Lavender Cottage en route for your detecting paraphernalia?'

Miss Busby felt a spark of excitement igniting. If they actually were to go ahead and tell McKay about the mysterious stranger, the more they could learn about him first, the better. She was now very much alert to the potentially catastrophic consequences for the young man and felt she should be certain of what she was doing. 'I popped my notebook and pencil into my bag this morning,' she said. 'We shouldn't require anything else.'

'Hattie and I need to go to Spring Meadows,' Enid added, as the sound of the church bells striking noon rang out on the warm breeze. 'If you could take us please, Adeline? We'll be late for lunch if we walk.'

'Oh. Yes. What's on the menu?' Adeline asked, momentarily distracted by the thought of one of Cook's Sunday roasts.

'Lamb, and then I have a tarot reading for Mrs Hopper. She becomes extremely agitated if one is tardy.'

'At which time I will be attending your Mr Waterhouse,' Hattie said.

'He's not *my* anything,' Enid replied archly.

Hattie smiled. 'Perhaps you could read my cards. I've never had it done.' She offered Enid a supportive arm as they headed towards the car.

'Hmm.' Enid sniffed. 'Perhaps I could.'

'I'm certain you will find Marjorie at home, Isabelle,' Hattie continued brightly. 'She rarely goes out. Just look for Midwinter Cottage. She is quite distinctive - her illness caused her to lose her hair years ago and she wears a very striking wig.'

'There we are then!' Adeline beamed. 'Come along, everyone, hop in the car.'

'It's such a treat to be driven in a Rolls Royce.' Hattie smiled.

Miss Busby called Barnaby as they arranged themselves in the sumptuous seats.

'He hasn't been in the lake, has he?' Adeline called out. 'Because his blanket isn't down.'

'He can sit on my lap.' Miss Busby discreetly removed a piece of pondweed stuck to his fur.

Fifteen minutes later, after dropping Enid and Hattie off at the gates to Spring Meadows, Adeline pressed her foot firmly down and the Rolls purred out of Little Minton to join the main road towards Stow.

'Such a glorious day for a drive,' Adeline said, fumbling in her bag beside the seat for her new sunglasses. Setting the amber-brown spectacles atop her nose, she added quietly, 'James would have adored this.'

Miss Busby took a moment before replying, 'Hunting down elderly women in wigs?'

'You know perfectly well that's not what I meant,' Adeline chided gently. 'But I appreciate you not letting me grow maudlin.'

'It afflicts us all at times,' Miss Busby said. 'But we have each other, Adeline, and our friends.'

Adeline nodded, and sniffed, eyes hidden behind the glasses. They drove in silence for several minutes, each lost in their own thoughts, before she declared, 'I am sorry, Isabelle, if you feel I've pushed you into investigating. It's just that things have been so *dull* lately. It's alright for you, you have Sir Richard close by now, and you'll soon be back to your crossword evenings, and trips to the theatre and so forth, once they have his symptoms under control.'

'*If* they can control them,' Miss Busby remarked softly.

Adeline turned to her. 'Once the tests are completed, and the consultants consulted, they should be able to alleviate some of them.'

'Eyes forward, Adeline,' Miss Busby reminded her. 'I know, and he is fortunate to be able to afford the best of help, but he seems to have gone downhill so fast. Have you no trips planned with Jemima and the boys?' she asked, trying to get back on a more positive footing.

'They went off to the Riviera for the summer, and then the boys started boarding school last week. I shan't see them until the first exeat.'

'Oh, what a shame. Well,' Miss Busby filled her voice with resolve, 'when Richard *does* feel better, you must come with us on our outings. We shan't let life pass us by.'

'Dash it all,' Adeline hissed.

Miss Busby looked at her in surprise, having expected a rather different response.

'We should have turned left there,' Adeline clarified. 'Hold on.'

She swung the large car around in the road, arms wresting the wheel as Miss Busby clung to both the door handle and Barnaby.

'There. Now, be on the lookout for Midwinter Cottage,' she commanded as they swept over the top of a hill. The lane wound down towards a wide circle of ragged looking stone cottages, their front gardens abutting a cart track running around a village green. Beyond that, the land spread in a patchwork of small fields edged by hedges and spinneys, and dotted with farmhouses and outbuildings in various states of disrepair. A river wound through the valley and on the highest hill, a large manor house stood surrounded by stately trees and gardens; its pristine beauty a stark contrast to the air of decay around it.

Adeline steered the Rolls down the dip and onto the track, motoring slowly past the cottages. These were in a sad state, and several appeared abandoned. Two villagers were busy scything the long grass on the green, but there was no sign of anyone sitting outside enjoying the sunshine.

'Not a very cheery sort of place, is it?' Adeline remarked as they crawled along, reading the names of the cottages.

'Perhaps Lady Compton decreed they must all remain indoors on Sunday,' Miss Busby said.

'She's dead,' Adeline replied archly.

'Then perhaps they're all off celebrating somewhere,' Miss Busby replied dryly.

Suddenly, a young man on a gleaming chestnut horse emerged from between two byres ahead of them. He cantered across the grass with elegant ease; a handsome profile, blond hair, an athletic build with broad shoulders. Wearing a dark jacket, jodhpurs and leather boots, he looked as though he'd ridden straight out of the past. They watched, almost mesmerised, as he turned away and exited onto another track.

'Well, I imagine that must be Lord Theodore himself,' Adeline sounded rather impressed.

'*Randolf,*' Miss Busby whispered, the young man's resemblance striking a memory. Adeline didn't hear her. Randolf had been her fiancé before he lost his life to typhoid in South Africa. He'd been the heir to the Bloxford estate, and the Earldom. She would have led a very different life, had he lived. Over forty years had passed since she last saw him… She gave herself a mental shake and turned back to reading the name boards on garden gates.

They passed a cottage proclaiming itself to be the post office, the red paint on the sign peeling, the windows dark and shuttered. Beside it stood a far tidier cottage, its slate roof showing signs of recent repair, and the windows gleaming bright in the sun.

Attached to it was an open byre, which was quite obviously a blacksmith's forge. The name '*Alfred Brownlow, Cold Compton Smithy*' was painted in white lettering on the black beam over the wide entrance. A huge fire was blazing on a raised stone base set against the rear wall, with various tools, hammers, tongs and the like hanging from hooks. An anvil stood on the worn stone flagged floor. The unique smell of woodsmoke, beaten metal and hot stones seeped into the car, bringing back memories of horses and carriages and an era now slowly ebbing away.

The next line of cottages also seemed in better state, and by far the cleanest and brightest of the row was a double-fronted house with a neat garden, white-painted picket fence, and a sign proclaiming it to be 'Midwinter Cottage'.

Adeline drove the front wheels up onto the green, waving aside Miss Busby's concern as she parked the car. 'It's not as if there's a cricket match in progress, Isabelle. And the ground is perfectly dry.'

Miss Busby let Barnaby out and allowed him a few moments to sniff about before taking his leash from her bag and attaching it to his collar.

'Well, it looks better kept than most,' Adeline noted as they observed the house. 'Rather pleasant, in fact.'

Miss Busby was more interested in the occupants of the cottage's large front garden, visible now over the neatly trimmed hedge as they drew closer. A pretty young woman with copper-coloured hair, an older man in worn country tweeds, and a rather plump old lady sporting an old-fashioned black wig under a white cotton cap tied firmly under her chin. She leaned on a simple hazel wood cane and regarded them through round spectacles on the end of her nose.

'I believe that may be Miss Marjorie Townsend!' said Adeline.

'I believe it is,' Miss Busby replied with a smile.

# CHAPTER 5

At the same moment as the bewigged Marjorie Townsend was revealed, the door of the cottage attached to the blacksmith's forge opened and a tall, muscular man with greying hair came out and strode along the track. Dressed in a linen shirt with sleeves rolled up to the elbows and a long leather apron almost completely covering black trousers and stout brown boots beneath. He carried a large iron pot of something delicious-smelling, and paused to gaze at the newcomers with dark eyes under thick brows.

'May I help you?' he asked, his voice as languid as his movements.

Adeline sniffed the air. 'Is that Brown Windsor soup?' she asked. 'I haven't had it in an age! It smells delicious.'

He nodded, replying, 'And a rich broth it is, too.' The man smiled at them both. 'Are you visitors?'

'I believe they are,' the elderly lady called out. The wig was noticeably faded at the front and mostly covered by the white cap. She was dressed in Victorian style; an unadorned dark frock buttoned to the neck and a paisley shawl around her shoulders. 'Are you looking for someone?'

'Miss Marjorie Townsend of Midwinter Cottage,' Miss Busby replied.

'Well, you have found her,' the lady replied, her faded eyes large behind the glasses, her plump cheeks pink from the warmth of the day.

Miss Busby placed her hand on the gate latch. 'May we enter?'

'Please do, it is most unusual to have unexpected visitors, and very welcome. May I enquire to whom I am speaking?' Her voice rose and fell and was a little breathless.

'Miss Isabelle Busby, and Mrs Adeline Fanshawe. We're friends of Nurse Harriet Delaney. She suggested we might find you here,' Miss Busby explained as Barnaby trotted in on her heels. Adeline came in behind, and the man with the soup brought up the rear.

'Hattie?' A smile lit her eyes. 'Oh, how lovely! Is she well? I am overdue a visit.' She advanced, tottering slightly as she leaned on the cane.

'She's very well.' Miss Busby's reply was cordial. 'But occupied with a patient this afternoon and unable to accompany us. She sends her regards.'

'Wonderful woman,' Miss Townsend went on. 'Infinitely knowledgeable, and a delight to converse with. Well, don't just stand there. Alfred has brought some Sunday soup. You must stay for lunch.' She turned to look up at the tall man still holding the pot.

'I'll let Lara put it on the dining room table and set the places.' He offered the lidded pot to the young woman. She took it with a sweet smile. A pretty girl with a heart-shaped face, large blue-green eyes, pale skin and a scatter of freckles across her small nose. She wore a white linen blouse with a long wool skirt in dark red. She'd tied her hair back in a simple plait which gleamed in shades of copper, amber and gold in the sunshine.

'Lara tends my garden each Sunday,' Marjorie Townsend said. 'You're a kind soul to help an old lady, aren't you?' She beamed at her.

'It's a pleasure, Miss Townsend,' Lara said in a light voice, then carried the pot through the open front door.

'Lara is our local beekeeper, and Alfred's niece,' Marjorie continued. 'Never one to shy from hard work, and kind with it.'

'That she is,' Alfred said, his voice resonating in his broad chest. He looked down at Barnaby, who looked up at him with liquid brown eyes. He bent to pat the dog's head. 'Nice little dog you have there.'

Such a transgression usually elicited a deep chesty growl from Barnaby – a result of his antipathy towards men in general, but he took it in good stead, and even wagged his tail.

'He's called Barnaby,' Miss Busby replied, relieved that he hadn't caused a minor fracas at such a delicate moment.

'Well, I'll be wishing you a good Sabbath, ladies,'

Alfred nodded amiably, then turned to amble back toward the blacksmith's forge.

Adeline was staring openly at the other man in the far corner of the sunny garden. He wore his tweed jacket over a moleskin waistcoat despite the warmth. Miss Busby assumed him to be the traditional sort who wore Sunday best on the Lord's day, come what may. He had nodded to them amiably when they entered the garden, then carried on cutting long beans from the tall plants growing in the vegetable patch.

'That is James Hooper,' Miss Townsend told them. 'He prefers Jimmy, do you not?'

'I do, and a rare good mornin' to you both.' He smiled and touched his cap.

'And to you,' Miss Busby returned.

'Rather unusual to grow vegetables in one's front garden,' Adeline observed.

'Well, it would be of no use growing them in the back,' Miss Townsend answered, eyebrows raised. 'The pig and chickens would eat every last shoot and stem. Which reminds me – Jimmy!' she called, 'did you feed Hamlet and the girls?'

He looked up. 'Yes Miss, they've all had the scrapings.'

'Good.' She nodded. 'They attempt ever more brazen breakouts if we forget.'

Miss Busby's eyes shone merrily. 'You have named your pig Hamlet?'

'I have. And the chickens are Jane, Mary, Catherine, Lydia, and Elizabeth,' she said proudly.

'The Bennet sisters, how wonderful!'

'*Pride and Prejudice.*' Miss Townsend nodded, her eyes twinkling behind the glasses. 'It is my very favourite book.'

'You have livestock *and* a vegetable garden?' Adeline asked, still seeming to struggle with the idea.

'Needs must,' Miss Townsend replied. 'We are all self-sufficient here. I am fortunate in having more space than most, so plenty of my vegetables go to my neighbours. But I doubt you came here to discuss runner beans and eggs.' She tilted her head to one side and regarded them shrewdly.

Miss Busby thought it best to come straight to the point, before Adeline began asking more questions about the pig. 'Hattie came to us regarding Lady Compton.' She kept her voice low. 'We wondered if we might talk to you about her.'

Her eyes widened in surprise. 'Really? How unexpected. Well, we may converse in comfort over lunch.'

'Absolutely.' Adeline beamed.

Miss Busby threw her a glance, then added, 'If you are quite sure there's enough.'

'Oh, there's plenty. Alfred always brings enough for tomorrow.' She led the way along the path, still tottering. 'But I find having the same meal two days in a row rather tedious.'

Lara came out at that moment. 'It's all ready for you, Miss Townsend.' She smiled.

'Bless you, you're a dear girl.' Marjorie beamed up at her.

'I'll help Jimmy finish off here,' Lara said and walked over to pick up the basket of beans.

'Come along, and bring your little doggie.' Marjorie moved towards the door. She seemed more confident indoors and paused in the wide hallway to put the cane in an umbrella stand next to the stairs. 'We're in the parlour,' she said and led them, and Barnaby, through to the sunny front room where a dining table was placed in the window with four padded chairs around it. Lara had put three bowls, plates and spoons on the embroidered tablecloth and a vase of sweetpeas next to the pot.

Miss Townsend sat down, then leaned over to stir the soup with a ladle. Miss Busby glanced through the open window at the pair still gathering beans.

'They take Sunday lunch mid afternoon with their folk, but I prefer to eat earlier,' Miss Townsend said and filled the bowls with thick brown broth.

Miss Busby picked up a spoon, and wondered how best to begin. 'Hattie mentioned, with regard to her ladyship, that–'

'Lady Compton shall not be missed,' Miss Townsend announced firmly, her homely demeanour suddenly becoming quite strict.

'Oh, yes, we had heard–'

'She was a pitiless tyrant. Jimmy used to be gamekeeper for the estate under the late Lord Compton.' She lowered her voice. 'He was trusted and respected by the old lord, but her ladyship was always disparaging him for no good reason. When she took over, he worked for her until he could bear it no longer.'

Jimmy straightened up and brushed down his trousers, apparently having finished his part in the task. 'I'll be away now, Miss Townsend,' he called out. 'I'll bring the pigeons plucked and dressed in the morning.'

'Thank you, Jimmy, that's most kind of you,' Miss Townsend called back through the open window, and waited until he'd gone out of the gate, and earshot. 'Jimmy lost his home in the village when he resigned his position. I believe Lady Compton was most pleased to have saved the expense of his wages.' She shook her head, the wig wobbling slightly. 'He rents a cottage in the next village now, but he always returns to us here. Our little community exchanges good for good, regardless of her ladyship's scheming. We may be poor, but we are rich in kindness.'

Miss Busby nodded and sipped another spoonful of broth.

'What does he do for work now?' Adeline asked, curious.

'Ah, well, he's rather switched sides.' Miss Townsend scooped up a spoonful of soup.

Adeline thought for a moment. 'Good Lord, not a poacher?'

The elderly woman's creased lips twitched briefly. 'He would not thank you for use of the word, my dear, although he still tends the birds and thins the deer herd when required. He simply doesn't take payment, rather he takes in kind and shares where there is a need.'

Adeline didn't appear convinced. Poachers in the county had a sinister reputation, but the man, Jimmy, had seemed polite and helpful, and Miss Busby wondered how much genuine need could, at times, be behind some of the more nefarious activities of the countryside.

'How long had Lady Compton been running the estate, Miss Townsend?' she asked.

'Marjorie, please. My pupils and my doctor call me Miss Townsend.'

Miss Busby nodded graciously.

'Ten years,' Marjorie continued. 'Since Lord Compton died. Rather suddenly, as it happens.'

'Really? What did he die of?' Adeline asked, leaning forward eagerly, her earlier distaste forgotten.

'The torment of his wife's company, I should think. He bled to death, according to the doctor,' Marjorie said wryly, then took another spoonful of soup.

'Really? How?' Adeline continued unabashed.

'He had an accident whilst out hunting. He was brought home and died of internal bleeding.'

'My husband was a surgeon, and even he would admit not all medical men possess the same ability,' Adeline said. 'I assume this doctor failed to spot it?'

'He did, and another good reason I don't trust doctors,' she remarked.

'Notebook, Isabelle,' Adeline said, gesturing to her bag impatiently. 'This may be important.'

Marjorie arched a brow in disapproval, whether at the

way Adeline chivied Miss Busby along, or at the idea of her words being noted down, Miss Busby was unsure.

'Would you mind?' she asked politely. 'It's just an aide-mémoire.'

'To what end?' The creases on her face deepened into a frown.

'Some possible enlightenment,' Miss Busby tried to phrase her words diplomatically. 'Hattie wondered if we might be able to set her mind at rest regarding a certain stranger seen recently in the area.'

'One who looks like Lord Theodore Compton,' Adeline added bluntly. 'Who we just saw riding across the green.'

Miss Busby sighed.

'And why not, he rides the estate most days,' Marjorie said, her warmth dissipating slightly. 'And I may add, it is not like Hattie to fall prey to rumour.'

'Indeed,' Miss Busby agreed. 'She was simply concerned as to whether the stranger's appearance was a coincidence, or perhaps something more…worrying.' She let the implications hang for a moment. 'And she mentioned you were the lady who told her about the gentleman in the first place…'

Marjorie's plump cheeks flushed, before she countered, 'I may have, but reporting a rumour is a rather different matter from subscribing to it.'

'You don't think this man is the boy's real father, then?' Adeline jumped in with both feet as Miss Busby finished her soup, put the bowl aside, and began taking notes.

'I am simply not in the habit of imagining every blond-haired, blue-eyed individual to be related,' Marjorie replied.

'And was that the sole resemblance?' Adeline pressed on, undeterred.

'I could not say.'

'Oh.' Adeline's shoulders dropped a little.

'He was reportedly spotted by the river. And as I rarely leave my home, I didn't see him myself,' she continued. 'Very few people did. But word spreads nevertheless.'

'I see,' said Miss Busby, adding, 'I do hope you don't think us terribly nosy; we're simply trying to set Hattie's mind at ease.'

Marjorie eyed the notebook with suspicion.

'It's something of an old schoolteacher's habit,' Miss Busby explained deftly.

Marjorie's thin brows arched, before the edges crinkled up and a smile once more took firm hold.

'You used to teach? How commendable! Whereabouts?'

Adeline emptied her bowl of soup and fidgeted impatiently in her chair as the pair began to discuss the profession they had both loved, swapping tales of the more colourful characters they'd taught over the years.

'You taught Alfred,' Miss Busby guessed. 'And Jimmy, and Lara.'

'I did, and I care for them all as much now as I did then. Dear souls, all,' Marjorie said as she placed her cleared bowl to one side.

'So you don't think it likely this stranger is related to Theodore?' Adeline asked.

'Oh, you must be aware of village life. One careless remark spreads like lightning. Did your pupils play Chinese Whispers in the schoolyard, Miss Busby?'

Miss Busby nodded, understanding at once.

'It is possible, though, isn't it?' Adeline countered. 'Particularly given that Lady Compton was absent from the environs for the birth.'

Marjorie tutted. 'That is a common practice. Would you risk your health to parochial medicine if there were greater resources available to you?'

'Lord Compton did,' Adeline riposted.

'Precisely, and the result was his demise.'

Adeline huffed, realising she'd set her own trap.

'But you are an advocate for Nurse Delaney,' Miss Busby pointed out. 'Who was summoned when Lady Compton returned to the manor with the baby.'

'I am indeed. Her presence in the village that day was a happy accident of Fate. There are few medical professionals in the vicinity,' she added, with a look to Adeline, 'who have her good sense.'

Miss Busby smiled.

'But Lady Compton's age,' Adeline objected. 'No babe in all that time, and then she simply disappears and reappears with one, whilst showing no–'

'Has anyone mentioned this stranger to the police, do you know?' Miss Busby interrupted, nudging Adeline's foot with her own. If Hattie hadn't shared her observations with Marjorie, she didn't think it was their place to do so.

'I very much doubt it,' Marjorie replied, giving them a direct look. 'The police have an entire estate full of suspects; they won't have the time or the inclination to chase a ghost. I assume this is what Hattie is concerned about? That this supposed stranger may have been responsible for the atrocity?'

'It's been preying on her mind since she read about the murder in the newspaper.' Miss Busby nodded.

'Tell her she must not give it a second thought.' Marjorie waved the notion aside as if it were no more than a passing fly on a summer's day.

Miss Busby tried to decipher this. 'The body was found in the grounds, I understand? Early on Friday evening?'

'That much was in the newspaper, Isabelle,' Adeline chided.

Miss Busby suppressed a sigh.

'And did the newspaper mention from which direction the shot was fired?' Marjorie asked.

Miss Busby sat up straight in her chair. 'It did not,' she replied swiftly.

Marjorie looked at Adeline, as if in challenge. 'The shot was fired from the direction of the Manor,' she went on. 'Which is a very good reason to tell Hattie not to concern herself. The mysterious stranger could not have been in any such location.'

'Who told you this?' Adeline demanded. 'If I may

ask,' she conceded a heartbeat later, reaching down to rub at her ankle after another warning tap by Miss Busby.

'The estate manager, Charles Walton, mentioned it. He called in yesterday to see if I was disturbed by the awful events. So thoughtful of him.'

'Another ex-pupil?' Miss Busby guessed with a smile.

'Indeed, and always with such good manners. He has built himself up from a very difficult upbringing.' Majorie nodded.

Miss Busby weighed the implications of this. If Lady Compton was shot from the house, it changed all their previous theories.

'Is Theodore more liked within the estate than his mother?' Miss Busby asked swiftly, placing a calming hand on Adeline's arm.

'Oh, infinitely so. He is a fine young man, he truly cares for the village and those within it.'

'And you think he will inherit it all?' Miss Busby asked, finding herself intrigued.

Marjorie nodded. 'Just as Lord Compton intended he should.'

Miss Busby tilted her head in confusion.

'Lord Compton adored the boy, and made provision in his will for the estate to pass to him when he reached the age of twenty-one.'

'And why didn't it?' Adeline asked.

'Because Lady Compton refused to allow it. She deemed the boy too young and inexperienced. They both agreed that he would take the reins when he reached twenty-five.'

'Which is next month,' Adeline stated.

'Correct,' she agreed.

'And do you believe she was now prepared to give up the estate to her son?' Miss Busby was turning over the facts.

'I doubt anyone thought she would, Theodore included, and how he would handle that has been the cause of much speculation.'

'I imagine it would be,' Adeline said.

'After all, what could he do?' Marjorie continued. 'Set lawyers upon his own mother? The coffers are allegedly empty, so neither could afford to go to law even if they wanted to.'

'So he shot her instead,' Adeline said and received frowns from both the other ladies.

'Why was she so determined to hang on?' Miss Busby asked, ignoring Adeline.

'Any number of reasons, I imagine,' Marjorie replied, her face quite animated. Despite the occasional flare up, she seemed to be enjoying herself. 'And she wouldn't listen to a word of advice from a living soul. She simply didn't trust anyone. Not after her husband's death, at least.'

'And prior to it?' Miss Busby wondered.

Marjorie thought for a moment.

'She was a little less fractious, I suppose, but her husband was a gentle sort and a calming influence.

With that influence removed, her true colours revealed themselves. Although widowhood changes a woman, of course. Some rise to responsibility, some crumble before it, and some, I'm afraid, are irrevocably corrupted by it.'

'And Theodore had to live with this woman every single day,' Adeline observed.

Miss Busby decided to ignore the obvious implications of that. 'Did he love his mother?'

Marjorie paused to consider. 'I believe so. He wouldn't hear a word said against her, although he's intelligent enough to recognise her mistakes. And fortunately for us, unlikely to repeat them.'

'I imagine the police must have a number of questions for him,' Adeline said archly.

'As they have for everyone at the manor.' Marjorie's eyes suddenly glinted behind the spectacles.

'But none of the household staff have been arrested?' Adeline asked.

'Clearly not, or I am sure we wouldn't be having this discussion,' Majorie replied curtly.

Silence fell for a moment. Miss Busby looked down at her brief notes and considered.

'And I should imagine no arrests are likely to be made in the foreseeable future,' she mused.

'You are very astute, Miss Busby. I am rather glad Hattie sent you to me!' Marjorie wasn't quite the grandmotherly type she appeared to be, there was a touch of steel beneath the homely exterior.

Adeline hadn't quite grasped the implication. 'Why

aren't any arrests foreseeable? Are the local police force so incompetent?'

'Not at all. They are thorough and considerate. Cold Compton is served by Stow Police Station,' Marjorie continued, 'although I believe a young hotshot inspector from Oxford has been called in. A Scottish fellow with quite the impressive record of convictions behind him.'

'Ha!' Adeline boomed. 'I think you'll find–'

'But that won't matter,' Miss Busby interjected, 'if I am reading the situation correctly.'

'It most likely will not.' Marjorie smiled. 'Which leads me to believe you are.'

'What?' Adeline looked between the two. 'Why not?'

'Because the murderer, if known, will be protected by the servants and the villagers,' Miss Busby said, puzzling it out. 'And if unknown, will likely remain so by dint of fellow sufferers minding their own business.'

Marjorie gave her an appraising look. 'I believe you are correct.'

'Well, *really*. I cannot imagine how such behaviour could be supported!' Adeline objected strongly. 'Anyone complicit in such criminality ought to hang their heads in shame. And the murderer himself ought to hang. I fail to see how you can possibly accept such a cover up–'

'My dear lady,' Marjorie interrupted, looking as though she thought Adeline anything but, 'if you had lived under the circumstances imposed by a despot such as Lady Compton, you would feel quite differently, I can assure you.'

'What circumstances?' Adeline challenged, her eyes flashing at the thought of the conspiracy.

'We heard Lady Compton permitted washing only to be hung out on certain days,' Miss Busby said, 'and that farm machinery not be used.'

'Hardly crimes to warrant murder,' Adeline scoffed.

'But of course we don't know the full extent of the difficulties you and your neighbours suffered daily at her hands,' Miss Busby went on, and looked to Marjorie.

'She was a tyrant.' Marjorie spoke firmly. 'All our young people have left the village due to her archaic notions and high-handed manner.'

'There is a young woman in your garden as we speak!' Adeline pointed towards Lara. 'And *is* it archaic to value peace and quiet, and the beauty of country views unsullied by rows of smalls blowing in the breeze?'

'The vicar tried to object to her draconian measures, and she harried him from the parish and refused to allow a replacement,' Marjorie retorted firmly. 'God himself has been evicted from our midst. She refused to permit electricity to be supplied to the cottages. Or mains water. One has to use one's own well and boil everything. Machinery is entirely forbidden, as are oil lamps. Any such are confiscated if seen and any 'culprits' who persistently break her rules are evicted. We must only use candles. Her idea was to force us to employ self-sufficiency, although she took advantage of every modern convenience up at the manor. The reality is that she kept us in poverty to keep herself in comfort.'

'Ah. Well.' Adeline shifted awkwardly in her chair. 'That is perhaps rather more… unkind,' she conceded. 'But what about all her charitable deeds in foreign parts? She couldn't have been a *total* monster.'

'Ha,' Marjorie scoffed. 'Posturing and self-satisfaction. You may rest assured that Lady Compton did nothing that would not directly benefit herself. The fact is, she made so many poor decisions that the estate is rumoured to be near bankruptcy, rendering supplies like electricity, mains water and gas completely unaffordable. Not to mention a sadistic desire for power and a pleasure taken in making the *little people* suffer.'

She paused for a moment, looking at Adeline. No objection was forthcoming in this instance.

'What youngster would stay in Cold Compton when other towns and villages offer them so much more?' she continued. 'And of course, their parents suffered greatly when they sought work elsewhere. They had no help on the farms, or assistance in their dotage, and no one to follow in their footsteps. Even the school has closed; there are no pupils left.'

'The school has closed…' Miss Busby echoed the words. 'How appalling. It is almost as though they have given up all hope.'

'Many of them have,' Marjorie replied, suddenly looking tired, and rather sad.

'Wasn't there anyone who could point out the consequences of her decisions?' Miss Busby asked.

'Oh, Charles Walton tried. Endlessly, as he would tell

anyone who would listen over a brandy in The Royal Lion. Before she ordered that closed, too.'

'She shut the school, the church *and* the village pub?' Adeline's eyes widened.

Marjorie nodded gravely.

'Good Lord,' Adeline muttered. 'I'm surprised she lasted as long as she did.'

'Yes, and that it had to come to this,' Marjorie said wistfully, then rose to her feet with some difficulty. 'Well, if you could please excuse me. I believe I am in need of some rest.'

Miss Busby made to help, but Lara noticed the movement at the table and hurried indoors to offer her arm.

'Thank you, dear Lara.' She turned back to them. 'Do give Hattie my best, and tell her she must set her mind at ease. It was a pleasure to meet you, Miss Busby.'

'Indeed,' Miss Busby replied with a smile. 'And a delight to meet you, Miss Townsend.'

'Well,' Adeline remarked as they left the house, 'she might have said it was a pleasure to meet me as well.'

Miss Busby had a smile as she fixed Barnaby's leash.

'The inspector must be told about this,' Adeline went on, rather haughtily. 'If neither villagers nor servants at the Manor can be relied upon to speak up, the culprit may very well get away with murder.'

Miss Busby made towards the gate. 'This is a close-knit community, Adeline. They've clearly been through the wringer. I think it best we leave the police to make their own enquiries from this point.'

'But Isabelle, there is a conspiracy of silence, and it whirls around the young lord–'

'No,' Miss Busby said decisively. 'I absolutely do not condone covering up a murder, if indeed that's what is being done. But that's for the police to discover, not us. We came for Hattie's sake, Adeline, and we can go back and tell her it's extremely doubtful the stranger would be able to shoot Lady Compton, unseen, from the Manor and so he could not be the culprit. There is therefore no reason to carry this tale to the police. And our involvement in the matter must now rest.'

## CHAPTER 6

'Well,' Adeline complained as they closed the gate to Midwinter Cottage behind them and made for the Rolls, 'if you feel able to sleep soundly in your bed knowing a murderer is at large, Isabelle, then who am I to–'

'I can't,' a quiet voice said from behind them.

Adeline jumped with a gasp. Miss Busby turned in surprise to see Lara behind them. She must have hurried from the cottage to catch up.

'I'm sorry, I didn't mean to startle you,' she said, her voice soft in the stillness of the warm afternoon. 'But I heard what you said, and I've hardly slept since the murder.'

'Oh, you poor soul.' Miss Busby's eyes shone with concern.

The young woman nodded, then looked down, biting her lower lip, her pretty face pale and troubled.

'Is there something we can do to help?' Miss Busby asked gently.

Lara looked up. 'It's just, we don't see many people

from outside the village. Other than the police, now, of course. And they're... well, the inspector, he's quite...'

'Gruff,' Adeline supplied. 'And about as useful as a wicker canoe, at times.'

Lara looked at her, then nodded. 'I'm not sure Miss Townsend was quite right in all she said. Not that I meant to listen, it's just...'

'What do you think she may be mistaken about?' Miss Busby asked, noting the shadows under Lara's blue-green eyes.

'She thinks the police won't learn anything because everyone will close ranks, but I'm worried that...that...' Her voice caught and Miss Busby reflexively reached into her bag for a handkerchief.

'Goodness me, whatever is it?' she asked, passing it to the young woman.

'Oh, thank you. I'm sure I'm just being silly, but...' she stammered, visibly trying to stiffen her lip and carry on. 'But I'm frightened the police are going to arrest Theo–' She swallowed a sob. 'Lord Compton, I mean. The inspector from Oxford was asking so many questions this morning, much more than the sergeant from Stow yesterday. Everyone in the village is talking about it, and how the Oxford man is very... that is, he's rather...'

Adeline took a breath; Miss Busby jumped in to cut her off.

'We've known Inspector McKay for some time,' she explained. 'He can be rather brusque at first, but you mustn't take it personally. It's just his way, but he is scrupulously fair.'

'Oh, I didn't realise you knew him…' She hesitated, suddenly wary.

'Indeed, Miss Busby has practically solved two murders for him. She is quite the accomplished sleuth,' Adeline sailed on. 'So whatever is upsetting you, you must let her help. Can we offer you a lift home? We oughtn't stand in the road.' She moved to open the back door of the Rolls for her. The girl looked startled. Miss Busby couldn't blame her; Adeline gathered momentum quickly once she formed an idea in her head.

'I…' Lara looked around, then at the car. 'Thank you.' She moved forwards but Barnaby jumped in before either could stop him. Lara smiled and climbed in beside him, then shuffled along to make room for Miss Busby, who decided not to remark on the lack of his blanket, as he was now perfectly dry.

'I'll be chauffeur,' Adeline said, getting in to start the engine.

Lara turned to Miss Busby. 'I was afraid…' She paused for a moment, collecting her thoughts. 'It's just that there's no one else, you see,' she suddenly blurted out.

Miss Busby waited; she had learned in her years of teaching that silence was often far more effective than direct questions. Some people simply couldn't bear to let silence run on.

'That is,' Lara continued, 'there are lots of people who could have killed Lady Compton, but there's no one quite as convenient to blame as Theo. And I'm worried no one will *say* anything to support him.'

'There, you see?' Adeline looked over her shoulder to Miss Busby in triumph. '*This* is what happens when people refuse to speak up. You poor girl,' she said to Lara. 'You have done the right thing in telling us.'

'What makes you think Theodore is more convenient to blame than anyone else?' Miss Busby asked.

'Well, he has the most to gain from Lady Compton's death, I suppose,' she answered softly. 'And everyone knows he's far nicer and far cleverer than she is…was, I mean, but I don't think anyone will speak up for him.'

'Speak up for him in what way?' Miss Busby pressed, the back of her neck tingling with a mix of excitement and dread as she waited for the answer.

'The staff up at the manor, they'll all speak for one another, for when her ladyship was shot. It was in the afternoon, and they'd have been working together. But Theo spends most of his time alone…' She sniffed, and rubbed at her eyes, as if to stop fresh tears from forming. 'I'm sorry, it's all just so awful, but what if no one will stand witness for him? As they would for…'

'As they would for each other?' Miss Busby remembered Marjorie's words, and the tingle now shot all the way down her spine.

The poor girl nodded, then the tears burst into sobs. 'What if they allow him to be blamed? He'll hang and everyone will be free of the Comptons once and for all… they've all lived in fear for so long, but he cared for them.

Even if he couldn't truly do very much. And he would never kill her... not even...'

The last muffled words were lost as she buried her face in the handkerchief, but Miss Busby understood.

'Was Lord Compton actually at the Manor the afternoon Lady Compton was killed?' Miss Busby persevered.

'No, but...' sobs escaped her and she struggled to contain them.

'Where is your cottage, Lara?' Adeline said kindly as she came to the end of the track circling the green.

'It's the old dairy cottage,' she replied in a hoarse whisper, still sniffing into the handkerchief. 'Near the manor, the lane on the right just before the gateway.'

Adeline put her foot down and they sailed along the tarmac.

'Do you really believe the people here would allow Theodore Compton to hang just because he's the Lord of the Manor?' Miss Busby asked.

Lara sighed. 'I hope they wouldn't but...well... if they had to choose one of their own, or...'

'What if he wasn't a lord?' Adeline said, watching Lara in the rear-view mirror.

'What?' Lara gasped. 'What do you mean?'

As they approached the lane towards the manor, a tall, thickset man in smart tweeds and a tattersall waistcoat stalked into the road ahead of them, his hand held high. Adeline hadn't been paying attention and slammed on the brakes. Barnaby slid to the floor and looked quite put out.

'This is private property.' The man leaned over the car to speak to Adeline as she wound her window down.

'So is my car,' Adeline retorted. 'Kindly remove your hand.'

He stood up and stepped back, a frown on his aquiline face. He had sandy hair brushed back from a high forehead, thick brows, and brown eyes glinting with intelligence.

'Mr Walton.' Lara opened the rear door and got out. 'These ladies have kindly given me a lift. They are friends of Miss Townsend.'

The frown barely lifted. 'Are they now? I've never seen them before. I suppose they just chanced to visit the village so soon after a murder occurred?'

'They were here on another matter,' Lara said, her face suddenly set in determination. 'Miss Busby was also a schoolteacher.'

'And a busybody to boot, eh?' Walton said.

Lara's cheeks flushed.

'You are Charles Walton?' Miss Busby climbed out of the car while Barnaby growled from the safety of the back seat. 'Miss Townsend mentioned you. I believe you to be the estate manager? She said you were always well-mannered. Perhaps that only applies when it suits you?'

He eyed her quietly, then nodded, abashed. 'Please accept my apologies, madam, but after the recent tragedy, you can understand that I am keen to defend his lordship's privacy.'

Miss Busby gave him the sort of stare only a teacher can. 'Very well, and I hope the police catch the culprit shortly.'

'There is a police inspector at the manor at this very moment, madam,' he replied.

That gave her pause, and Adeline leaned over in her seat. 'We really must be going,' she said. 'Lara?'

'I...I think I'll go to the big house and speak with his lordship,' she said. 'I can walk.' She was already edging away.

'Very well,' Miss Busby said and slid into the front seat of the Rolls. 'I hope we will see you again, Lara,' she called after the young woman.

'Yes, and thank you.' She waved and extended her stride almost into a run along the road, her long red skirt flowing with her movement.

'Adeline,' Miss Busby said as she pulled the door closed. 'We must not be seen by Inspector McKay. If you drive at your customary pace, we'll be gone before he can catch sight of us.'

'I don't see why we couldn't just go and speak to him,' Adeline complained as she started the engine and crashed the gears into reverse.

'Because someone may see us.'

'And what if they did?' She turned the car in the narrow lane, nosing it into the hedges, forward and back before aiming down the way they'd come.

'Then they certainly won't talk to us any further.'

'Does it matter?' Adeline was dismissive, but put her foot down on the accelerator anyway. 'If we aren't...

Oh!' She turned to Miss Busby and beamed. 'So we *are* going to return?'

'Eyes front, Adeline,' Miss Busby instructed, before admitting, 'I don't know, but I see no reason to limit our options.'

'Well, you've certainly changed your tune. You were quite cross with me earlier,' Adeline pointed out.

'Yes, but that was before–'

'...*That's for the police to discover,* you said,' Adeline quoted, with unnecessary emphasis.

'And so it is. But if the villagers and servants are truly falsifying alibis for one another, yet refuse one for Theodore, then he is in peril. An innocent man must not face the noose simply because he is higher born.'

'If they are all falsifying alibis, no-one will believe any of them,' Adeline pointed out. 'Not even when they are genuine. And anyway, he may not be higher born.'

'No, but as far as they're concerned, he is. It may not be anything sinister,' she was quick to emphasise, lest Adeline became carried away. 'It's more than likely they've all had to stick together for so long that they don't know any other way. Nothing unites people like a common enemy, after all.'

'Unless one is of a different class, apparently,' Adeline sniffed, before wrenching the car to a halt as a roan horse pulling a trap appeared around the bend.

'I think it would be more of a reflection of the way they were treated by the late Lady Compton,' Miss

Busby replied as the horse trotted towards them. 'You can't blame them for–'

But Adeline wasn't listening. 'I don't see how playing fast and loose with the truth for one's own ends could be seen as anything *but* sinister,' she interrupted. 'And did you hear how easily Lara lied?'

'When she said we weren't visiting Marjorie Townsend about the murder?' she replied. 'But it was the truth— we were there about the stranger.'

'Hmph.' Adeline didn't agree. 'And she was eavesdropping all the time we were talking.'

Barnaby popped his paws up on the back window to warily watch the beautifully groomed horse as it trotted past the car. The driver, a rather grizzled old man in a dark tunic and tattered cap, regarded Adeline with a wary eye in the exact same manner as the dog.

'Well really, you'd think we were some sort of invaders,' she muttered. Once man and horse had turned the bend, Adeline thrust her foot back down and they soon reached the turning for the main road. 'Where are we going? The station at Stow?'

'No, back to Lavender Cottage.'

Adeline turned to her in surprise. 'Aren't we going to speak to the police? If nothing else, we have uncovered great moral turpitude, Isabelle!'

'Nonsense, Adeline.'

'But everyone is lying! And Marjorie Townsend, for all her moralising, was dismissive of the whole idea of even seeking the culprit,' Adeline protested. 'If we don't tell the police, no one else will!'

'It does seem that way, I agree, but we must be careful - we only have conjecture at present,' Miss Busby reminded her. 'And I may be seeing Inspector McKay this evening,' she admitted, rather reluctantly, hoping Adeline wouldn't try to–

'Where? What time? I shall come with you.'

Miss Busby sighed. 'I think he may be going to Rowena's for her drinks party,' she explained. 'It's tonight, at eight.'

'Rowena who?'

'The woman who has moved into Mary's old cottage.'

'Oh, *her*. Hardly a woman, Isabelle. More of a petulant youth.'

'She must be in her mid-twenties!' Miss Busby objected.

'Yes, a youth. At least as far as you and I are concerned.' Adeline doubled down.

Miss Busby felt she could have done without the reminder.

'Very well then,' Adeline conceded with a dramatic sigh as she turned the car towards Little Minton. 'What time shall I meet you?'

Miss Busby thought carefully for a moment. If she admitted she'd prefer Adeline didn't go, it would hurt her feelings. But if another task needed attending to at the same time…

'Actually, I wonder if you might take on something more pressing,' she suggested, 'and drive to Spring

Meadows to tell Hattie and Enid all that Marjorie and Lara told us.'

'I'd hardly call that pressing,' Adeline scoffed.

Miss Busby's mind churned through the gears, as did the Rolls as it tackled a steep incline.

'If we're to go back to Cold Compton and perhaps talk to Lara in more detail, it would be useful to have Enid and Hattie's opinions on the matter.'

Adeline considered. 'Very well,' she relented, brightening as they crested the hill and picked up speed on the other side. 'I shall go to Spring Meadows at seven, and bring them both to drinks at eight. *Excellent* idea, Isabelle.'

# CHAPTER 7

Miss Busby woke with a start at the sound of a car horn. She quickly rose from her armchair and went to look through the sitting room window. Several gleaming vehicles were already parked in the narrow lane outside Lavender Cottage, and the newest arrival had nowhere to go. Unperturbed, the driver – a young woman in a striking silver sequinned dress and matching headband – simply turned the engine off and hopped out, laughing, as she abandoned the vehicle in the middle of the road.

*A girl after Adeline's heart*, Miss Busby thought with a wry smile.

Looking at the clock on the mantel, she saw that it was already seven forty, and her light doze after tea had turned into an hour long nap. Annoyed with herself, she hurried upstairs to change; she didn't want to be late as she was hoping to catch Inspector McKay before Adeline's arrival.

Barnaby eyed her with suspicion as she returned to the living room looking rather smart in a dusky pink twin set, maroon skirt, and her single row of pearls. She had even added matching drop earrings that Richard had recently bought her.

'I won't be long,' she told the little terrier.

Barnaby hung his head, his stout little shoulders drooping, his brown eyes as doleful as only a dog's can be.

Miss Busby looked at the clock again. It was not quite eight.

'Quickly, then,' she sighed, fetching his leash from the hall and opening the front door. 'Once around the common and then home.'

She kept a watchful eye out, lest more of Rowena's guests arrived in powerful motorcars - several of which were now parked haphazardly in the cart track circling the green. She spotted the sedate grey Alvis belonging to Inspector McKay as he crawled slowly around the track, before finding a spot some distance away.

'Well done, Barnaby.' Miss Busby bent to ruffle his ears. 'The walk was an excellent idea! We shall have him all to ourselves for a moment.'

Arranging herself on a direct path to intercept, she met him as he walked toward the leeward cottages.

'Miss Busby!' He looked up, surprised. 'You look very nice.'

'As do you, Inspector.' She smiled.

Casually dressed in cream trousers and a crisply pressed white shirt open at the neck, he looked rather more dashing than his customary grey suit allowed. His red hair was freshly trimmed, his face clean-shaven, green eyes sharply alert in the evening sunshine.

'Thank you.' He cleared his throat awkwardly. 'Are you going somewhere?'

'Yes. I'm glad to bump into you though. How were things at Cold Compton Manor today?'

He narrowed his eyes. 'What happened to being "resolute in staying out of the whole business"?' he asked.

Miss Busby wished people would stop quoting her. 'Circumstances rather drew me in, I'm afraid. I had lunch there with a fellow retired teacher.'

He smiled. 'That must have been pleasant for you both.'

The man had a fondness for teachers, she knew, his mother having been of the profession.

'It was, and most illuminating,' Miss Busby replied.

His brows narrowed at that. 'I haven't heard from your friend, the nurse,' he added, glancing down as Barnaby trotted over to see if he was in possession of any biscuits. 'I checked my messages at the station before I left. You mentioned she had something to tell me?'

'Ah, yes, but I think it moot now.'

'How so?'

'Given that Lady Compton was shot from the direction of the manor,' Miss Busby explained, 'it's unlikely Nurse Delaney's concern will prove to be relevant.'

He was silent for a moment, his face showing surprise, then annoyance, then resignation so quickly Miss Busby had to look down to hide her amusement.

'I don't recall any mention of direction being made in the newspaper report,' he said.

Miss Busby was delighted he seemed to be skipping his usual disapproval and dire warnings regarding the consequence of "civilians" meddling in such matters. *Third time's a charm*, she thought, thinking back to his reactions on the last two cases they'd had in common.

'My counterpart in Cold Compton is rather well informed,' she said. 'You of all people, Inspector, should know never to underestimate the resourcefulness of a teacher.'

'Aye, perhaps, but I'm afraid your friend has overestimated her resourcefulness in this instance,' he countered. 'Local police may have assumed the direction of the shot to be from the house given the position of the body, and bandied such assumptions about,' he added with irritation, 'but forensic examination made it clear that Lady Compton was shot from the woods bordering the grounds.'

It was Miss Busby's turn to look surprised.

The inspector's eyes suddenly sparked amusement. He seemed to rather enjoy being on the front foot. It was, she realised, the first time he'd got the advantage of her in an investigation. 'I led the forensic investigation myself,' he continued, a rare note of pride in his voice as he stood a little straighter. 'The murderer wanted us to *think* the shot came from the manor, but the blood splatter on the grass tells a different story.'

Miss Busby's heart sank. If the shot had come from the woods, then any one of the villagers could have been responsible. As indeed could the mystery stranger. They were back to square one.

Spurred on by her continued silence, the inspector added, 'Rearranging the body after death was a clever move on the part of the murderer, but not clever enough to fool the eye of a trained professional.'

'Goodness, yes. I see.'

The inspector blinked, as if he'd been expecting something more. It was his turn to look thoughtful, before asking, 'Why would the direction of the shot have been relevant to Nurse Delaney's information?'

'Oh, I ought to let her tell you herself really, but—'

'Alastair! What are you doing out there? You're late!' Rowena's shrill voice echoed along the lane. Miss Busby turned to see the distant figure of her new near neighbour waving impatiently from her front garden. Dressed in a carmine-coloured frock, far shorter at the knee and considerably lower at the neck than Miss Busby would have advised, her bright jewellery glittered at her neck, hands, and ears in the last rays of the evening sun. *The girl is a veritable magnet for magpies*, Miss Busby thought, *or perhaps something of a magpie herself.* She turned back to the inspector and arched a disapproving brow.

He reddened as he waved a hand in acknowledgement. 'An old friend from my university days,' he muttered in explanation. 'I ought to be getting along. But neither you nor Nurse Delaney should concern yourselves,' he assured her. 'Matters at Cold Compton will be resolved shortly. First thing tomorrow, in fact.'

'You're ready to make an arrest?' Miss Busby asked in surprise.

A riff of jazz music drifted on the breeze. The inspector made a point of checking the watch on his wrist.

'But… who?' Miss Busby asked.

He smiled with a glint of mischief in his eyes. 'Have a lovely evening, Miss Busby.' And with that he strode determinedly towards the cottage, now lively with music and light.

Miss Busby watched him in astonishment. In previous cases, she and Adeline had been leaps and bounds ahead of the man.

*Well, it only makes sense that he's improving,* she reminded herself. He'd been new to the role last December, and was now more settled and proving his competency. Perhaps her soul searching as to whether or not they ought to become involved had been misplaced. He was clearly doing perfectly well without her.

But did he know about the stranger? Or the fact the villagers may have been colluding to fabricate alibis?

The sound of yet another motorcar approaching distracted her from her thoughts; she called Barnaby and turned on her heel. Arriving back at Lavender Cottage, she went through to the kitchen to find Pud impatiently awaiting her.

She was just arranging cold cuts onto plates for the animals when a loud rap on the front door sounded.

'I had to park miles away!' Adeline announced as she came through.

'Good evening, Adeline,' Miss Busby greeted her with a smile.

'It was not "miles" at all, it was 500 yards at most,' Enid admonished from behind. 'And if I can manage it, so can you, Adeline. Isabelle, you look lovely,' she observed, with a tad more surprise than Miss Busby appreciated.

*I really must make an effort more often*, she thought.

'As do you both,' she returned the compliment. Adeline had plumped for a dark-green and gold dress, ankle-length and elegantly cut to make the best of her generous curves, whilst Enid had chosen a peacock blue blouse with a saffron-yellow skirt and matching silk tunic.

'The party is in full swing, I hear,' Adeline remarked as the three of them walked the short distance to Rowena's cottage.

'Yes, and when she said "drinks" I didn't imagine anything on quite this scale,' Miss Busby said, glancing at the cars lining the lane. 'It's a wonder they all fit in.'

'They don't!' Adeline complained, having to turn sideways at one point to pass a car.

Mary's old cottage, like Miss Busby's, was a modest two-bedroom affair with a low thatched roof and pretty lattice windows. When no one responded to their polite knock on the open front door, they walked through into the hallway to see almost every inch of space packed with gaily dressed young men and women chatting animatedly. A large gramophone on the dining table was responsible for the music that emanated into the garden and beyond. They continued out to the back in search of their hostess and a quieter spot.

Enid took a sharp intake of breath as she noted a group of youngsters dancing at the bottom of the garden.

'Mary's lawn will be ruined,' she remarked with horror.

'Nonsense. It's perfectly dry. And look, they've removed their heels.' Adeline pointed to a row of carelessly abandoned shoes by the rose bed.

Miss Busby reached for Enid's hand and gave it a quick squeeze before letting go. She knew Enid missed Mary dearly and that this would somehow seem rather disrespectful.

'Mary liked young people; she would have loved seeing the place so full of life,' Miss Busby remarked.

'Perhaps on rare occasions,' Enid retorted. 'And I do hope this is a rare occasion.'

Miss Busby hoped the same, but didn't say so. 'Look, there is sherry, and glasses.' She tried a diversion. An outdoor table set up under the kitchen window was covered with a fresh white cloth and a myriad of bottles and glasses of all sizes.

'Never mind the sherry, there's a rather expensive cognac,' Adeline noted, before a pretty piece of carved marble caught her eye. 'Good Lord, is that the bird bath I gave Mary? I do hope it won't be knocked over in this crowd.' She marched off to commandeer a young man to move it to a safer spot down in the orchard.

'It looks as if we are expected to help ourselves,' Miss Busby said and poured two small sherries, one of which she passed to Enid. 'Shall we raise a glass to Mary?'

Enid did so. 'May she rest in peace,' she murmured.

Neither Rowena nor the inspector, Miss Busby noted with a flicker of concern, were anywhere to be seen.

'There don't appear to be any vacant seats,' she remarked, just as Rowena finally appeared from the kitchen.

'Miss Burby! I didn't imagine for a moment you would actually come.' She laughed, before declaring, 'Vicky, Kelvin, do get up. Make way for the olds,' she demanded of two startled young people. They instantly sprang from their chairs under the magnolia, then gave polite grins before amiably wandering off.

Miss Busby didn't have time to object to being labelled an "old" before she was ushered to a wrought-iron chair, with Enid at her side.

'Oh good,' Rowena carried on. 'You've got drinks. There are nibbles coming soon. I've ordered them from the tea rooms in Little Minton.'

'It's not Miss Burby, it's Miss Busby,' she managed, as the girl finally drew breath. 'Enid, this is Rowena. Rowena, this is Mrs Enid Wheatley, a great friend of the former owner of your cottage.'

'Who will no doubt be turning in her grave at the state of her lawn,' Enid remarked pointedly.

Rowena was momentarily stunned into silence, before she gave a sparkling trill of laughter. 'Well, I shall have the gardener fix it tomorrow. Will that suffice?'

'I suppose it will have to.' Enid aimed sharp eyes at the young woman, looking her up and down. Miss Busby braced herself for comments regarding the length, or lack thereof, of the dress, but Enid surprised her by simply nodding approvingly. 'That is a very attractive dress. Enjoy your youth while you can, it does not last long.' She glanced at the girl's left hand, and asked, 'Are you living here alone?'

'Yes, for now, and it's only rented anyway. I'm rusticating,' she spoke archly, then glanced up, over their heads. 'Oh, *Lord*.' She was looking into the kitchen. 'Alistair's surrounded by the pack. Alistair!' she called, darting off as swiftly as she'd appeared.

Miss Busby twisted in her chair to see Inspector McKay surrounded by four young ladies, all apparently hanging on his every word.

'Whirlwind of a girl,' Enid pronounced. 'Her manners need work, but there's a promising spark there. You shall have your hands full with that one, Isabelle.'

'*I* shan't,' she replied, watching as Rowena cut through the other young women and took the inspector by the arm to lead him away. 'But others might.' Lucy sprang to mind. 'Why isn't Hattie with you?'

'She was tired and didn't feel up to it. There had been quite the list of minor ailments requiring investigation,' Enid explained, before taking a sip of sherry. 'We dropped her at home after Adeline told us about your adventures. Strange sort of village, Cold Compton. I'm not at all surprised they are closing ranks. I suspect whoever killed the woman shan't have to buy their own drinks ever again.'

'Possibly…it's rather difficult to say,' Miss Busby replied hesitantly. Enid looked at her sharply.

'You don't think so?'

'I'm starting to wonder if there might be rather more to it all... Oh, here's Adeline now.'

'Didn't you pour me one?' she asked, looking at their glasses.

'I wasn't sure what you would like. Perhaps something non-alcoholic?' Miss Busby suggested, thinking of the Rolls and the unusual amount of traffic around the narrow country lanes.

'I shall only have a small one, Isabelle, don't fuss.'

A glass of rich amber cognac in hand, Adeline returned to join them and sat in the remaining chair.

For a moment all three sipped contemplatively, watching the young people dance as the sun disappeared behind the orchard and hills beyond.

New voices rang out from the kitchen, along with the clattering and clanking of plates, before the delicious smell of savoury treats filled the air.

'Evenin' Miss! Whatchoo' doin' here?'

Miss Busby turned in surprise at the familiar voice, to see young Dennis, the local postman, smiling widely at her from beneath his tousled brown curls. 'Your dog int' here, is he?' he added, looking around nervously.

He was wearing a wrinkled white shirt, a badly tied red tie and grey shorts that came to just below the knees. His grey socks were rumpled round his ankles. He didn't look much different from when she'd taught him in his school days.

'How lovely to see you, Dennis. And no, Barnaby is at home. Rowena is allergic to dogs.'

'Good,' he declared. 'I brought the food up in the post van. Maggie from the tea rooms asked me to.' He puffed his chest out proudly. 'She gave me sandwiches and vanilla slices for my trouble.'

'Wonderful.' Miss Busby smiled up at him. She knew vanilla slices were his favourite.

He looked around the garden, then dragged fingers through his untidy curls. 'Have you seen Miss Rowena?' he asked eagerly.

Miss Busby narrowed her eyes. An attractive young woman in a short frock wasn't good for young postmen, in her opinion. 'Her attentions are occupied, I believe. Oughtn't you to be taking the van back to the post office?'

'I s'pose,' he sighed.

'I suggest you do so, before your sandwiches wilt.'

'Yes, Miss. Night, Miss,' he said, trudging back towards the kitchen dejectedly.

'Isabelle,' Enid chided.

Adeline laughed. 'That was rather stern.'

'It's no laughing matter. I shall never get my post in the mornings if Dennis is constantly patting his hair and putting his eyes back in his head,' she told them.

The smell of food attracted the young dancers, and they soon began drifting toward the kitchen, leaving a welcome moment of peace in their wake.

Miss Busby took the opportunity to tell Adeline and Enid about Lady Compton's body being moved, and the inspector's hint at an impending arrest.

'Well, I wish we'd known sooner. We have just told Hattie it couldn't have been her mysterious stranger!' Adeline remarked. 'She'll think us enormously incompetent when she hears the very opposite is now true.'

'Yes, the timing was rather unfortunate,' Miss Busby admitted.

'If he's about to arrest someone, Hattie's information will be redundant,' Enid pointed out. 'He clearly believes he has found the culprit.'

'Hm,' said Miss Busby, trying not to think about the fact that the inspector had initially arrested the wrong person on two occasions prior.

'He's never beaten us to the murderer yet,' Adeline noted.

'It's not a race,' Miss Busby said. 'But I do wonder… why would the murderer go to the trouble of making it look as if Lady Compton was shot from the direction of the manor?'

'To *frame* one of them in the house, is that how you say it, Enid?' Adeline asked.

'It is exactly that.' Enid, who had a fondness for American crime novels, nodded authoritatively.

'Well, it explains why the inspector was up at the manor today,' Adeline continued.

'But he won't know about the locals fabricating alibis,' Miss Busby remarked, 'or that they might not do so for Theodore. The young lord may be the only one without an alibi.'

'That is assuming there truly is some sort of conspiracy going on,' Enid warned, adding, 'Have you met anyone from the manor?'

'Yes, Charles Walton, the estate manager,' Adeline said.

'What do you know of him?' Enid asked.

'Miss Townsend said he had built himself up from a difficult position,' Miss Busby answered. 'I expect there's a butler and probably a housekeeper too.'

'I would wager the Rolls that the lower staff have given each other alibis,' Adeline said. 'There are class distinctions between the positions, as you well know.'

'I shouldn't think there are many staff *left* up there, the way things have reportedly been mismanaged. And would any of them have access to a shotgun?' Enid mused. 'Or the faintest idea how to use one?'

'Well, I very much doubt the housekeeper–' Miss Busby tried.

'It's the *principle* of the thing,' Adeline insisted, warming to her theme. 'It fits perfectly with how Marjorie described things. The murderer was trying to protect himself and his compatriots not only by killing the woman, but also by turning the body around. There's no point avenging them all from a cruel mistress and then leaving them in danger of the noose, is there? And there's no point in *our* telling the inspector about them fabricating alibis now; if he has the arrest planned, then I doubt anything we say will change his mind. No, we shall do best to wait and see who he hauls in, and then act!' She looked around. 'Where is he, anyway?'

'Inside. Rowena has him,' Enid said.

Adeline thought for a moment. 'But what about Lucy?'

'Indeed.' Miss Busby was tight-lipped.

Adeline pushed the sleeves of her elegant green and gold dress up a little way towards her elbows. 'Enid, hold my cognac,' she said, passing her drink across and stalking towards the cottage.

'Oh, dear.' Miss Busby sighed, rising to her feet to follow.

'It might be best to leave her,' Enid said, looking down at Adeline's glass. 'That way you can't be held responsible for any upset. But perhaps, while you're up, you wouldn't mind bringing me one of these?'

Miss Busby, momentarily torn, sighed and took Enid's empty glass back to the drinks table, returning with a fresh glass of a very conservative amount of cognac in exchange.

Enid took a sip and smiled.

'I really ought to rescue Rowena,' Miss Busby fretted, looking over her shoulder towards the kitchen.

'Nonsense, the girl is clearly capable of looking after herself. And it will do Adeline good to meet her match.'

'Poor Lucy, though,' Miss Busby mused sadly. 'I thought she and the inspector were rather a lovely match. Richard said they've seen each other several times since the party.'

'Best not to get too involved where matters of the heart are concerned,' Enid cautioned. She took another sip of the cognac, closing her eyes as she savoured the flavour. 'This really is delicious. You ought to try some, Isabelle.'

'No, thank you.' Miss Busby gave a small shudder. 'I fell foul of brandy at Lannister House in the spring and am in no hurry to repeat the process.'

Enid smiled, before inquiring after Richard's health, adding, 'I haven't seen him in an age.'

'I've hardly seen him myself,' Miss Busby replied with a sigh. 'He's suffering terribly with his arthritis.'

'Cruel affliction. I'm beginning to feel it myself in the hips. Cook brings Mr Waterhouse henbane and hemlock, it eases the joints. I'll ask her for some for Richard.'

'Aren't they rather poisonous?' Miss Busby asked, alarmed.

'Only if you don't know what you're doing.' Enid glanced down at her wristwatch. 'I oughtn't be back too late. Mr Waterhouse has his heart set on defeating Mrs Hopper and her sister in tomorrow evening's bridge tournament. I shall need my wits about me in the morning. He has several practice rounds and a lengthy warm-up in mind.'

Miss Busby contemplated a somewhat risqué rejoinder, but decided against it. She also decided against any further sherry.

'Well, that's given them both something to think about,' Adeline announced, returning to the duo and swiftly finishing her drink.

'What happened?' Miss Busby asked with a sinking feeling.

'The young madam's nose is out of joint, that's what. I addressed the inspector and asked after Lucy's health, and work, as well as enquiring as to her whereabouts this evening. His cheeks turned as red as his hair, and Rowena's brows shot skyward. She had eyes like thunderclouds when I left. I think it might perhaps be time we headed home,' she added, rather shiftily, gathering their glasses and returning them to the table.

Enid chuckled. 'The romantic lives of the young can be rather convoluted. Do you know, I think that cognac may have given me an idea...' she added as they made their retreat.

'Did you have some?' Adeline asked, surprised.

'Yes, it was very pleasant; rather rich, and sweet with honey tones. I wonder if it might be nice to have some hives at Spring Meadows...'

Miss Busby raised a brow.

'For cognac?' Adeline asked, confused.

'I was thinking more for porridge. Why not visit the young beekeeper tomorrow?' They left the cottage and stood together for a moment in the pale light of the harvest moon. 'I shall be busy with bridge practice,' Enid continued, 'and I'm rather tired, but if you went to chat with her alone, away from interfering estate managers and the like, I wonder if you might find her rather more...illuminating.'

Miss Busby considered. Things had certainly changed – this business with the body having been moved, and unanswered questions regarding Theodore's parentage. A further chat to Lara surely couldn't hurt, and the young woman would no doubt relish the extra income from her honey.

'Yes, I suppose we might,' she replied.

Adeline grinned. 'You can never go wrong with a decent cognac!'

# CHAPTER 8

Miss Busby felt as though she'd done an entire day's work by eight o'clock the next morning. Having put her washing in to soak when she'd got home from the party, she'd woken early to rinse and mangle it before breakfast, pegging it out on the line while the birds sang and the sun broke through the dawn mist. Pud had ambled out to check for mice in the hedge at the bottom of the garden, but Barnaby hadn't stirred until she'd come in to make tea and spread butter and jam on toast - a firm favourite of his (particularly strawberry.)

She shared a slice with him at her old wooden table in the garden, a long cardigan over her dress as she sat and enjoyed the tranquillity of the village. It had felt rather different last night, as though the modern world had intruded with all its raucous energy; full of music and laughter and youth, but it appeared the youth in question were not early risers, and all was back to normal this morning. There was a balance, she thought, between the old ways and the new. Quiet little Bloxford was unlikely to change much, despite Rowena and her frenetic friends. Cold Compton had to embrace some of the changing world, albeit in the country way – choosing what was needed to lighten the load rather than indulging in passing fads and fripperies.

She let her gaze drift to the orchard beyond the garden. The autumn apples were ripe and ready to harvest. She ought to collect some of the windfalls for pies and possibly a crumble. She was even contemplating homemade apple brandy when Pud flushed a startled pheasant through the hedge and into the garden. Barnaby flew into a frenzy, little legs propelling him forward, barking with excitement. His jaws closed just inches from the bird's long tail as it flapped its way to safety, squawking in protest.

Pud returned to his mousing duties, unperturbed, as Barnaby returned jauntily to her side. The bird had got Miss Busby thinking. She took her breakfast dishes into the kitchen, then fetched her notebook and pen from the davenport desk and settled into her comfortable armchair by the fireplace. She'd made some brief notes last night, as the music had kept her awake, and she turned to them now. She wrote at the head of a fresh page: *Lady Compton's Murder.*

Then she continued on to a new paragraph;

*Lady Compton was shot in the afternoon, but not found until evening. (Shots were not unusual in daytime on the estate, but did the household hear it?). The shot came from the direction of the woods, but her body was turned to* look as if shot from the manor house. Why? To implicate a member of the household? Or to protect a villager?*

She made a subheading: *Suspects.*

She paused to think. The people she and Adeline had met yesterday weren't exactly suspects. But they might know something.

*Miss Marjorie Townsend*, she wrote, *retired schoolteacher. Knows everybody and is a 'leader' of sorts in the village. Would she have incited murder?* Miss Busby stopped and smiled at such a ridiculous idea, then continued writing. *Marjorie was keen to dismiss the idea that the mysterious stranger could be involved, yet likely knows Lady Compton's secret, and if the stranger is indeed the boy's father, then Theo is not the late Lord Compton's child either. So Theo is not a lord, nor can he inherit the estate. Are they all trying to protect Theo? If so, from what? The secret of his birth? Or worse, the murder of his 'mother'? This would refute Lara's fears that they would not protect him – unless she knows he truly did murder Lady C.*

She sighed - it was all questions and conjecture. And rather a lot of writing.

*Lord Theodore Compton*, she continued. *Currently the most likely suspect. Not at the Manor the afternoon of the murder. Sighted briefly, nothing known other than the question mark over his birth and he appears to be thought well of.*

Then: *Lara. A very pretty girl. There aren't many youngsters left in the village. Plus, her cottage is very close to the manor and she expressed a great deal of concern for him. Could she and Theo be sweethearts?*

*Alfred Brownlow,* she continued, after a quick pause to ease a twinge of tension in her wrist – *Blacksmith. Appeared capable and strong, caring and protective. Lara is his niece. He would likely know how to handle a shotgun.*

*Jimmy Hooper, ex-gamekeeper turned semi-ethical poacher.* She paused, looking down at his name as the image of the bird flew in her mind once more.

'Who would have been shooting on the estate if not the gamekeeper/poacher?' she asked Barnaby as he plopped himself onto the rug beside the unlit fire. 'Marjorie didn't say anything about a replacement, and she said Jimmy still "thinned the herd", which I suppose means no one else is doing it.'

She tapped the top of the pen on her chin for a moment, then continued:

Motives - *Theo.* She underlined his name.

*Lady Compton had prevented Theo from taking over the estate. Did he want to take over? It was run down, if rumours were to be believed, so if he were of a responsible nature, he probably would. His 25th birthday is next month,* she added. *Is that relevant? Possibly. Has he met the stranger, and is this man his real father? This affects Theo's whole life. But if Theo were a killer, why not shoot the stranger who jeopardised his inheritance?*

*If Lady C is not Theo's mother, she has been lying to him all his life. And he may loathe her for all her cruel acts. Would he now have less compunction about killing her? Is it the reason he killed her? Or did the stranger incite him into killing her for his own reasons?*

She paused once more, stretching her hand and hoping arthritis wasn't hovering on her own horizon.

Other potential motives, she continued – *Lady C's tyranny finally became too much for someone and they shot her? In which case it could be anyone in the village capable of handling a shotgun. Which would be most of them probably. They shot her from the woods and turned the body to imply it was someone in the house.*

She stopped there. Richard was on her mind following the twinges in her wrist and her thoughts of arthritis. Enid had mentioned a herbal concoction their cook was going to offer him. It sounded rather dangerous, and she thought she ought to warn him. She glanced at the clock on the mantelpiece to make sure it wasn't too early, then went into the hall to telephone him.

A man's voice she didn't recognise answered with a rather haughty, 'Sir Richard Lannister's residence.'

'Oh, good morning,' she said, surprised. 'May I speak to Sir Richard please? It's Miss Busby.'

'Sir Richard is resting, ma'am. May I take a message?'

Finding herself rather wrong-footed, she tried, 'Is Lucy there?'

'Miss Lannister returned to Lannister House last evening, ma'am.' There was a pause, then, 'If there's nothing else?'

Recovering herself, Miss Busby said, 'To whom am I speaking?'

'I am Mr Montague, ma'am. Sir Richard's new valet.'

'Well, I am Miss Busby, Sir Richard's old friend. Please

tell him I should very much like to see him when he feels up to it.'

'Very well, ma'am. Good day.'

*Well,* Miss Busby thought. *A valet.* And he took it upon himself to answer the phone, rather than allowing the butler to do so. Although perhaps the 'valet' was actually a male nurse employed to care for Richard? Was he so much worse?

She toyed with the idea of telephoning Lucy, but the young woman would likely be out and about reporting. And her brother, Anthony, would probably still be working at the newspaper office where he'd taken the reins in Richard's stead. Resigning herself to wait and see, she went through to the kitchen to wash the dishes and put some scraps down for Pud. He had given up on mouse hunting and arrived for the certainty of ham and chicken on a plate.

The washing lifting lazily in the breeze outside caught her eye, and another thought sparked. 'Who on earth would traipse round Cold Compton insisting women take down their washing on a bright and sunny day?' she asked the ginger tom. 'Surely not Lady Compton herself?'

Pud offered no help whatsoever. Drying her hands, she closed the back door before heading upstairs to change. On the way through the sitting room she stopped at the davenport and added: Washing? Some sort of village warden acting on Lady C's orders? to her notes.

She tucked her notebook, pen, and a pencil into her bag, along with Barnaby's leash, and the pair left the cottage to wait for Adeline in the lane. The inquisitive little terrier spotted the bright red post van parked by the green and ran straight towards it, jumping in through the open door and settling himself in the front seat. Surprised to see it so early, Miss Busby looked around to find Dennis standing outside Rowena's gate, staring at the cottage with a look of unadulterated longing.

*Ah*, she thought.

'Dennis,' she called, 'I wonder if you might do me a favour.'

His eyes didn't leave Rowena's front door.

'Dennis!'

He jumped, startled, before hurrying over to her.

'Mornin' Miss. Lovely day, in'it?'

'Beautiful,' Miss Busby agreed. She caught a waft of citrus and creosote and saw that Dennis's unruly curls had been greased into submission with liberal amounts of Macassar oil. His jacket – usually abandoned from May onwards – was smartly buttoned, and a clean tie fixed in place over a pressed white shirt.

'You look very smart,' she told him. 'Is there any post for me?'

'No, but there's lots for Miss Rowena.' He showed her a thick handful of letters, some postmarked Edinburgh.

'And is there something wrong with her letterbox?' she asked.

'No, Miss. I was just…that is 'ter say, I thought she might…'

'I doubt you'll catch her much before noon, Dennis,' she told him, with a note of kindness. It wasn't hard to understand why the lad would be moonstruck by Rowena; young cosmopolitans of her variety were rarely seen in the Oxfordshire countryside. 'The music went on until late last night.'

His face fell, then he blushed red.

'Why don't you hang onto them for a moment?' she suggested. 'You can keep yourself busy, picking the windfall apples from my orchard, as many as you can gather. That ought to take you a while, then you can come back here and deliver the letters.'

'Oh, but Miss! I don't want 'ter get my uniform dirty!'

'Nonsense. The ground is perfectly dry.'

He wavered in indecision.

'Leave them at my gate,' Miss Busby continued. 'I'll make a crumble, or perhaps a pie, later. I shall save you some.'

He thought for a moment, and then his eyes lit up. 'I could give some apples to Miss Rowena!'

Miss Busby doubted she was the baking sort, but nodded all the same. 'That's a very generous thought, Dennis.' Leaving the young man grinning, she called Barnaby down from the van and they strolled around the green until Adeline sailed into sight in the Rolls.

'I've had a thought,' Miss Busby said without preamble as she and Barnaby climbed aboard. 'Hattie said Lady Compton had blonde hair and blue eyes. She was a widow, and probably still attractive, so perhaps she had a lover and there was a falling out?'

'A lover?' Adeline said in a similar tone to that of Lady Bracknell, remarking, "a handbag?".

'This is the modern age, Adeline, and there's no need to adopt affectations between us,' Miss Busby lectured. 'It's a perfectly natural process.'

'*Hmph,*' Adeline huffed. 'Well, lover or not, it all sounds rather extreme. She can't have been much younger than us, Isabelle. It's hardly likely.'

'Age is no barrier to love.' She was thinking of Enid's comments regarding the convoluted romantic affairs of the young. The old weren't really any different; youngsters were just starting out, of course, but older ladies who had lost their husbands were also starting over, in a way.

'Love, yes, but *lover* implies something else. One must be realistic, Isabelle, that sort of activity is a thing of the past at our age, and one does not kill over mere affection.'

'Look at Mr Waterhouse. He moped after Enid for months before she relented.'

'Perhaps, but he's hardly likely to have shot her if she hadn't,' Adeline remarked as she swung the car around a particularly tight corner.

'No, I suppose not,' Miss Busby conceded. 'But what if this stranger who's been seen about the place isn't Theo's father at all? What if he was a beau of Lady Compton's? It can happen, Adeline,' she admonished, as her friend turned towards her in disapproval. 'Eyes front and centre. There are any number of rabbits about this morning,' Miss Busby reminded her.

'I am perfectly capable of spotting rabbits,' Adeline huffed, before taking the road into Little Minton from entirely the wrong side of the road.

Miss Busby muttered something under her breath.

'What if the stranger is *both*?' Adeline suggested as they motored through the High Street and took the turning onto the main road towards where Stow lay in the distance.

'Hmm?' Miss Busby had lost herself in the view. The pretty country town was a collection of handsome stone buildings burnished by the sun into a rich amber hue. Adeline slowed down as they negotiated Stow's bustling market square and sped up again when they emerged from the narrow streets to head towards the hills and dales surrounding Cold Compton.

Who, she'd been wondering, would check the windows for oil lamps in Cold Compton? Would they walk the streets alone in the dark? Or would the view from the manor give away any rebels in the village? Were there any rebels left? Perhaps they'd all fallen into the habit of compliance…all bar one, that is…

'What if the man is both a beau *and* the father of the boy, Isabelle?' Adeline continued, jolting Miss Busby from her musing.

'It's possible, I suppose. We ought to ask Lara if Lady Compton was known to have a romantic interest in anyone.'

'And who it might be,' Adeline replied. 'Or we may even ask Theodore, but I suppose McKay is already in the process of arresting him.'

Miss Busby arched a brow.

'Well,' Adeline sniffed, 'who else *could* he be arresting?'

'Anyone at all,' Miss Busby replied. 'He has clearly investigated matters more closely than us in this instance.'

'Well, we've only just started,' Adeline replied. 'And Lara may indeed have had good cause to worry. McKay could have found out about Lord Theo's true birth, and suspect that he shot his supposed mother in vengeance. Or found out about the beau, and shot her in anger and disgust. Or–'

'We shan't get anywhere by simply guessing,' Miss Busby said firmly.

Adeline returned her attention to the road until they reached Cold Compton. The village appeared the complete opposite of the quiet, almost deserted place it had appeared on Sunday.

'Adeline, look!'

'Oh!' Adeline pulled the car to the side of the road, and they both gazed ahead in surprise. The two largest fields were a hive of activity. A long line of men were rhythmically swinging scythes, cutting down the golden wheat. Working closely behind were women in country clothes and straw hats, bending to gather cut stems and tie them into sheaves. Others were stacking them on end to dry in the sun.

'Every able villager must be out there,' Miss Busby said, eyes wide.

'And more,' Adeline remarked, squinting against the sunlight. 'Some of those men look quite young. They can't be from the village.'

'And they're doing it all by hand. Not even a horse-drawn binder to cut the wheat.'

'But the despot is dead!' Adeline exclaimed. 'Surely a neighbouring farmer could provide them with the equipment now?'

'Perhaps they don't like to ask for help,' Miss Busby mused.

'Or perhaps they have an ingrained respect for the old ways of doing things. Even for all their complaining about it,' Adeline wondered. 'It's rather beautiful,' she went on, watching them for several moments. 'The way they work together, Isabelle. It's almost like a ballet. I can't remember stopping to watch wheat being cut by hand in years, can you?'

Miss Busby shook her head. 'It reminds me of my childhood,' she said. 'Although we thought nothing of it then, of course. It was simply how things were done.'

'Well, there may have been some method to Lady Compton's madness after all,' Adeline declared. 'She certainly brought the villagers together. Such *community*, Isabelle. And such beauty, utterly unmarred by modern menace.'

'But it's backbreaking work,' Miss Busby objected. 'Can you imagine? And there's no beauty in the abandoned cottages we saw yesterday, or the barns and outbuildings falling to wrack and ruin.'

Adeline sighed. 'No, I suppose you are right. But I do think she may not have been quite as unhinged as we thought. Even if she didn't go about things in the best way,' she was quick to add. 'I mean, *look*, Isabelle. It's like a Constable painting come to life.'

The pair stepped out of the car and silently took in the view for several peaceful minutes, Adeline's red and blue floral dress catching the gentle breeze and billowing in the early sun.

The sound of hooves rang out on the road behind them. They both turned around as the beautiful roan horse and dour looking driver they'd seen yesterday approached. A tall man, but thin and stooped with a weathered face, his thick hair white beneath the tattered cap, dark eyes glinting beneath snowy brows.

'Good morning,' Miss Busby called. 'What a handsome animal.' If she'd hoped the compliment would elicit a smile, she was disappointed.

'He 'int mine,' the man replied, drawing to a halt beside them. 'Where 'ud I get the money for an animal like this?' He looked down somewhat accusingly, before softening as he regarded the gleaming flanks of the horse. 'He's handsome right enough, though. Chester, he's called. Alfred lends 'im to me. I groom 'im, it's the least I can do. Alfred Brownlow, he's the blacksmith.'

'We met Alfred yesterday,' Miss Busby replied.

'Good man, is Alfred,' he said. 'Village would stop altogether without 'im, nor get any post if he didn't lend me Chester.'

Miss Busby noticed that the cap perched on his head resembled Dennis's, although it was barely recognisable as such.

'Post?' Adeline said. 'Don't you have a van for the mail?'

'Do you see one?' the man asked, sounding irritated once again. 'It's workhorses we have. And a workhorse I've become, delivering the mail every day, with no help from no one but Chester here.'

'Oh.' Adeline seemed momentarily lost for words.

'That must be very tiring,' Miss Busby remarked.

'Exhaustin'. And with rheumatoids.' He held up his left hand, the knuckles showing the painful, tell-tale swelling.

Miss Busby thought of Richard again, and tried to imagine her good friend having to work when in such pain. Her heart went out to the poor man before them.

'Have you no family who might be able to help?' she asked.

'My boy's moved away with his own wife an fambly, and I don't blame 'im one bit. There's nowt for the youngsters here. But it leaves me on my own and I've no money to stop workin', so here I am, and that's that.'

He frowned down at the women, as if they were somehow responsible.

'I'm Miss Busby and this is Mrs Fanshawe,' she tried another tack. 'We visited Miss Townsend yesterday.'

'Did ye now?' His head tilted to one side as if assimilating this new information. 'Well, I'm Ernest Jones. Postman. Pleased to meet both you ladies,' he said gruffly, then reached up to touch his cap.

'And we are pleased to meet you, Ernest,' Miss Busby replied, while Adeline looked nonplussed.

'Where're you headed, then?' he asked. 'Off up the manor, I'spose?'

'No,' Miss Busby replied. 'We're on our way to see Lara. Regarding bees.'

He seemed equally surprised by that and paused for a moment, as if in indecision. 'Well, that won't do ye no good.'

'Why not?' Miss Busby asked.

'Lara ain't there. On account of her being taken away this mornin' fer murderin' Lady Compton.'

# CHAPTER 9

'I can't imagine what the inspector is thinking,' Miss Busby said as they got back into the car, hushing Barnaby as they did so. 'Lara seemed a perfectly charming young woman, and her concern for Theodore was quite touching.'

Adeline raised her eyebrows. 'The girl was hiding something, Isabelle,' she pointed out. 'We must keep an open mind, as you yourself are so fond of reminding me.'

Miss Busby sighed, whether at Adeline's suspicion, or at the fact her friend could be right. *This must be why police inspectors are always so gruff,* she thought. *Constantly suspecting absolutely everybody must take its toll.*

'Marjorie will be terribly upset, she's very fond of the girl.'

'To Midwinter Cottage, then?' Adeline asked, starting the engine now the horse and cart were safely past.

'I think we should go to the heart of the matter,' Miss Busby suggested after a little thought.

'The manor?'

'Yes, perhaps to get the lie of the land, and a look at the woods where the shot was fired from.'

'Ah, the scene of the crime.' Adeline's eyes lit up. 'Right you are.' She pulled out and headed enthusiastically towards the top end of the village and up the long, gently sloping hill to where the manor sat proudly looking out over all.

They wound slowly between overgrown hedges, branches of hawthorns reaching out to tap the sides of the car, wild roses still showing pink amid bright red hips and haws and long thorny briars bowed down with gleaming blackberries.

'How close should we get?' Adeline asked, slowing to a crawl as the imposing stone manor came into view.

Miss Busby looked about and noted the dense woodland of oak, ash and elm forming a border to the left of the house.

'That must be what they call the woods. It's smaller than I imagined. Drive a little further so we won't be visible from the house, and we'll have a walk. We may be able to see where Lady Compton's killer took the shot.'

Adeline looked ahead to the trees, then back over her shoulder to the manor house, where black iron gates stood invitingly open onto a wide gravel driveway. 'We could—'

'We're not equipped with an excuse to call,' Miss Busby cautioned.

'Oh, I suppose you are right,' Adeline said and powered the Rolls forward then turned into an open farm gate a hundred yards or so further on and tucked them as tightly as possible under the overgrown hedge. Or rather, into it. Spiny branches and twigs barred Miss Busby's exit completely.

'You'll have to come out my side,' Adeline said, opening the door and offering a hand.

Having performed the manoeuvre with as much dignity as she could muster, Miss Busby straightened her skirt and let Barnaby out the back. The little terrier immediately darted under the hedge and into the trees.

'There must be an opening somewhere,' Miss Busby said, wishing their own route were as easy.

They set off, following the hedge as it curved away from the road where an old wooden stile led into the woods.

Eyeing it warily, Adeline removed her heels before mounting the worn wooden step and launching herself over.

Miss Busby felt a surge of pride in her friend – never one to let an obstacle halt her progress. She followed, accepting Adeline's once more proffered hand to dismount. A narrow path led through the trees.

Barnaby was ahead of them, zigzagging about, ears pricked and tail aloft.

'Squirrels,' Adeline supposed.

'I shouldn't think so, he's not looking up,' Miss Busby observed.

The wood ran parallel to the manor gardens. They followed the beaten path, breathing in the scent of rich earth, moss, and leaf mould. Sunlight played through the canopy, the leaves already tinged with bronze as autumn crept in. The path weaved between massive trunks to a winding brook and simple plank bridge. They paused to watch trout swimming lazily against the slow current, the water crystal clear and quite deep with a silted muddy bottom.

'Beautiful views from here,' Adeline said as they gazed at rolling fields of wheat, hay, and barley bordered by sprawling hedges. 'Quintessential Cotswolds. And that's the chestnut Theo was riding when we saw him yesterday.' She pointed over to the horse peacefully cropping grass in the meadow behind the house.

'Look there, Adeline,' Miss Busby pointed. 'Among the irises, there are spent cartridges.'

Adeline leaned perilously over the steep bank. 'Ah yes, and most are quite old by the looks of them. This must be a well-used shooting spot.'

'Which might explain why nobody in the house was alarmed to hear a shotgun go off.' Miss Busby nodded.

'Really?' Adeline was less convinced. 'A shot from here would echo around these hills.'

Miss Busby looked back to where the roof of the manor could be clearly seen. 'You may be right,' she sighed. 'Should we try to get closer to the house?' Miss Busby looked at a narrow deer path wending through thick undergrowth covering the ground beneath the trees.

'We have come to observe, Isabelle, so let us observe,' Adeline said determinedly and surged off along the track.

'There doesn't seem to be any way into the wood other than the way we came in,' Miss Busby said as she pushed a fern frond aside.

Adeline was negotiating a fallen log. 'I'm really not dressed for this,' she muttered.

They arrived at a spot where the undergrowth thinned enough to give a clearer view of the house and gardens. Miss Busby looked down at the churned ground. 'There's been any number of people here.'

'The police,' Adeline immediately deducted. 'This is where the fiend must have taken his shot!'

'It must indeed,' Miss Busby remarked, peering between two leafy branches.

A wide strip of sloping manicured lawn separated the copse from a laurel hedge running parallel to the side of the house before it widened further into a sweeping garden planted with carefully placed islands of shrubs and flowers.

'Isabelle, there's a dark stain on the grass,' Adeline said too loudly, then lowered her voice to a whisper. 'It could be blood.'

Miss Busby stood on tiptoe. 'There's not very much.'

'They'd have doused it with water to wash it away once the body was removed.'

'Yes,' Miss Busby spoke slowly. 'And that high laurel hedge could explain why they didn't find the body for a while.'

Adeline shuffled forwards as far as the undergrowth allowed. 'There don't appear to be any windows looking down from this side of the manor. One, perhaps,' she amended, craning her neck for a better view of the fine stone house not a hundred yards away. A closer view showed signs of neglect, weeds in the guttering, rotten window frames in the top floor attic, one chimney leaning perilously inwards.

'Even so,' Miss Busby reasoned, 'staff ought to have been moving about, particularly the gardeners. How on earth could her body have lain there unnoticed for so long?'

'Wait here,' Adeline suddenly ordered and then made a dash across the lawn, her head bent. She paused at the dark stain, leaned over for a better look, then scooted back.

'Adeline!'

'Oh don't fuss, Isabelle. And it is blood! I'm certain of it,' Adeline declared, her cheeks flushed with excitement. 'Now, I think the most sensible thing to do is go and ask them what happened.'

Miss Busby's eyes widened in alarm. 'What if they've already seen us?'

'I sincerely hope they haven't, we would make the most ridiculous sight.'

Miss Busby looked about and stifled a laugh. Adeline was quite right, a couple of ladies of a certain age would appear quite comical peering through bushes and sneaking across the grass.

'Come on.' Adeline marched off. 'If we're caught, we can say we're looking for Barnaby,' she called back.

Miss Busby smiled. 'Good thinking,' she said. 'Although, now I come to think of it,' she added with a note of concern, 'where is he?'

They called for the dog as they walked back to the stile. They found him delightedly nosing a grubby cricket ball around at the foot of a tall elm.

'Where did you find that?' Miss Busby asked, bending to pat him.

He looked up at her, tail wagging in anticipation.

'It's too heavy to throw, it might hurt you. And too big for you to carry,' she added. 'Leave it now. Come on, we have a job for you.'

Adeline bent to pick up the ball and wiped soil from its shiny red leather. 'It's almost new. We ought to take it, Isabelle. It may be evidence.'

Miss Busby suspected it was more a case of the boys being able to make good use of it when they visited their grandmother, but didn't see the harm. Adeline carried it with her all the way back to the car to place on Barnaby's blanket.

They walked cautiously out onto the road. On being given assurances he was a good boy, Barnaby obligingly darted toward the open iron gates and raced up the gravel driveway towards the manor. Adeline made to follow, but Miss Busby held out a hand. 'We ought to give him a head start,' she said, counting slowly down from ten before they began walking towards the drive.

Miss Busby glanced up at the front of the house where a dozen windows had a full view of their approach.

'Barnaby,' she called softly, adding a, 'Wherever has he gone,' for good measure in case anyone was watching. She called a little louder as they walked around to the left side of the house by the laurel hedge. 'Barnaby?'

'Two windows on this side,' Adeline whispered, looking around furtively and putting Miss Busby in mind of an exceptionally brightly dressed cat burglar. She looked up to see one narrow window on the first storey, presumably a landing, and one equally narrow on the ground floor, partially obscured by a bed of hydrangea bushes in late bloom. A plain wooden door was next to the ground floor window. Just as Miss Busby was observing it with interest, it opened to reveal Jimmy, the former gamekeeper. He was accompanied by a short, slim woman in a black dress with a large bunch of keys hanging at her waist.

Her eyes widened in surprise at the sight of them as Jimmy stopped in his tracks. It was hard to tell which of the four was more startled.

Adeline was first to recover. 'What are you doing here?' she asked Jimmy. 'You said you haven't been employed at the manor for years.'

'Adeline!' Miss Busby admonished. 'That's none of our—'

'That's alright, Miss,' Jimmy said, recovering in turn. 'It's no secret,' he told Miss Busby kindly, before turning to Adeline and straightening up to give her a determined reply. 'I came to ask the young lord for my job back. Had to leave him a bit of time to grieve, but the estate is in need of putting in order and the young gentleman needs someone he can trust by his side.'

'Jimmy, who is this?' the woman asked. She had a pleasant face with even features, her honey coloured hair was lightly touched with grey and tied back in a neat bun. She took in the imposing sight of Adeline in her colourful dress and ox-blood heels. 'And what business is it of hers where you do or don't go?'

'I am Mrs Fanshawe, and this is Miss Busby, and we are investigating a murder.' Adeline puffed out her chest.

Miss Busby groaned inwardly.

'You and everyone else,' the woman replied, clicking her tongue. 'We've had nothing but trouble up here all morning. Young Lara came to deliver the candles and honey and she'd no sooner arrived than that police inspector drove up and ordered her to go to the station with them...' Her voice suddenly cracked; she cleared her throat and raised her chin.

'On what grounds?' Miss Busby asked before she could stop herself.

'Suspected murder I suppose,' the housekeeper replied, her voice tight. 'Although it couldn't possibly be Lara, she was with Miss Townsend that afternoon, along with Jimmy.' She nodded to indicate him. 'Now, I'd say as the pair of you are no detectives, and you're certainly not from the village, so I can't imagine you've any reason being here.'

'Now, Emily,' Jimmy began calmly, 'these ladies are friends of Miss Townsend.'

'Yes!' Miss Busby was quick to add. 'We had lunch with Marjorie yesterday. And we're not investigating the murder,' she shot a dark glance at Adeline, 'as much as asking a few questions to try to help a dear friend in distress.' She laid it on rather heavily, and remained sufficiently ambiguous in the hope of avoiding further contretemps.

'Is that so?' the woman asked, looking from Miss Busby to Jimmy and back, as if weighing the truth of the matter.

Jimmy nodded. 'It is.'

'Well, I can't see as what you could possibly ask that I haven't answered a hundred times already.' She sniffed, and softened slightly. 'I'm Miss Emily Shepherd. Housekeeper here.'

'Good morning, Miss Shepherd.' Miss Busby smiled, grateful for the chance to start again. 'I must apologise for startling you. We were simply walking among the trees when my dog ran off.' She indicated the woodland they'd been trailing through. 'We think he came this way.'

'Oh, now bless you, there's nothing more upsetting.' The housekeeper looked genuinely concerned. 'What sort of dog is he?'

'A Jack Russell,' Adeline said. 'Rather rotund. The shaggy type.'

'Oh, I had a Jack Russell growing up! Bertie, his name was.' She clasped her hands to her chest, seeming an entirely different woman now than mere seconds before.

Dogs, Miss Busby thought, often had a way of doing that to people.

'I haven't seen him, I'm afraid,' Emily went on, 'but there's chairs on the terrace around the back.' She pointed around to the rear of the house. 'You're welcome to sit and wait, if you'd like. Hopefully he'll realise you're there and come back.' She moved to lead the way. 'Lord, I haven't thought about Bertie in years...' She shook her head with a smile. 'What's your little dog called?'

'Barnaby,' Adeline said.

'We have a ham bone left over in the kitchen. I could fetch it, it might encourage him to come to you.'

'Oh, please don't trouble–' Miss Busby began.

'No trouble! Jimmy will help.' She tapped his hand. 'And cook made some lemonade fresh this morning. I expect you're tired from your walk in the woods...' She stopped and frowned. 'But whatever were you doing in there?' she asked, probably realising they were dressed in an unlikely manner for a rural ramble.

'Hiking,' Adeline deadpanned.

'Well, you really shouldn't,' she chided. 'That's private property. If Mr Walton had caught you, there'd have been the devil to pay. He can't abide trespassers.'

'What's he going to do, shoot us?' Adeline instantly countered.

'Of course he wouldn't,' Emily retorted, her tone more defensive than angry.

'You don't get many strangers up this way?' Miss Busby asked kindly, trying to moderate the sudden spat.

'We don't. We're in the middle of nowhere. And Lady Compton isn't - wasn't - the sort to welcome visitors,' Emily said, her shoulders falling as she looked away, anxiety pulling at her lips.

'There was a stranger seen about the place some time ago, though, wasn't there?' Adeline pressed as they walked along the side of the house. 'By the river.'

The woman's eyes darkened as she focused back on Adeline. 'Is that so?' she asked.

'Yes, he caused quite a stir by all accounts.' Adeline wasn't about to be put off.

'You mustn't think us horribly nosy,' Miss Busby jumped in. 'The reason we came to Cold Compton yesterday was to discuss the matter with Miss Townsend, you see. Our friend, Nurse Delaney, is also a good friend of hers, and...' Miss Busby trailed off. The housekeeper's face had suddenly drained of colour.

Jimmy rested a supportive hand lightly under her elbow. 'Now then, Emily, let's fetch that lemonade, shall we? We'll be right with you, ladies,' he called over his shoulder to Miss Busby as he steered the woman back towards the door. 'Make yourselves comfortable on the terrace. Maybe you can call for your dog? There's a brook at the far end of the lawn, he might be playing by the bank. There's ducks and all sorts down there.'

'Yes, of course, thank you.' Miss Busby blinked as Jimmy held the door open and ushered the housekeeper quickly through.

# CHAPTER 10

'Well!' Adeline exclaimed as they went to sit on the set of white cast-iron chairs set about a dainty round table on the terrace overlooking the rear garden. A tranquil spot, the lawn and flower beds running down to the brook, an old bench on its bank and the fields and meadows beyond. 'What do you make of that?'

Barnaby appeared from behind a lavender border, watching them, ears pricked and head tilted. Miss Busby gestured towards the brook. 'Good boy, run along and play,' she called softly. He stared back at her, tail wagging. 'Squirrels! Barnaby, find the squirrels,' she tried. 'That way!'

The magic word did the trick.

'The poacher and the housekeeper!' Adeline's eyes brimmed with mischief. 'They are quite clearly besotted with one another.'

'They do seem comfortably companionable, yes.'

Adeline arched a brow. 'Isabelle! There could be conspiracy at work here! The woman didn't like me mentioning our mystery man, and she almost fainted when you mentioned Hattie Delaney's name.'

'I expect she's tired of it all,' Miss Busby pointed out. 'It was odd, though,' she mused.

'She was shocked. I think she knows something.' Adeline nodded.

'About the murder, or–' Miss Busby began, but stopped as the sound of footsteps signalled the reappearance of Jimmy, with a large bone in his hand.

'Here we are, Miss,' he said, placing the bone a little way down the lawn. 'Maybe he'll smell that and come running. Although we'd best not mention it to Cook.' He grinned and pulled out a handkerchief to wipe his hand.

'Of course.' Miss Busby smiled. 'Is Emily alright? I do hope we didn't upset her.'

'Oh, Emily's made of sterner stuff. She'll be along with the drinks shortly.'

'How long has she worked here?' Miss Busby asked.

Jimmy thought for a moment. 'Getting on for thirty years now, it must be. Started out as a young maid, and worked her way up to Housekeeper.' There was a note of pride in his voice.

'Admirable,' Adeline proclaimed. 'Well done that girl.'

'Yes,' Miss Busby agreed. A spark had just ignited in her brain which was revving at low throttle.

'I'll just nip and see if your little dog is by the brook,' Jimmy announced and ambled off down the garden.

'Lemonade, m'ladies,' a deep male voice behind them announced.

Their heads spun around. It was the butler, standing very upright, dressed in the usual starched white dickie, bow tie, collar and cuffs and a faded black tailcoat rather too long for him. He set a tray down with two glasses and a jug full of ice-cold lemonade, on the table.

'Mr Chadwick insisted he serve,' Emily said, her tone kind and warm. She was obviously fond of her elderly colleague.

'Indeed, Miss Emily, and I am very honoured to do so.' He bowed his head with old-fashioned good manners.

'Oh, Mr Chadwick.' Emily put her hand to her cheek. 'There are biscuits in the pantry and I've gone and forgotten them.'

'Do not be concerned, Miss Emily, I will fetch them,' the butler intoned. 'It will be my pleasure.'

'Why not bring more glasses and we can all sit together?' Miss Busby called after him.

'No, no, I can't…I mean, I really shouldn't,' Emily said, placing a glass in front of each of them and pouring the lemonade.

'I don't think anyone would mind,' Miss Busby said kindly. 'Why don't you sit down, at least.'

'Oh, just for a moment then.' Emily sank onto the chair opposite. 'I'm sorry, I… well. You can imagine, I'm sure. It's all been a bit…' she struggled, tiredness showing clearly in the lines creased around her eyes and mouth.

Miss Busby smiled sympathetically. 'There's really nothing to apologise for,' she assured her.

'The inspector coming back up here this morning and taking Lara away was the last straw. It's questions, questions, questions with him, til you've half a mind to wonder if you killed the woman yourself.'

'Yes, he's like that,' Adeline remarked, spotting a kindred spirit.

Emily looked up in surprise.

'He has a reputation for being rather unrelenting,' Miss Busby said, before Adeline could puff her chest out and announce that they'd solved murders together in the past. Their being in league with the man would win them no friends here.

Emily nodded and folded her hands in her lap.

'You must be delighted that Jimmy has his job back, at least,' Adeline said. 'And he'll get his cottage as well, I suppose?'

'Well, the two do go together. Hillcroft belonged to Jimmy's father, and his father before him. And it's of no use to anyone sitting empty and rotting away like it is. Pure spite from her ladyship, that was. Jimmy'll fix it up like it used to be… but he hasn't got his position just yet,' she said. 'He came over today to ask his lordship, but he isn't here to ask.'

'Why, where is he?' Adeline asked.

'He had Sykes drive him and Alfred in the Morris Cowley to the police station. They took off just after Lara was taken.'

'Sykes?' Miss Busby queried.

'He's the chauffeur and gardener,' Emily explained.

'Though he's not much of a gardener. He's happy enough driving cars around, but doesn't give a fig for plants.'

'Why not?' Miss Busby asked.

'Oh, he thinks he's above that now. He was gardener here when the old lord was alive, but he was made up to chauffeur when the master couldn't drive himself any more.'

'And who tends the gardens now?' Miss Busby asked, then added, 'They're quite beautiful.'

'They are, and that's thanks to his lordship. He likes things kept in order.'

'Really–' Adeline began but Miss Busby cut her off.

'But why would Lord Theodore not drive himself to the station?'

'His lordship wanted to stay with Lara but then Alfred wouldn't be able to get back to the forge, and he's needed there, 'specially during harvest.'

Adeline blinked. 'His lordship is helping the girl when she's just been arrested for killing his mother?'

'She wasn't arrested, she was taken for questioning,' Emily said. 'Of course his lordship would help her; it's only natural he'd go right to her aid.'

Adeline's brows shot up. 'The Lord of the manor and the village beekeeper?'

'And why not?' Emily looked up sharply. 'What could be more natural than two young folk falling in love?'

Adeline raised both brows. 'And did Lady Compton find it natural?'

'I– well…' Emily floundered, lifting a hand briefly

to her mouth as if she could somehow usher the words back in. She cleared her throat. 'I didn't say they *had* fallen in love; I only asked what could be more natural.'

'Of course,' Miss Busby said, seeing the woman's distress and not wanting Adeline to riposte. 'It must be difficult for them as the only two youngsters left in the village.'

'Yes, and I have already noted that, too,' Adeline ploughed on regardless. 'Miss Townsend told us that the young had all been driven out. But here's Lara, with her work, home, and family. Why does she stay, when all the others have left?'

Emily locked eyes with her. 'Labourers and the like are ten-a-penny. Beekeeping's different, it's a skill. Lara's good at what she does, and the village would grind to a halt without Alfred. Lady Compton would have struggled to replace Lara and Alfred both, and if one went, the other'd follow.'

*Meaning,* Miss Busby thought, *Lady Compton perhaps hadn't been quite as inept as people seemed to think.* 'When we met Lara yesterday,' she said, 'the poor girl seemed very concerned that Theodore didn't have an alibi for the time of the murder.'

Emily waved a dismissive hand. 'He was working around the manor, cutting wood and tidying the garden until late morning. We all saw him. Then he rode out and took his lunch to eat down by the river. Fishes down there sometimes too, when he's not too busy discussing estate matters with the local farmers.'

'Rather lowly work for a Lord, cutting wood and so on,' Adeline pointed out.

Emily raised her chin. 'Lowly, is it? Practical, I'd call it. He was never one for shutting himself away inside when there was proper work needed doing. Not like his mother.'

'I thought Mr Walton was the estate manager,' Miss Busby said. 'Why would Lord Theodore be discussing estate matters?'

'Because he's been learning how to run the estate,' Emily answered sharply.

'But he doesn't actually have an alibi.' Adeline wasn't giving up on the topic.

'Do you think someone might have told the inspector about Lara's friendship with Theodore?' Miss Busby asked, trying a diversion.

'Of course they wouldn't,' Emily scoffed, before quickly adding, 'there's nothing to tell,' with a slight flush to her cheeks.

'And Theodore wasn't here when she was taken away by the inspector?' Miss Busby pressed.

'No, he was grooming his horse in the field. Little Harry was sent to fetch him, but they'd taken Lara by the time he came, so he ordered Sykes to get the car. Then they went to fetch Alfred, and he won't stand for it,' she went on firmly. 'He's a devil when riled; he'll tear that station apart with his bare hands to bring Lara home if he has to.'

'Will he?' Miss Busby said, surprise lifting her tone. 'He seemed rather gentle when we met him. He brought Miss Townsend soup.'

The butler reappeared with a plate piled with cherry and oat biscuits and two more glasses on a smaller tray. 'I took the liberty of supplying additional glassware, as requested, ma'am.' He placed the tray down. 'I apologise for the delay, but Cook has discovered the ham bone has gone missing and I was forced to explain the situation.'

'Oh, dear, I am sorry.' Guilt reddened Miss Busby's cheeks.

'Don't fret, she likes a bit of drama,' Emily laughed. 'She'll settle down soon enough.'

'I must agree,' Chadwick said. 'But the mood has not quite passed and I am afraid I am obliged to calm her disquiet, if you will please excuse me?' He bowed again and left with a quiet tread.

'Trying to keep the peace?' Adeline remarked with a smile.

'He is, and he's plenty of experience of it.' Emily smiled back. 'Cook is Mrs Chadwick, and has been married to Mr Chadwick for nigh on fifty years. She's apt to fly off the handle sometimes, but they rub along comfortably enough despite the problems these last years.'

Miss Busby smiled. It was interesting to see the inner workings of the house.

Jimmy returned, without Barnaby. 'Ah, so you agreed to sit down.' He smiled fondly at Emily.

'And I'm glad I did, it's brought a bit of comfort. Come on Jimmy, sit here beside me and I'll pour you a drink too.' She reached for the jug.

Adeline was watching them, noting, as Miss Busby did, that they seemed very much at ease with each other.

'There were a great many people working in the fields as we drove up,' Miss Busby turned the conversation.

'Some of them are strapping young men!' Adeline threw in.

Emily laughed. 'They come up from the hamlets; there's more than usual this year, now that word's spread about her ladyship having died.'

'Do you think one of them might have killed her?' Adeline asked, suddenly struck by the idea.

'For a few days' extra work? They'd have done it before if that were the case,' Jimmy said, taking a long drink of his lemonade. 'There's easier ways to find work. But I'm sure Lara will be home before we know it, and that'll be an end to it.'

Miss Busby suspected it wouldn't be quite that simple. *McKay must have a very good reason for holding her*, she thought to herself. And given Marjorie Townsend's attitude toward the murder, it was unlikely McKay would accept any alibi she'd given as to Lara's whereabouts.

'But surely there won't be an end to it until they find the culprit,' Adeline said.

'Well, I don't see as how they'll ever find him now,' Emily said, matter-of-fact.

'Why not?' Adeline asked.

'That inspector's convinced it's one of us from the house. He's spending all his time here asking the same questions over and over instead of being out there looking for the real villain. If I was the murderer, I'd be pleased as punch knowing that no-one was on my tail. Or rather, nowhere near it,' she added.

Adeline picked up the plate of biscuits and proffered it to the housekeeper, reverently. Miss Busby hid a smile; hostilities appeared to be over – Adeline had found an ally.

'Thank you, Mrs Fanshawe.' Emily smiled and took one. 'There's not one of us has done anything wrong.'

'Innocent until proven guilty,' Jimmy added, drawing his shoulders back. 'No one's in danger here.'

Miss Busby took a sip of lemonade, and a moment to enjoy the view of the hills and vales stretching to the horizon while she gathered her thoughts. She thought she caught sight of a stubby white tail moving like a periscope through the tall grass where the woods met the brook.

'Miss Townsend mentioned,' she opened, hoping the name would forgive the indelicate question, 'that Lady Compton's body had remained undiscovered for quite some time.'

She thought she saw Emily flinch.

It was Jimmy who answered. 'She fell to the side of the house,' he said, eyes flicking to the housekeeper. 'On the other side of the laurel hedge. No one walks round that way, do they Em?'

Emily shook her head, then took a sip of lemonade.

'Surely someone must have realised Lady Compton was missing,' Adeline pointed out.

Emily began coughing, patting a hand to her chest as though the lemonade had gone down the wrong way.

'Who was in the house that day?' Miss Busby asked.

Jimmy looked to Emily, who recovered her breath but continued patting her chest in exaggerated fashion

'Cook ought to have put more sugar in the lemonade,' she said.

'It's delicious,' Miss Busby said, quite certain lemons weren't the issue.

'Yes. Just catches you a bit at the back of the throat,' she said in a tight voice. 'We were all here, except for Sykes and Mr Walton. They go into Stow on Friday afternoons for provisions.' She raised her fingers to count. 'There's Mr and Mrs Chadwick and little Harry the boot boy, he's their grandson, and there's me. We're a small staff, and her ladyship ran us ragged.'

'Were there any visitors last Friday?' Miss Busby asked. She'd noticed the side lawn was visible from parts of the drive as it curved up towards the house.

'None. The inspector's already asked,' Jimmy said.

'Someone must have seen her lying on the grass from the landing window,' Adeline pressed. 'She would have been visible over the hedge from there.'

'No one's got time to stand watching at windows. Her ladyship always wanted everything just so. We'd have been out on our ears if we'd been standing about.'

'Did you see the body?' Miss Busby directed the question to the housekeeper, who reddened.

'I did, but I don't think I should answer you further.' She turned defensive.

'Why?' Adeline was direct.

'I…well…' Emily said.

'It'll do no harm to tell them, Em,' Jimmy said quietly.

She nodded, her lips tight. 'She was lying on her front on the other side of the hedge. We never heard a thing. We were busy working about the house as usual until we went to the kitchen for lunch at one o'clock. Then we all stayed there, sitting round the table preparing the veggies for dinner while Cook baked bread and biscuits.'

'Would you have heard the shot from the kitchen?' Miss Busby asked.

'No.' She shook her head. 'It's below stairs, you can't hear a blessed thing down there, what with these big stone walls.'

'You would have heard the shot while you were above stairs though?' Adeline asked.

Emily nodded. 'We would.'

Adeline gave Miss Busby a look of triumph.

'And how long did you all remain down in the kitchen?' Miss Busby prompted.

Emily looked at her hands wrapped around the glass of lemonade. 'Until three o'clock. Her ladyship never ate lunch, she liked to look after her figure, but she'd take tea at three. Mr Chadwick began preparing her usual tray, then I said it was strange she hadn't rung the bell. So I went up to her parlour – that's where she liked to work on her accounts and such. I knocked on her door but she wasn't in there. Then I went looking round the house. The drawing room, the blue room, her bedroom, other bedrooms and the bathrooms. She wasn't anywhere. Then I went outside…and I found her.' She sighed. 'I could see straight off she was dead. Blood everywhere, soaking her clothes and hair. She'd been shot in the back of the head and fallen face first,' her voice trembled over the words and she cleared her throat again before continuing. 'It looked like she'd been walking towards the woods when it happened. It felt like it wasn't real. I couldn't move for a minute, then I ran for Mr Chadwick.'

'Did you touch the body?' Miss Busby asked a question that she thought sounded quite official.

'No.' She shook her head. 'Mr Chadwick leaned over her, it made him dizzy to see her like that. Then we went in and talked about what to do…We didn't know where his lordship was, so we decided to wait until he came back.'

'And that's when the police were called?' Adeline asked.

'It was. His lordship did it himself, and I told the inspector all what I've just said to you.' Emily spoke quietly. Jimmy stretched a hand out to squeeze hers.

Miss Busby exchanged glances with Adeline - this tale had the ring of truth to it.

'And nobody else in the neighbourhood heard the shot?' Miss Busby asked. 'Surely a gun going off so close to the house would be remarked upon?'

'There's always someone shooting on the estate,' Jimmy

replied. 'Rabbits, deer, hare. The villagers will take something for the pot if they can, or be trying to keep the foxes down. I doubt anyone would even notice it.'

Miss Busby mused for a moment, thinking of the cartridges in the brook, then continued, 'When was Lady Compton last seen alive?'

Emily looked away, obviously not wanting to reply.

'They all heard raised voices in her parlour upstairs,' Jimmy told them. 'Mr Sykes shouting at her. Disgraceful, acting like he was her equal. Then he slammed the door and stormed out, and drove Mr Walton to Stow. It put everyone on edge.'

'The argument was just passed noon,' Emily added. 'We stayed out of her way afterwards because she'd have been in a nasty mood.'

'We encountered Mr Walton.' Adeline went off at a tangent. 'Where is he today?' She looked around as though expecting him to appear.

'In the dower house, he lives there and has his office there too,' Emily explained. 'And now he says he's snowed under, what with her ladyship dead. Official papers and all the like.'

Miss Busby nodded. 'And you were with Miss Townsend and Lara at that time, Jimmy?'

Jimmy shifted uncomfortably in his seat. 'Around that time, yes.'

'I was surprised to hear that,' she continued. 'Miss Townsend said you and Lara came each Sunday to help in the garden. Why were you there on Friday?'

'I…we…' he stuttered, then looked at Emily.

'Now I don't think you've any right to be asking us questions like this,' Emily said. 'If you've finished your drinks, I'll take the tray.' She stood up, busying herself with clearing the table. 'I ought to be getting back to work, and you'll be wanting to look for your dog, I'm sure.'

'He might have gone back into the woods,' Jimmy said. 'I'll help you look. It's best you don't go in there on your own.'

'Oh, there's no need, look!' Miss Busby feigned surprise, pointing to where she'd last spotted the periscope tail. 'Barnaby!' she called. There was a rustle of movement, and the terrier appeared. 'Come here! Where *have* you been?' Miss Busby admonished as lightly as possible, while Barnaby made a beeline for the knucklebone and grabbed it eagerly between his jaws.

'I'll see you out, then, Miss,' Jimmy said, bending to ruffle Barnaby's ears as he trotted past with the bone, ears perked, tail aloft as though he'd caught it entirely himself.

'Thank you for the refreshments,' Miss Busby said, noting that Emily looked flushed, before the sound of tyres on gravel diverted their attention.

'Is that his lordship back already?' Emily hurriedly put the tray back on the table and rushed past them. Miss Busby and Adeline followed, Jimmy lagging warily behind.

A bottle-green Morris Cowley pulled up directly outside the front door, and a short man dressed in dark clothes with a leather driving hat and goggles masking his features, emerged. Alone.

'Oh, no,' Emily whispered, then turned back to Jimmy. 'You'd best go out through the woods. Go on. I'll see the ladies out.'

Jimmy didn't need telling twice. He hurried back towards the laurel hedge and out of sight.

Miss Busby paused to watch him go - it was obvious he'd often used that route. She turned to follow Adeline, heading towards the drive.

'Who's that?' The driver's thin, reedy voice matched his appearance. As he pulled the helmet and goggles from his face, his features came into sight, sharp and ferret-like, with a long nose and small, dark eyes. His dark hair stuck up in all directions, and he looked just the sort of man, Miss Busby thought, one would cross the street to avoid.

'Two ladies looking for their dog,' Emily said. 'They've found him now. Where's his lordship? Is he with Alfred and Lara?'

'They're going back home, left 'em at the crossroads.' Sykes caught sight of Barnaby, and his lip curled. 'That dog shouldn't be on the lawn. Her ladyship wouldn't have it. Go on, get off with yer!' he called angrily.

Barnaby let out a low growl, barely discernible from behind the bone.

Adeline *harrumphed*. 'There is no need to raise your voice.'

'This is a manor house, not a common park. And I'll do as I like with my voice in my own village, and suggest you go back to yours if you don't like it!'

'Really!' Adeline readied herself for the fray. 'Well, I–'

'Adeline, we are leaving,' Miss Busby insisted, waving a feigned apology to the unpleasant man. 'We're sorry to have bothered you,' she told Emily, and took Adeline's arm to hurry her past the car. They paused as the front door creaked open.

Mr Chadwick, the butler, came out and paused on the top step, rigidly upright, his brow furrowed with anger.

'Keep walking,' Miss Busby whispered.

'Alright, but slowly, I want to hear what's said,' Adeline hissed in reply.

'I suppose you let them in, did you Chadwick?' Sykes accused him.

'I did not.' The butler spoke coldly. 'Where is his lordship?'

'His lordship,' Sykes said, as he slammed the car door shut, 'has got himself arrested for murder after insisting the girl was let go. And they know about the argument. Someone's been talking.'

'Good *Heavens*,' Adeline whispered, their pace having slowed to that of a snail.

'It wasn't anyone here,' Chadwick replied angrily.

'Well don't you go round saying 'owt,' Sykes snarled back. 'There ain't no-one here in charge now 'cept me and don't you forget it.'

'Come *on*,' Miss Busby insisted. Sykes' manner, as well as the butler's barely restrained fury, made her extremely uncomfortable, and they walked back to the Rolls as quickly as Adeline would allow.

# CHAPTER 11

'Well!' Adeline exclaimed, opening the back door for Barnaby to hop in. 'Was it our young lord after all? Committing matricide to gain his inheritance? Or perhaps to save the village, if the coffers truly have run dry. And I wonder what that argument was all about?'

Adeline installed herself in the driver's seat and started the engine. 'Stay right there, Isabelle.'

Miss Busby waited while she reversed out of the hedge. The Rolls lunged backwards, then slammed to a halt as Adeline put her foot on the brake and called, 'In you get.'

Miss Busby opened the passenger door, ready to climb in. 'We are in no great rush, Adeline.'

'Miss, Miss! Wait a moment!' Jimmy swung himself over the stile and hurried towards them. 'Have they got Theo?' he called.

She paused, hand still on the door handle. 'I'm afraid so.'

He pulled off his cap and rubbed a hand over his forehead as he reached her. 'I feared as much when I caught sight of Sykes alone in the car. Do you know where Lara is?'

'Sykes said he dropped her and Alfred off at the crossroads,' she told him.

'Ah, well that's summat,' he said but looked sorrowful nonetheless.

'We had intended speaking to Lara originally, about some hives for Little Minton,' she said. 'But I shouldn't imagine that's something she'll want to concern herself with, under the circumstances. Perhaps we ought to call back another day.'

'Well, that's as may be, but I'm sure she'll want you to help his lordship,' Jimmy said, speaking slowly as if unsure of his words, 'and p'raps you might want to stop by the barley meadows next to Grange Farm. Folk are harvesting there today. If you were to drive down here,' he pointed to where the road wound back down into the valley, 'until you come to an apple orchard, you'll see the track on the left.'

Miss Busby tilted her head in polite enquiry.

'And... well. There'll be farmhands from Barton there,' he explained haltingly. 'They'll have started work early this morn, and should be breaking for lunch about now.'

'Barton?' Adeline leaned over the passenger seat to ask, 'What relevance is Barton? And where is it?'

'It's only a little hamlet, Miss,' Jimmy said, bobbing down to peer in the car to address her. 'A few miles west of here. If you were to ask at the fields for Henry

White,' he turned back to Miss Busby, 'you might like to talk to him.'

Miss Busby, no stranger to nervous pupils standing before her with both information to divulge and concerns for the consequences, waited patiently for him to expound.

He clutched his tweed cap and gazed at the ground. 'We went to school together. Miss Townsend taught us both. And, you see, if you were to address him as "Huckleberry", he'll know you were sent by a friend.'

Miss Busby had the distinct impression Jimmy was doing his best to send them in the right direction, but couldn't for the life of her see to what end.

'Lara'll be heartbroken, she dotes on the young master, but if you were to speak to Huck, it might…' He trailed off, scratching his head.

'Might what?' Adeline's patience was less robust. 'If there is something we need to know, tell us and be done with it. The air of secrecy hanging over all of Cold Compton is helping none of you!'

'We only want to help, Jimmy,' Miss Busby reassured him.

'I know, Miss, and I wouldn't normally be one to say anything, but it seems the matter's getting outta hand.'

'Do you think,' Miss Busby asked, carefully picking her own words now, 'that if an alibi were to be found for Theodore, the matter would be resolved?'

He hung his head. 'It oughta have been found sooner.' He looked increasingly uncomfortable, his cheeks flushed with what Miss Busby took to be shame.

'Why wasn't it?' she asked softly.

'We had to look after our own, Miss, and happen we thought the gentry would be safe. Lord knows they are in everything else.'

Miss Busby felt a wave of sympathy for the man. He looked perfectly wretched.

'I understand,' she said softly.

He nodded, and took a breath, before bending back down to look at Adeline. 'You know about the stranger,' he said, 'and so I 'spect you know why he caused such a "stir", as you put it?'

Adeline nodded.

'Well then. You oughta talk to Huck.' He straightened and faced Miss Busby. 'Tell him the young master's been taken and the stranger needs to be told. There's not one of us wants to see his lordship suffer any more than he already has. He's a good man. Young, and a bit idealistic maybe, but neither of those are faults. And that's all I oughta say on the matter.'

With that, he took a step back from the car, as if he'd just completed an uncomfortable, but necessary task.

'What do you know of the argum–?' Adeline called, but Jimmy turned and rushed away.

'Come on, let's find this track,' Miss Busby said, slipping into the car seat and pulling the door closed.

'Aren't you concerned it may be a fool's errand?' Adeline asked as she shifted the gears noisily. 'All this alibi business is nothing but lies covering for what could well be more lies. We ought to go straight to

Stow and tell the inspector. It's as if none of them want to be helped.'

'They don't,' Miss Busby replied. 'Or rather, they didn't. In a way, they all got exactly what they wanted with the death of Lady Compton. Now that Theodore has been arrested, however, things have changed.'

'But why? The woman remains dead either way.'

'Yes, but there does seem to be genuine affection for the young man. And support.'

'Particularly amongst beekeepers,' Adeline remarked with a look of disapproval.

Miss Busby narrowed her eyes.

'Remember our last case,' Adeline cautioned. 'Love between the classes can have terrible consequences, Isabelle.'

'Very well, if you prefer a more practical outlook, then without Theodore to take over the manor, the estate - and indeed the village - it will probably be sold. And then there is the possibility, however narrow, that they may all end up in even worse hands.'

'Indeed. Better the devil you know,' Adeline said. 'Pity they didn't think of that, instead of burying their heads in the sand. Inspector McKay ought to know, though.'

'I think he already does,' Miss Busby admitted. 'He seems a step ahead of us at every turn.'

Adeline *harrumphed*. 'How did he find out about this argument?'

'He does have a police badge, Adeline,' Miss Busby said. 'It's much easier for him to question people!'

'Well, it never used to be,' she grumbled in reply.

'We've known the locals in our last two cases,' Miss Busby reminded her. 'On this occasion, we don't, we are strangers here. Come on, let's find this Huckleberry chap. Maybe we can surge ahead.'

That did the trick. Adeline reached for her sunglasses, took a firm grip of the steering wheel and put her foot down.

The narrow, winding lane dipped back into the valley, and as they took a tight bend, with Adeline grazing the verge on the wrong side of the road, the apple orchard came into view. Adeline slowed as the pair of them cast about for any sign of the track.

'There!' Miss Busby called, spotting the opening in the thick hedgerow.

Adeline pulled the car to an abrupt halt. Barnaby's knucklebone clattered to the floor. The little dog looked down at it in consternation.

'Best climb out while I try to park off the road,' Adeline warned.

Miss Busby dismounted and let Barnaby out, while Adeline attempted to park without obstructing the narrow lane.

'These roads are not at all suited to my car,' she complained, giving up and leaving the rear end jutting out.

'Perhaps we should have asked Ernest if he could take us in the trap,' Miss Busby said and eyed the cart track warily. Typical of ancient roads, it was formed of loose stones flattened and worn from centuries of use, with a dividing line of grass along its centre. Brambles and wild roses formed rough hedges either side as the track ran up a low hillock behind a cluster of workers' cottages to a large farm, presumably Grange Farm. Men and women were busy working in the fields surrounding it.

'We couldn't ask Ernest to help,' Adeline began. 'He might guess at our task and then where would we be? I'm beginning to think we can't trust any of them. Emily said Jimmy and Lara were with Miss Townsend the afternoon Lady Compton was shot, but it didn't ring true. No wonder McKay took Lara in for questioning if they are lying to the police. And we only have Emily's word the staff were all together in the kitchen when the woman was killed.'

Miss Busby was struggling to keep up with Adeline's determined pace. 'It's the age-old problem,' she replied. 'People will only ever tell the police so much, for a myriad of different reasons. Some may be perfectly innocent, some may be protecting loved ones, and some are protecting their own black deeds.' She looked back towards the road, where the manor could just be seen dominating the valley. 'And it's never easy to see which is the case.'

'Either way, their carryings on will make it difficult for the inspector to find the true culprit,' Adeline grumbled. 'Imagine no one telling him that Theo and the beekeeper are enamoured with one another. They are all of them hampering a murder investigation as if it were nothing.' She stumbled, narrowly avoiding a rut. Miss Busby pointedly ignored a moment of most unladylike language, as Barnaby trotted over to the nearest brambles to investigate a freshly dug hole. 'And here we are, tramping through the wilderness in search of yet another villager who will no doubt also lie to us,' she complained.

'Barnaby, leave it,' Miss Busby commanded as he thrust himself up to his shoulders into a badger hole. 'You'll get your nose bitten.' She turned back to Adeline. 'Huckleberry isn't from Cold Compton,' she pointed out. 'And nor is the stranger he may lead us to.' She sighed. 'This estate has been shrouded in lies for goodness knows how long. It will require more than a little patience to dig out the truth.'

'Then how does the inspector suppose he has found it so soon?' Adeline said, rather breathless now.

This, Miss Busby knew, was what rankled her friend the most. McKay being ahead of the game.

'He had a head start,' she pointed out. 'And the benefit of forensic experience.'

They walked on in silence for several minutes, taking in the sunlit beauty of their surroundings as the track wound behind the cottage gardens, neatly tended and heavy with rhubarb, gooseberries, and plums ripe for picking. Pigs snuffled in stone-walled pens, chickens scratched and pecked among the bushes, a cockerel ruffled his feathers and crowed loudly. For every tumbledown building and overgrown verge, there was homegrown fare and a deep sense of community. For every closely guarded secret, a kindly word and close kinship. Adversity, it seemed, had bound them more tightly together. The scene of simple country life began to lift Miss Busby's mood.

'Why did McKay hold the beekeeper and then let her go?' Adeline began again. 'Lara was certainly keeping something from us, and this closeness of hers with the young lord is extremely suspicious, no matter what the housekeeper says.'

'Adeline…' Miss Busby cautioned.

'I am not being heartless, Isabelle. I consider myself as modern a woman as any, but a Lady is dead and the matter cannot be ignored: the two young people are world's apart in status, and any closeness, no matter how innocent, could cause concern for either family.' She walked in silence for a moment. 'Indeed, how innocent can it be, if they felt they had to keep it a secret from the inspector?'

'I'm sure they simply deemed it a private matter,' Miss Busby said.

'Well, given this morning's events, it's likely he has found out. The most obvious scenario is that Lara had designs on the boy, and his mother found out, leading to an ultimatum.'

Miss Busby nodded. It wasn't an unreasonable theory. 'Are you suggesting then that Lady Compton had acted to stop it?'

'Yes,' Adeline said, without a hint of hesitation. 'It's perfectly obvious Lady Compton wouldn't have approved of such an affiliation.'

'And so, rather than ejecting the young beekeeper from the village, you assume she simply forbade the relationship?'

'Possibly… If she'd ejected her, she would have lost her blacksmith as well as her beekeeper, remember.'

'At which point Lara, objecting to Lady Compton's objection, shot her?'

'It's perfectly plausible,' Adeline argued. 'People have done worse for love.'

'Leaving Theo with no alibi and as primary suspect to the murder?'

'Well. Yes. But I doubt she thought that far ahead.' Adeline pulled Miss Busby aside from a deep cartwheel rut gouged into the track. 'Do watch your step, Isabelle. Oh!' She stopped, eyes wide. 'That's why she moved the body! To divert suspicion from Theo!'

'I doubt she would have been able to move a dead weight,' Miss Busby pointed out. 'And the inspector has let her go, don't forget.'

'Well, then, she had help…from her uncle Alfred of course! In fact, he may have been the one to shoot the woman. He doubtless knows his way around a shotgun.' Adeline remained undeterred. 'McKay let the girl go because the uncle did the deed.'

'And arrested Theodore because…?'

Adeline huffed, and considered. 'If you really must have me solve the whole thing, Isabelle, then I imagine he arrested Theodore to draw the uncle into confessing. He doubtless will not be able to stand by and see his niece's beloved hang! There! I have overtaken you as primary sleuth!'

Miss Busby laughed, and Adeline beamed as they companionably crested the top of the hillock.

Both women stopped short at the sight that unfolded before them, as Barnaby barked excitedly and raced ahead.

'Isabelle, how wonderful! We have found lunch!'

# CHAPTER 12

A large hay cart was static further along the track, two handsome shire horses, tethered on long leads, were cropping grass on the verge. A trestle table heavily laden with thick loaves of homemade bread, a large ham, butter, hunks of cheddar, and what looked to be dishes of chunky relishes and pickles had come into view.

An older woman wearing a simple blue dress, sturdy boots and a wide hat to keep the sun off, was setting pottery plates and tumblers at the far end of the table, before adding a large brown jug.

'Good afternoon!' Adeline called to the woman, who was now pouring from the jug and filling the tumblers. 'I don't suppose we might trouble you for some water? I am Mrs Fanshawe, and this is Miss Busby. Jimmy Hooper sent us,' she added, at the woman's look of surprise at seeing Adeline's comfortable figure in her striking frock and heels in the middle of a country harvest.

'You're friends of Jimmy's?' the woman said, then relaxed into a smile. 'Come and sit down. I'm Irene,' she added, gesturing to a simple wooden bench. Adeline eyed it warily, but Miss Busby thanked her and obliged.

'Whatever did Jimmy send you all the way down here for?' she asked, hefting the jug. 'It's not water, mind,' she continued, pouring them each a tumblerful. 'Although I might be able to find some for your dog.' She smiled down at the little terrier staring intently up at her. 'It's our own cider, with Lara's honey added. Best kept secret in the county. There, you try that now and tell me it isn't.'

She looked at them expectantly, one hand on her hip. Adeline narrowed her eyes in suspicion, before taking a cautious sip.

'Good Lord!' she exclaimed, eyes widening.

Irene nodded approval, before looking to Miss Busby.

'Jimmy suggested we might find Henry White here?' she said.

'Henry's in the second field, he'll be along any minute. I can fetch him now if you're in a hurry?'

'No hurry,' Adeline murmured, before taking another appreciative sip.

Irene smiled as she looked back at Miss Busby.

Miss Busby looked down at the tumbler. 'It's very kind of you,' she said, 'but I don't normally—'

'Oh, be a devil, Isabelle,' Adeline encouraged. 'It's utterly delicious.'

Miss Busby obliged before Adeline could think of another argument. 'Oh, that *is* delicious!' she exclaimed.

Sweet and refreshing, there was a fizz to the drink that tickled the tongue and woke her taste buds.

'We always have a good batch ready for harvest,' Irene said. 'Are you hungry?'

'Ravenous,' Adeline declared.

Miss Busby arched a wry brow. Adeline had eaten rather a lot of biscuits at the manor.

'It was a long walk!' she retorted.

Irene began attacking a crusty loaf with a knife, then sliced each of them a thick piece of cheese, another of ham, and unceremoniously added a dollop of chutney for good measure. Barnaby had been exploring new smells, but now returned to sit by the table, ears pricked and nose twitching.

'Are you sure there's enough?' Miss Busby asked, as the first few men jumped the ditch at the end of the field and came forward to take their plates.

'There's plenty. The lads brought some loaves with them, Esther down at Lower Farm makes the chutney, and the butter's fresh churned this morning. You tuck in, my dears.'

'Thank you!' Adeline seemed delighted with the simple fare and Miss Busby found her enthusiasm infectious.

The farm labourers gave the unknown pair curious looks, but Irene murmured something to them in turn and each nodded respectfully as they filled plates and tumblers. Several bent to offer Barnaby a small piece of cheese or ham en route, and took seats either at the table or under the shade of the surrounding trees. Miss Busby looked around and saw a fallen log below the trees, and asked Irene if they might take their plates and sit in the cool shade.

'Well, of course you can. There's blankets on the wagon. Take one and make yourselves comfortable. I'll send Henry over soon as he appears.'

Adeline looked at the uneven ground and frowned. 'I was quite happy on the bench.'

'Yes, but we shan't be overheard on the log,' Miss Busby pointed out as they made their way over. 'And we needn't stay long.'

Adeline perched on the log as elegantly as she could manage, before attacking the food with gusto.

They had each cleared their plate when a short, wiry man, dressed in rough-spun trousers held by wide braces over a shirt that may once have been white, approached them holding a chipped enamel bowl.

'Af'ernoon. Heard you was lookin' for me,' he said, putting the water-filled bowl down beside them. 'Irene says t' give it your dog.' He took off his flat cap and twisted it nervously in his hands as he looked down at them. 'I'm Henry White.'

'Good afternoon, thank you for sparing us a moment, Henry. Would you like to sit down?' Miss Busby asked, smiling up at him.

He glanced back towards the table. Barnaby trotted over to drink from the bowl.

'Do join us,' Adeline said jovially, the tangy chutney having cheered her considerably. Or perhaps the cider. '*Huckleberry*,' she added in a dramatic stage whisper.

Henry's mouth fell open.

'Begging your pardon, but how is it you know Jimmy?' he asked, looking at Miss Busby. Adeline seemed to frighten him a little.

'We have a mutual friend in Miss Townsend.' Miss Busby glanced over Henry's shoulder, to make sure no one was able to overhear. 'Jimmy suggested you may be able to help with a matter concerning Lord Theodore Compton.'

'Theo?' He smiled and the tension lifted from his face. 'O'course, Miss.'

'Do you recall a gentleman visiting Cold Compton in recent weeks?' Miss Busby asked.

He furrowed his brow. 'I'm sure lots of 'em do, Miss, but I'm only here at harvest time, so I'm not sure as I can—'

'This one bore a striking resemblance to Theodore himself,' Adeline added.

Miss Busby wasn't sure the word *striking* had been used, but it certainly seemed to have the desired effect.

The sun-flush from the fields faded from his cheeks, leaving Henry pale and nervous before them.

'Theodore may be in trouble,' Miss Busy said gently. 'But you mustn't worry. Jimmy is keen to help him. We would like to talk to this stranger, if we may. Do you think that's something you could help us with?'

'I couldn't say... that is, I don't rightly know who you mean, Miss.'

'Perhaps a newcomer to Barton?' Miss Busby pressed, hazarding a guess from the little Jimmy had intimated.

'Why does Jimmy know you as Huckleberry?' Adeline asked, catching the poor man even more off guard.

'I...he... It was my favourite book, Miss. As a nipper. *Adventures of Huckleberry Finn*. Miss Townsend used to read it to us, if we was good in our lessons. Me and Jimmy both. We was in the same class.'

'Jemima and the boys were always more in favour of Tom Sawyer,' Adeline said.

Miss Busby thought she perhaps oughtn't to have any more cider.

'Oh, I liked Tom too, Miss,' Henry said. 'Only, Huck, well, my Dad liked a drink or two, y'see...'

Miss Busby felt a tug at her heart as she nodded in understanding. She had read the book to many of her pupils in her time.

'I'm surprised he told you,' he went on quietly. 'There's only him and Miss Townsend left in the village who know me as Huckleberry, now. I used to pretend to be Huck, see. When things got so as you'd want to pretend to be someone else.'

Adeline put down her mug with a small 'Oh' of sympathy.

'He suggested we use the name to show we are trusted friends,' Miss Busby said. 'We shouldn't have asked anything further about it, I'm sorry if we were intruding.'

'It dun't matter, Miss. But it must be serious, then,' he said. 'About the young Lord?'

'It may be. He has been arrested this morning for the murder of his mother. If he's innocent, as I'm sure

Jimmy believes him to be, I think this stranger may be able to help.'

'Well, of course he's innocent, Miss!' Henry looked bemused. 'Theo kill his mother? I never heard anything so daft. Wasn't he the only one in the village who supported her!'

'Inspector McKay is a most determined individual,' Adeline cautioned. 'And he would not arrest the man without good cause.'

Henry scratched his head. 'Determined or not, he can't fix up a man for a crime he didn't do, can he?' Henry shook his head, as if to clear it, before continuing, 'I'm sure the master'll be home in time for his tea, Miss. Didn't that policeman arrest Lara this morning? Seems he dun't rightly know what he's doin'. He musta changed his mind pretty quick.'

'He only took her in for questioning, but if some new evidence has come to light…' Adeline let the thought hang for a moment.

'We're not sure what has gone on, Henry, and everyone seems so concerned for both Lara and Theo, but so reluctant to talk to us. We would like a word with the stranger, if possible. We don't mean him, or Theo, any harm. I'm quite sure Jimmy wouldn't have sent us to you unless he believed that.'

Henry hung his head, worrying at the rim of his cap with nervous fingers.

'There ain't no harm in Kaleb Brakspear,' he said quietly. 'He only wanted to see…well, it in't my place to say, Miss.'

'That's perfectly understandable,' Miss Busby assured him. 'Perhaps you could tell us where we might find him, and then we can ask him for ourselves.'

'I dunno…' Indecision twisted his features.

'It's better we find him before the police do,' Adeline added sternly.

Henry was quiet for a moment, then murmured, 'Like in the book, when Aunt Pol found Huck?'

'What?' Adeline's brow furrowed in confusion, but Miss Busby thought she caught his meaning.

'True identities do have a habit of being revealed,' she said softly. 'Both within fiction and without.'

Henry rose to his feet and replaced his cap on his head. 'You might like to look on the very edge of Barton, Miss. Past the bridge and beyond the thicket. There's a rundown old cottage in amongst the overgrowth back there. And now if you'll excuse me, I 'spect they've finished loading the first wagon and I've to take it back to the stackyard. They'll be held up if I don't.'

'Is that on the way up to the main road?' Adeline asked hopefully. 'Because we would rather appreciate a ride with you.'

## CHAPTER 13

'Thank you, Henry,' Miss Busby said, giving him a warm smile as he hopped down and held out a hand to see her safely down from the worn bench seat of the laden wagon.

'Hello?' Adeline called rather sharply from the other side.

Henry dashed around to help her.

Miss Busby picked a stray barley stalk from Adeline's hair as Henry bade them farewell and clicked the reins to move the horses on.

'Well,' Adeline said, brushing down the front of her dress. 'To Barton, I presume? And if this Kaleb fellow turns out to be the suspicious sort, we must go to Stow.'

'Yes. Although you might like to freshen up first, if that's the case…'

Adeline raised a hand to her hair in alarm, feeling the damage the bumpy ride up the track had caused.

'It's not that bad,' Miss Busby tried. A smile, then a laugh, escaped her, and Adeline followed suit.

'If James could see me now.'

'He would be extremely proud of your spirit of adventure,' Miss Busby replied, her blue eyes shining.

'Yes, I rather think he would,' Adeline agreed as she marched over to the Rolls, still perched awkwardly on the verge, and installed herself behind the wheel once more.

'Henry's directions were quite clear,' Miss Busby said, letting Barnaby into the back. 'We drive up through the village and onto the main road, take the first turning on the left, and look for a sharp right, then up to the old Barton bridge.'

Adeline gamely manoeuvred the front end of the car into the narrow lane and they set off once again.

'We are drawing closer to uncovering the mystery,' she proclaimed, reaching for her sunglasses as the road widened before them. 'The poacher has let the cat out of the bag. Or the rabbit out of the hat, rather.' She turned to Miss Busby with a satisfied smile.

'Perhaps the housekeeper, more than the poacher,' Miss Busby mused.

'How so?' Adeline asked, turning to her.

'Eyes forward,' Miss Busby cautioned.

Adeline *tsked*, but obliged.

'Jimmy said Emily has worked at the manor for the best part of thirty years, and started out as a maid,' Miss Busby continued.

'Yes, I should imagine a lot of them do.'

'They are a small staff, and she has known Theo all his life.'

'Isabelle, there is nothing remarkable in that. Many servants– Oh!' The penny dropped. 'You think she may be the young maid who let Hattie in to see Lady Compton and the baby that day?'

Miss Busby nodded. 'I think it was clear by her reaction when we mentioned Nurse Delaney. The entire village may know, or suspect, the truth of Theodore's birth and are guarding the secret.'

'Because Theodore would not inherit if he were known to be illegitimate,' Adeline reasoned as they approached the main road. She gave a perfunctory glance over her shoulder before making the left turn. 'And we would be back to the notion of the estate being sold and fresh devils potentially waiting in the wings. For all this talk of kindness and community, Isabelle, these people are perhaps rather self-centred at heart.'

'Oh, I think we probably all are, if you dig deep enough,' Miss Busby reasoned. 'But the difference here is that they are community-centred, rather than self.'

'You are endlessly determined to see the good in people,' Adeline said, turning to her once more.

'So are you, Adeline,' Miss Busby remarked. 'Underneath it all. And I think we have just missed our turning.'

Adeline wrestled the car around and they crawled slowly forward until a narrow, overgrown farm track could just be seen bordering the field.

'Good Lord, is it safe?' Adeline asked, peering through the windscreen with concern.

'Henry said it should be passable this time of year,' Miss Busby replied, a note of doubt in her voice.

Adeline nudged her wheels onto the track, and the Rolls slowly began to bump along it, scraping the hedgerows either side en route.

'He did say it was little used,' Miss Busby added, as a particularly deep rut almost sent Adeline's sunglasses flying. Then smiled at the incongruous sight they must be making, for the second, or perhaps third time, this day.

'Good, because we shall be in trouble if we meet anything coming the other way.'

'I suppose… all the… farm traffic will… be at Cold Compton…until nightfall,' Miss Busby managed as they bounced along.

Adeline concentrated her attention on the track until, after a torturous mile, a dense hazel thicket signalled the end of the road. A small stone bridge stood to the right over a stream.

'We'll have to walk from here,' Miss Busby said, letting a rather shaken Barnaby out of the back.

Adeline stood and began to straighten her dress and hair once more, before eyeing the thicket Miss Busby was headed towards. She sighed and gave it up as a lost cause.

'I do wish I had known we would be indulging in such rural pursuits, Isabelle,' she called. 'I wouldn't have worn these heels for a start.'

'Would you rather wait in the car?' Miss Busby called.

There was a short pause, then, 'No. I'm sure I shall manage.'

Miss Busby smiled as she held back a branch to let her friend through. 'It's not too bad here, look,' she said, finding a narrow path.

'I can smell woodsmoke,' Adeline remarked, picking her way around nettles and brambles.

Miss Busby looked up to see a thin tendril of smoke rising ahead. 'We aren't far. Barnaby, this way!' she called.

They concentrated on their footing in silence for a while before rounding a mass of brambles to reveal the remains of a crumbling cottage before them. Tumbledown in the extreme, an oak tree had forced its way through the back half of the house and grown up through a broken section of the roof. The front half, however, showed makeshift curtains hanging in the window, and a line had been hung between two branches to the side of the house. Several personal items of clothing hung there, drying in the breeze.

Adeline turned to look at them with distaste. Miss Busby followed her gaze.

'Well,' Adeline sniffed, 'It *is* Monday, I suppose.'

'May I help you, ladies?' a soft voice called. Both women turned to see a tall, strongly built man standing in the now open doorway of the cottage. A navy woollen jumper over an untucked shirt, fringing dark trousers. Heavy, unlaced boots appeared to have been thrown on in a hurry, and his thick blond hair was pushed back from a mature face. He observed them with icy blue eyes from behind the gun aimed directly at them.

# CHAPTER 14

Barnaby emerged from the thicket and began barking insistently at the aggressor.

'Barnaby, come here!' Miss Busby called, frightened for the little dog.

'That is a Lee-Enfield rifle,' Adeline hissed amidst the commotion.

Miss Busby failed to see the significance. A gun was a gun, and an image of Lady Compton lying shot on the lawn filled her mind. Were she and Adeline about to meet the same fate? Not to mention Barnaby. She took a quick breath, and tried to keep her voice even as she called, 'Good afternoon. We are looking for Kaleb Brakspear.'

'You've found him,' the man replied, his voice equally even.

Barnaby stopped barking, but kept up a low growl from his mistress' side.

'That is an Army issue weapon,' Adeline hissed, more urgently. 'Be careful, Isabelle, if he stole that from a military man he may well have–'

'You've a good eye, if a terrible whisper,' he called. 'The rifle's my own.'

'Then would you mind lowering it?' Miss Busby asked, her voice shaking only a little. 'I'm sure you can quite clearly see we pose no threat. We simply want to talk.'

He studied them in silence for a moment, before saying, 'You're not from Cold Compton. You're too well dressed, with your hair nice. Look very well fed, and all.'

Adeline, who had raised a hand reflexively to her hair, bristled. 'Well, *really*, I–'

'And I'd say as I've had more to fear from coddled women pushing their noses in than I ever have from someone pointing a gun. So before I lower it, why don't you tell me what you want to talk about?'

Miss Busby's head spun. She thought to say that Henry White had sent them, but then worried the poor man might suffer retribution. She didn't mention Jimmy for the same reason. Perhaps the inspector? *Oh, Lord*, she thought. *What have I done–?*

'We are here to ask if you are Theodore Compton's true father, and if you killed Lady Compton,' Adeline said firmly. 'And if it *was* you,' she added, 'you needn't get any ideas. There are several people who know exactly where we are, and what we intend to ask you. If anything happens to us, they will know precisely who is responsible.'

Miss Busby's jaw dropped in tandem with Kaleb's. '*Adeline!*' she whispered, her tone part horror, part admiration.

Kaleb lowered the gun, and raised his eyebrows.

'Well now, a lady who speaks fair and square, is it? That's a rarity and no mistake. Although, I'm not so sure as to that last part. But I admire your bravery, Miss…?'

'*Mrs* Fanshawe. And this is Miss Busby.'

'Well then, Mrs Fanshawe and Miss Busby, I suggest you both mind your business and go on home.'

Adeline opened her mouth to object, but floundered. She turned to Miss Busby, to see her friend's shoulders hunched and trembling. Her eyes widened in alarm. 'Isabelle! Are you alright?'

'I…I'm so sorry. I think it's the heat…' Miss Busby's voice was hoarse, and she swayed unsteadily on her feet. Barnaby began to whine. Adeline took her elbow, and looked to Kaleb.

'Fetch some water,' she called. 'Please. My friend is unwell. Isabelle!' She took both elbows now, standing in front of Miss Busby and looking down at her with deep concern. 'It's all this walking. We've hardly stopped to draw breath today. We should have washed our hands of the young lord the moment we were first lied to. Water, *please*!' she called back to Kaleb, who was watching them with a mixture of caution and curiosity. 'If you hadn't aimed that gun at us…' her voice quavered.

'It's not loaded.' Kaleb leaned the rifle against the door of the cottage and stepped towards them. 'You'd best come inside,' he said, holding a hand out to Miss Busby. Barnaby began barking again, and Adeline glared at the man. He gestured through the open front door. 'Go on and sit down. I'll fetch a cup of water from the well.'

Adeline steered Miss Busby through the door, Barnaby glued to her heels as she fretted terribly over her friend. Kaleb strode off quickly around to the back.

'Adeline, don't be silly,' Miss Busby said quietly, her voice perfectly strong and controlled.

'Isabelle! You... you were *faking*!' she whispered.

'Yes,' she admitted. 'I got the idea from Emily's reaction earlier this morning.'

'But...I was worried!' Adeline objected.

Miss Busby took her hand, and squeezed it, before bending to ruffle Barnaby's ears. 'I'm sorry for that, but I couldn't see how we should manage to talk to him otherwise.'

'Well...yes...I suppose, but now what?' Adeline hissed, exasperated.

'We ought to sit down, as he said, and I'll pretend to recover. Slowly. I'm sure if he meant us harm, he would have acted by now.'

Adeline *harrumphed*. 'He could be fetching an axe, or some such,' she muttered.

'Nonsense,' Miss Busby tutted and sat down. She looked around the dim interior, as Barnaby made a thorough investigation of the floor. Floral wallpaper, peeling and spotted with damp, a fire burning in the iron cooking range set in the wide inglenook. Blankets and cushions had been arranged neatly on a bed which doubled as a sofa, and a wooden table stood in the centre, surrounded by three wooden milking stools. A bible rested on a shelf fixed to the wall, alongside several small wooden ornaments in various states of carving - a folded pocket knife beside them. One was clearly a horse, the other, she thought, had the shape of a beehive, although it was unfinished. The last, she couldn't discern.

Barnaby turned around three times before lying on the threadbare rug beside the range.

'You are both far too trusting,' Adeline muttered, taking the stool beside her as Kaleb's heavy footsteps announced his reappearance.

'Here,' he said, passing a tin mug filled with clear, cold water to Miss Busby.

She nodded her thanks and took a sip as Adeline looked on suspiciously.

'I've another cup if you'd like some?' Kaleb asked.

Adeline lifted her chin. 'I am not thirsty. Thank you.'

'You feeling better?' he asked Miss Busby, concern in his voice.

'A little, yes,' she said. 'I still feel rather dizzy, I'm afraid.'

'Hm.' He took the third stool, doubt furrowing his brow.

'If you hadn't aimed your rifle at us, this wouldn't have happened,' Adeline repeated in heavy reprimand.

'If you hadn't come asking questions you've no business asking, then you're right, it wouldn't have.'

*Touché,* Miss Busby thought. 'If I may just finish this and sit for a moment, I'm sure we shall be on our way in no time.'

'That you will,' he agreed.

Miss Busby glanced at the shelf. 'Are those your carvings?'

He nodded.

'The beehive is most unusual.'

Adeline followed her gaze. 'Oh, Lord, not bees again.'

'You spoke of the young lord,' Kaleb said, pushing himself back from the table and crossing one long leg over the other. 'What is he to you?'

'A thorn in our side,' Adeline declared.

'A friend of ours is concerned for Theodore,' Miss Busby said, ignoring her. 'She has known him since he was a babe, and had heard of a stranger near the estate not long before his mother was murdered.'

'Had she now? And what's her name, this friend of yours?' Kaleb asked.

His eyes showed intelligence in his face, which was still handsome, despite the deep lines carved into it. Miss Busby supposed Theodore would look much the same, albeit younger. Lara was certainly a pretty girl. They must make quite the couple.

'Nurse De–' Adeline began.

'I don't think that's relevant,' Miss Busby cut in.

'I should say it is,' Kaleb said, his eyes narrowing. 'If this nurse friend of yours is spreading rumours about the place.'

'*She* isn't,' Adeline went on. 'But there are rumours. And with no one in Cold Compton capable of telling the truth, we had no idea what to believe. We simply went to the village to allay Nurse, *ahem*, our friend's concerns,' she corrected herself, 'and found a community shrouded in falsehoods and misery.'

'Then why not just make your way home again?' he retorted.

'Adeline, that was unfair,' Miss Busby admonished. 'We found a community who cares deeply for one another, but they are afraid. As am I.'

'Afraid of what?' Kaleb asked sharply.

'Afraid a terrible injustice may occur,' Miss Busby answered solemnly.

'Well, if it does, what concern is it of yours? You don't live there.'

Miss Busby blinked. 'Are we only permitted, then, to care for our direct neighbours?'

'That's plenty more than some manage,' he replied.

'Perhaps,' Miss Busby said, taking another sip of water. 'But how sad, all the same. We have made a friend in Miss Townsend, and were charmed by young Lara. Jimmy has been most pleasant to us, and a nice woman from Grange Farm was kind enough to give us lunch. It didn't seem to matter to any of *them* that we aren't neighbours.'

'You are wearing your rose-tinted spectacles again, Isabelle,' Adeline cautioned. 'It certainly mattered when it came to them hiding things from us.'

Kaleb eyed the pair thoughtfully. 'But one of them must've told you where to find me. You're not likely to have stumbled down here by accident.'

Miss Busby gave a nod, and a sad smile. 'Their concern for their young lord rather loosened tongues this morning. Particularly now that he has been arrested.'

'What?' Kaleb said in shock. 'Theo's arrested? When?'

'A little before lunch,' Miss Busby said. 'That is the possible injustice which concerns me. *Us*,' she added, with a look at Adeline.

Kaleb pinched the bridge of his nose, before dropping his head into his hands and letting loose a long, painful sigh.

'Lara was taken into the station in the first instance,' Miss Busby went on to explain. 'And Theo went there with Sykes and Alfred–'

'Sykes?' Kaleb's head shot up. 'That sneaking lickspittle.'

Miss Busby looked up. 'He did seem rather…objectionable,' she said. 'He drove Lara and Alfred back to Cold Compton, and brought the news that Theo had been arrested for the murder of his mother.'

'Theo never killed his mother,' he said quietly. 'She died months ago.'

'Ah,' Miss Busby said softly, after a respectful pause, allowing the truth to sink in. 'I'm sorry to hear that. But I wonder if now might be the time to tell someone?'

'Yes,' Adeline added. 'This deception has gone on far too long.'

'Deception is it?' he suddenly raised his voice. 'Aye, and you'd know, would you? You do-gooding women are all the same. You go about, interfering, making out you're all charitable and respectable when underneath it all you're destroying people's lives without a thought.' His voice thickened with emotion. 'There are plenty of folk who truly *are* charitable and respectable, but because they're not rich, no one sees it that way.'

'How *do* they see it?' Miss Busby asked, holding a hand up to silence Adeline.

'They see it as an opportunity, don't they?' His eyes found hers, a mixture of anger, resentment, and something else she couldn't quite put her finger on. 'A chance to take what they want, throw a few coins about to make themselves feel virtuous, and off they go - not a care in the world for what they've left behind.'

'And what *have* they left behind?' Adeline asked.

'Pain!' he shouted, startling her. 'Heartbreak for the hole they left in our lives that couldn't ever be filled. And lies and deceit that'd tear a family apart even if the heartbreak didn't. Swanning in, full of privilege and entitlement and just… *taking*…our own…our own…'

Miss Busby placed gentle fingers on the man's arm. 'Your own son,' she said. There was no hint of a question. It was obvious from his distress. 'Lady Compton took your baby son, didn't she?'

Silence fell between them. Kaleb was clearly trying to hold back the tears, his head in his hands. Adeline reached into her sleeve for a handkerchief and blew her nose. Barnaby went to Kaleb and pushed his nose against his knee. He dropped a hand to the dog and ruffled his ears.

'Where were you, when Theo was taken?' Miss Busby asked gently.

'Far away,' his voice softened. 'Lost, so they thought. I'd signed up for the navy; Tess - my wife - and I wanted lives of our own. We didn't want to live in servitude to Lord Granville and his family. We thought that I'd be able to earn enough for us to move away somewhere.'

Miss Busby recalled Lady Compton's family home was the Granville estate. 'What was your work there?' she asked, observing that telling his tale appeared to calm him.

'I looked after his Lordship's hunters. Fine horses they were. I'd wanted to join the cavalry as an ostler but the recruiting officer said they only had jobs in the navy... Well, they sent me sailing off to fight in Crete, near enough right after I joined. Green as anything and scared half to death.'

Adeline blew her nose again and said sombrely, 'I'm sorry I accused you of stealing the rifle.'

'S'alright,' he replied gruffly. 'I bought it a long time ago from the Army and Navy Store. Needed it to keep the foxes out of the henhouse.'

'Tess must have been worried sick for you. I remember when Randolf, my fiancé...' Miss Busby trailed off. Even now, after all this time, it was still hard to think of.

'You lost him to war?' Kaleb asked.

Miss Busby nodded, looking determinedly down at her skirt and trying to keep her emotions in check. 'His regiment was sent to fight the Boers. He died shortly before he was due home for our wedding.'

The painful parallel in their circumstances sat between them for a moment, heavy in the silence.

'I'm sorry to hear that,' Kaleb said.

She waved a hand, trying to dismiss a sadness that had never completely left her.

'Neither me nor Tess had any other family. She found out she was carrying after I'd left. She was frightened, she wrote to me and they were going to let me come home to see him born,' Kaleb went on quietly. 'Said as the revolt would be over and done with plenty before then. But our ship was hit, and sunk, and they thought us all drowned. Sent word back home saying as much. Only we were lucky, me and a couple of the other lads had managed to hold on to some of the wreckage. Drifted a ways, but we clung on and kept our heads down. Didn't look like nothing more than lumps of wood floating about. We got ourselves picked up by some Greek fishermen, but it took weeks to get back to the fleet, and when we did, it took even longer for the news to get home. By then, Tess had already...' His voice caught.

'She thought she'd lost you,' Adeline finished the sentence for him. 'And she let the babe go.'

'She had no choice,' Kaleb went on. 'The money we'd saved was going nowhere, and I'd only just joined the navy, she knew she'd never get a penny from them.'

'How *awful*,' Adeline exclaimed softly.

'When I finally got back home, Tess was in a terrible

state. She told me she'd lost the baby. I thought she'd miscarried, and she never said otherwise. I was heartbroken, of course, but I never thought it was her fault, and never understood why she always seemed to blame herself. If anything, I thought it was *my* fault.'

'Don't be silly,' Adeline sniffed. 'How could it possibly be your fault that your ship was hit?'

'If I hadn't gone away, or had ideas of us living a life of our own, we'd have had our boy. I put that above us being together,' he scoffed, 'that's all it comes down to - having ideas above our station.' He dropped his hand to Barnaby's head again, rubbing at the wiry fur around the dog's solid little neck. 'Do you have children?' he asked, straightening up and taking a breath.

'Yes,' said Adeline, at the same moment Miss Busby said, 'No.'

'A daughter,' Adeline went on, 'Jemima. And I am blessed with two grandchildren.'

'Blessed is right,' Kaleb said, nodding with a sad smile.

'But Miss Busby has taught no end of children, and been like a mother to many of them,' Adeline added.

'I had none of my own,' she told Kaleb, then sighed. 'I fear we may have all judged one another rather harshly.'

Silence fell again.

'Happen I was wrong about you,' Kaleb said. 'Lady Compton soured everything for me, you understand? Even in death, she's still tormenting my family. My boy, Theo.'

Miss Busby thought how people could change when their family was threatened. Even the gentlest of souls would fight tooth and nail for those they loved. 'And Tess?' she asked softly. 'How did she die?'

'Scarlet fever,' Kaleb said. 'This May just gone. She's free of Lady Compton's cruelty now, and her own guilt.'

'I'm so sorry,' Miss Busby said. Adeline blew once more into the handkerchief.

'She was never the same after I got back,' Kaleb carried on. 'Never strong, like she was before I went. And with the babe gone… I didn't know why, then, but I think it ate away at her. Keeping the secret all these years. Probably wondering what his life was like.'

'How did you discover the truth?' Miss Busby spoke quietly.

'It was when she fell poorly. Once the doctor said what was wrong with her, Tess shut herself away and wouldn't let me near. Locked the door and screamed to be left alone, said she had to keep me safe,' Kaleb went on. 'I broke the door open, but she got so upset that I didn't dare do anything *but* keep away. I thought maybe she could fight it off, but she wasn't strong enough. She wrote a letter, tucked it away so I'd find it after she was gone. Told me everything. How the Granvilles' daughter, Lady Compton, had come home, and came to visit with the family nurse. They offered Tess enough to pay for my funeral and cover her rent for as long as she wanted to live on the estate. And they hinted she wouldn't be allowed to stay if she didn't agree. Well, she knew she couldn't find work, and there was no way to bring up the babe on her own. And where else was she going to live? She had no money, nowhere to go, no one to go *to*. So…there it is. I came back, but Tess's shame kept her silent. Wouldn't none of the neighbours speak up neither, they were afeared of saying anything.' He stared, unseeing, at the table. 'All so some rich woman could have what she wanted.'

# CHAPTER 15

Silence fell once more as each of them considered the circumstances, and the consequences of Kaleb's story in sorrowful silence.

Miss Busby broke it. 'Did you continue working for the Granvilles? When you returned from Crete?'

Kaleb sniffed, and shook his head. 'Tess didn't want to stay, and we'd planned to leave anyway. Didn't seem no point taking a backwards step. The navy gave me leave to get over my injuries - I'd taken a fair battering in the sea. While I was still mending, I found us a little place in Hayling Island.'

'Hampshire?' Adeline asked, eyebrows raised.

He nodded. 'One of the navy lads told me about it. Rent was hardly anything if you were signed up and could show your papers. I thought the sea air'd do Tess good, but…'

'There are some wounds it can't heal,' Miss Busby said.

'Happen so,' he murmured, lowering his head. 'She'd fallen into herself. I found her a doctor soon after we moved, and he said she had melancholia. Gave her laudanum for it. I thought p'raps we'd have another babe, but…' He shook his head. 'I never understood it, not until she left me that letter. If she'd only told me…'

'I suppose she thought the boy would have a better life as a lord,' Adeline said. 'She may have thought she was protecting him.'

'From what?' Kaleb looked up sharply. 'His own kin? What better life could a boy have than the love of his own true parents?'

'She knew you'd go to him,' Miss Busby mused. 'She was protecting you, as much as Theo. The poor soul must have been distraught.'

Kaleb sighed.

'And yet she confessed, at the end,' Adeline said, as if trying to chivvy him. 'Because he was a grown man, by then, do you think?'

He shook his head. 'Happen she couldn't meet God with what she'd got on her conscience. She was a believer, went to church when she could.'

'How did you manage to find Theo?' Miss Busby asked, not wanting the poor tortured man to drift any deeper into sadness.

He took a moment before replying.

'Would you like some water?' Adeline asked, reaching for the now-empty tin mug.

'No, thank you,' he said, a tight smile lifting his features. 'It's all overgrown out there and I wouldn't want you to trip. But you're kind to ask.'

Adeline sat back with a nod.

'The Granvilles only had one daughter,' he continued. 'She wasn't difficult to find; everyone knew she'd married the old Lord Compton.'

Miss Busby sighed. It felt as if they had done a week's worth of investigating in the space of a day. It had only been a few hours earlier, she realised, that she had hung her washing out and made notes. And even then she had felt tired. Now her brain was abuzz, but her heart heavy.

'And you didn't hesitate to seek him out?' Adeline was indefatigable.

'Of course not.' Kaleb's eyebrows rose. 'He's my flesh and blood. My only child.'

'But surely you didn't expect him to leave the manor?' Adeline pressed.

'I didn't expect anything,' Kaleb replied, pushing his shoulders back and sitting a little straighter. 'Only thought as the boy should know the truth, and that I'm here for him if ever he needs me.'

'And how did he react?' Miss Busby asked, intrigued.

'Shocked, at first, like you'd expect. But then in a heartbeat it was almost like it was a relief to him,' Kaleb said. 'As if he knew he'd never quite fitted, and now he knew why.'

'And did the two of you talk about what he wanted from your relationship?' Miss Busby's blue eyes shone as she leant forward, compelled by the man's tale.

He nodded. 'I gave him some time to let it all sink in. It's no easy thing to have dropped on you. I told him I'd find a place nearby, just for a little while, and he came to see me a few days later.'

'What did he say?' Adeline asked eagerly, equally compelled.

'He said as he'd like everyone to know I'm his father,' Kaleb said proudly. 'And that's what I want, too. He's a fine young man, anyone'd be lucky to call him their own. But Lady Compton was alive then. I feared that if he confronted her with the truth, she'd throw him out. He could've come to Hayling Island with me then and there, but she'd be even harder on the villagers because of it. I've seen what they're suffering. It was the same on her folks' estate, but folks here are older, they can't get jobs in the towns, nor afford the rent there, neither. Theo was worried about it, and so was I. My Tess and me had wanted to escape all that. It'd be a dishonour to her memory to make their suffering worse.'

'So you both decided to do nothing?' Adeline guessed.

'Yes, he wanted time to think. He had intended to take on the estate on his birthday next month,' Kaleb replied. 'But now someone's killed her, and you needn't go thinking it was one of us,' he went on, with a meaningful look to Adeline. 'Theo was with me down by the river from eleven o'clock the day she was shot. He'd come early, he was upset because he'd argued with her that morning.'

'*He* argued with her?' Miss Busby said. They'd only heard mention of the argument between Lady Compton and Sykes.

'What about?' Adeline asked.

'That doesn't matter. What matters is that he couldn't've killed her,' Kaleb said firmly.

'Word has got out about you being in the area,' Miss Busby said. 'And there do seem to be…suspicions…'

Kaleb's expression darkened. 'Sykes. He was Lady Compton's enforcer in the village. He loved the role and kept a watch on everyone. A snake if ever there was one.'

'Enforcer?' Miss Busby asked.

'The decrees!' Adeline realised. 'Isabelle, we wondered how she enforced her draconian rules, remember?'

'Yes, of course.' Understanding dawned. 'He would check for lamps in windows, and washing hanging out to dry when it shouldn't have been?' Miss Busby asked.

Kaleb nodded. 'He'd report back to her ladyship. I don't think he found out about me. He'd have caused havoc if he did. Most folk wouldn't talk, but…' He shrugged. 'Anyway, I was going to go home, and come back and forth to see Theo sometimes. It was the best we could think to do.'

'And what do you think would be the best action to take now?' Miss Busby asked.

'He must go and tell the police he was with Theo,' Adeline interjected, as if it were perfectly obvious.

'Tell the police?' Kaleb stood up, anger in his eyes. Adeline leaned back in alarm. 'And then what? If I go to the police and tell them the truth, it will bring all that to an end. He'll have nothing. And who's left to look out for the villagers then?'

'You needn't say you're his father,' Adeline replied.

'We look alike, that's how Theo understood I am who I said. The police'll guess in an instant,' Kaleb replied. ''Specially if they've already heard the rumours.'

His words sank home, and Adeline turned to Miss Busby.

'I understand what is at stake.' Miss Busby chose her words carefully. 'But he has no alibi for Lady Compton's death, other than you.'

'You think they'll believe us, given we're kin who've been part of a lie all these years? And given what you've heard? Who has a better motive to kill her than either of us?'

That gave her pause. 'Then what is the alternative?'

'I don't know.' He seemed confounded, his face dropping. 'Someone needs to find out who killed her. Cause it weren't me, and it weren't Theo.'

'And the best person for that is Isabelle,' Adeline immediately said. 'She has already uncovered two murderers – with some help from myself,' she added.

Kaleb looked at Miss Busby, doubt clearly written on his face. 'You've uncovered murderers?'

'Unlikely as it seems–' she began.

'Of course she has, and it was done properly, by helping the police find the right track,' Adeline pronounced. 'And don't forget, we found you, and even the police haven't been able to do that.'

Something like hope gleamed in Kaleb's eyes. 'But could you do that without the police finding out the truth of Theo's birth? Because it will condemn him if they do.'

'I really don't—' Miss Busby began.

'Of course we could,' Adeline decided.

Miss Busby closed her eyes and thought for a moment, her mind spinning as the morals of the issue danced. 'Only if Theo agrees,' she insisted. 'And that will depend on whether or not we can gain access to him at the police station.'

'We shall talk the inspector around,' Adeline declared. 'We always do. We will help you, Kaleb. And your son,' she added.

Kaleb was silent a moment, before taking Adeline's hand, startling her, as he said, 'You are a very kind lady, Mrs Fanshawe, and I'm sorry as how I ever lumped you in with the likes of Lady Compton. Both of you,' he added, turning back to Miss Busby.

'Well, let's see first, shall we?' Miss Busby replied. 'And you will have to decide what to do for the best, when the matter is concluded.'

'I will, Theo and me both,' he assured her.

Adeline didn't say a word when they got in the car. She seemed deeply affected by Kaleb's story, and, Miss Busby suspected, ashamed of her initial assumptions. *It's so easy to make them*, she thought. *We're all guilty of it from time to time.*

Miss Busby held on to the door handle as she was buffeted along the track, deep in thought. When they turned onto the metalled road, she glanced at Adeline and chided, 'You really ought not to have told him we can keep all this from the inspector.'

'Why not?' She remained unabashed. 'It has no bearing on the murder, if they were together at the time. And we know Kaleb isn't lying, that level of distress simply cannot be fabricated.'

'Yes,' Miss Busby murmured in agreement. 'He was certainly suffering.'

'And we are entitled to our secrets. Lord knows the Scot keeps enough of his own when it suits him! That young madam, Rowena, for a start!'

Miss Busby smiled, and drifted back into a contemplative silence, glancing out of the window at the view that unfolded before them. Mature woodland rose and fell with the hills, punctuated by farmland and water meadows, meandering brooks, and hedgerows alive with colour. *Such beauty*, she thought, *here for everyone to see - rich or poor, childless or surrounded by family; we are so very fortunate. If only we remember to look.*

The purr of the engine lulled her as they drove over the hill and the smooth road carried them closer to Stow, and the police station.

Adeline fumbled for her sunglasses as bright rays bounced off the road ahead. 'So when Lady Compton realised she couldn't have children,' she said, still working over the details, 'and the estate would consequently be left without an heir, she went home to her family estate and selected Tess as the most likely candidate, paying the poor girl off as described.'

'And threatening her as well,' Miss Busby said.

'Indeed.' Adeline nodded. 'And the woman truly

thought she could return to Cold Compton, suddenly in possession of a babe clearly not newborn, and have no questions asked?' Adeline continued.

'Her family must have had enough funds and power at their disposal - it could have been as simple as making any other transaction.'

'Like buying a horse?'

Miss Busby winced. 'Yes, I suppose. Although a horse's mother can't reappear several years later confessing his true parentage.'

'But in thinking the father dead, and knowing the girl had no family of her own, they banked on her shame and poverty holding her silent. It's despicable, Isabelle,' she concluded. 'No amount of money or status should enable someone to destroy a family in that manner.'

'It happens, Adeline, and Tess obviously thought the child better off,' Miss Busby said softly. 'And there's nothing we can do about it now. But we have a chance, perhaps, to set the balance straight in this instance. We'll have to be careful, though. It won't be easy to keep Kaleb's secret.'

'Lady Compton managed it for twenty-four years - we should be able to do so until the murderer is behind bars.'

'Speaking of which, how on earth are we going to persuade the inspector to let Theo *out* from behind them?' Miss Busby wondered.

Adeline didn't speak for a while. 'Are we quite certain he's innocent, Isabelle? Because her being killed is really quite convenient.'

Miss Busby sighed. 'I suppose that's what we will have to discover.'

They turned off the main road and onto Stow's busy High Street. Lined with bustling shops, it was crowded with people enjoying the late summer sunshine. Adeline had to sound her horn twice in quick succession to clear the road of a group of excitable children enjoying penny licks from an ice-cream cart.

'There's the station,' Adeline said, 'but I'll park in the market square - it will be easier.' She did so, leaving the car rather impressively angled to take up room for three vehicles before she turned off the engine. They sat for a moment. 'If Theodore didn't kill Lady Compton, and it wasn't Kaleb, then who on earth was it?'

'Sykes seems to engender a fair amount of dislike,' Miss Busby mused.

'Yes. And he looks the sort,' Adeline agreed, before exclaiming, 'Isabelle! He was the chauffeur!'

'Yes?' Miss Busby said, raising a quizzical brow.

'What if he was the one who drove Lady Compton back to Berkshire to purchase the babe in the first place? We know he was engaged by the old lord. Sykes could have known about the deception from the outset!'

'It depends on when he was taken on,' Miss Busby said, opening the door and clipping Barnaby's leash to his collar. Stow was a busy market town and he had a mind of his own when he wanted to.

'Yes, but *Emily* wouldn't have shot her. She barely looked strong enough to hold a pistol, never mind a shotgun, and she went into a paroxysm of fear just thinking of the matter. Sykes may have known *more* than all the others. Where the babe was taken from, for example. Perhaps even how much was paid. He may have been blackmailing Lady Compton for years!'

'Then surely killing her would have removed his source of income.'

Adeline *tsked*. 'You are not thinking this through, Isabelle. Perhaps she refused to pay him any longer. Perhaps she had heard Kaleb had turned up and knew the game was up. Or perhaps, if the estate is as indebted as people say, she simply had no more money to give him.'

Miss Busby considered as they walked. 'But why would he have continued working for her, if he were blackmailing her?'

Adeline floundered a moment, before rebounding with, 'to keep up appearances. And he seems the sort to enjoy enforcement, don't you think?' she added, gaining steam.

'But he wasn't at the manor on Friday afternoon. He went to Stow with Charles Walton, the estate manager,' Miss Busby reminded her.

'Ah yes, there is that. Oh,' she sighed in irritation. 'There is so much still to uncover.'

They passed a bookshop, a baker, and a butcher's to arrive at the black railings and privet hedge surrounding the police station. Miss Busby paused to let two young schoolgirls in neat uniform and straw boaters, to make a fuss of Barnaby before looping his leash over one of the railings. She told the dog to be a good boy before following Adeline through the front door.

'Aha!' Adeline exclaimed.

'Bobby,' Miss Busby smiled, delighted to see the young sergeant.

'Hullo, Miss.' He seemed rather startled as he looked up from writing in a notebook open on the scarred and ring-stained counter top. 'What are you doin' here? You're not looking for the inspector, are you?' he added, 'Only he's in an awful mood.'

'*Imagine* my surprise,' Adeline muttered.

Miss Busby shot her a look. 'We might ask what *you're* doing here,' she countered. 'Can Little Minton spare your talents?'

'Oh, yes Miss, there's nothing goin' on there. The inspector has asked me to be his sergeant on the case. It's a real honour it is.' He suddenly grinned, reminding her of the schoolboy he had once been. 'Anyway, what with detaining that young lady, and now the lord, there's loads to do. I'm runnin' here, there and everywhere. And the lord's got Mr Maurice Medley advising him. He's a top-notch lawyer, and tough with it. Friends they are, they went to school together. Drivin' the inspector mad, he is, sayin' we've got no right to hold his lordship on account of us not havin' any evidence. And the inspector's saying he needs time to *find* the evidence, only Mr Medley's sayin' as how he's had *plenty* of time, and if there was anything incriminating, then anyone with a brain would've found it by now. And it all got a bit heated, and… Oh, I probably shouldn't be sayin' this, Miss, should I?' he faltered, his round cheeks flushed.

'Probably not,' Miss Busby agreed with a smile. 'But it's only us, Bobby. And we were hoping to speak to him about Theodore as a matter of some urgency.'

Bobby looked nervously at the door behind him. 'I don't think you'd be able to, Miss, he'll be a couple of hours at best. Likely a lot longer,' he added quietly. 'I reckon the inspector wants to keep the lord in overnight to sweat a confession out of him. It's what those London police do. I've read about it.' He shared a conspiratorial look.

'Doesn't he have any other suspects?' Adeline asked.

'Not really, Miss,' Bobby said. 'They all give each other alibis. Driving him mad, it is. He's convinced most of them are lying but there's no provin' it, see. The young lord's the only one without one.'

'Aha!' Adeline exclaimed. 'That's what we've come to discuss. This arrest is unjustified—'

'Oh, he ain't arrested,' Bobby interrupted. 'He's just detained. Same as the lady we had in this morning. Can't arrest no-one without proper evidence, y'know. It's habeas corpus, that is. I had to learn it for my sergeants exam.'

'Not arrested… Oh.' Adeline suddenly deflated.

'Thank you for your help, Bobby,' Miss Busby said swiftly. 'We'll leave things for today. I wonder if you might ask the inspector to telephone me at his earliest convenience tomorrow?'

'Yes, Miss, I will. Thank you, Miss!' Bobby nodded.

They exited back out into the sunshine.

'Oh, Isabelle.' Adeline turned to her. 'We've told Kaleb that Theo has been arrested, and it's not true.'

'So I realise.' Miss Busby went to unhook Barnaby's lead. 'But we were merely repeating what Sykes told Chadwick. Perhaps he thought it was the case.'

'Or he said it on purpose to upset everyone. What a nasty piece of work.'

'Yes, but—'

'We should go back in,' she declared. 'Tell McKay, or that lawyer fellow, that Theodore has an alibi, and then they'll have to release him. We could drive the young man home. Once he knows we've met Kaleb, I'm sure he'll talk to us.'

'Who do we say has provided this alibi?' Miss Busby asked.

'A…a woodsman,' Adeline blustered. 'We wouldn't be lying, there is a tree growing through Kaleb's cottage, after all!'

'Yes,' Miss Busby continued patiently, 'and the inspector would go straight there to ask Kaleb to verify the alibi. Kaleb would be completely unprepared. And don't forget about the family resemblance. No, Adeline, this isn't the time. If the inspector is occupied and in a bad mood, he's not going to speak to us. You know how he is when he's feeling badgered.'

'But he'll have to, if we—'

'No,' Miss Busby replied firmly. 'Theodore has his lawyer fighting his corner for now, and we can move on tomorrow. I suspect he'll be home by then, and it'll be much simpler for us to talk to him.'

'But he could be home much sooner if—'

'Perhaps, but home is where I'd very much like to go now, Adeline, if you don't mind,' she replied. 'It's been a long day, and I'm suddenly very tired.'

Adeline looked longingly towards the station, before back to Miss Busby with a sigh. 'Oh, very well.'

# CHAPTER 16

Several cars were once again lining the narrow lane leading to Lavender Cottage. Rowena, it seemed, had company once more.

Adeline huffed as she made a great deal of thrusting the car into reverse and muttering about having to park on the green, before Miss Busby suggested, 'Would you mind just dropping me here? I'm feeling rather wrung out.'

Adeline turned to her in surprise; the car lurched forward before she quickly found the brake. 'But we need a plan of action. And Enid and Hattie will want to hear about Kaleb!'

Miss Busby thought for a moment. 'If you feel up to it, why don't you pop over to Spring Meadows to see Enid? They play bridge on Monday evenings. Hattie's rather good at it, and she may well be there. Cook's suppers are always a treat, too.'

Adeline considered. 'Well, yes, but are you sure you're quite well?' she asked, peering at her friend with concern.

'Perhaps that business with the rifle shook you up more than you thought.'

'I'm fine,' Miss Busby assured her. 'The music went on until late last night, and I was up early this morning.'

'That wretched Rowena,' Adeline growled. 'You ought to give her a piece of your mind.'

'It was only one night,' Miss Busby said. 'I'll have an early night tonight and be firing on all cylinders tomorrow.'

'Well, what if she plays music again tonight?' Adeline objected. 'You cannot let these things go, Isabelle. She will take over.'

'It was a housewarming party! She won't be having one every night,' Miss Busby admonished.

Adeline glanced pointedly at the cars.

'I'm sure they're simply friends helping her move the last of her things.' Dismounting, Miss Busby opened the back door for Barnaby, who wrestled his knucklebone out with him.

'Tell him to mind the paintwork!' Adeline shouted, a little too late.

She was about to close the door when she noticed the cricket ball lying on the floor. It must have fallen off the dog's blanket. 'That reminds me,' she said, 'would you ask Enid if Mr Waterhouse's old valet can remember who he played cricket with at Cold Compton? I'll telephone you tomorrow to see how you got on.'

'And the very minute the inspector calls?' Adeline pressed.

Miss Busby nodded, standing back as Adeline executed an eight-point turn and motored off into the distance.

Walking past the cars and up the lane to her cottage, Miss Busby noted that one of them was familiar: Sir Richard Lannister's black Austin Twenty. Her heart gave a leap and she quickened her step, almost tripping over the apples Dennis had left on her doorstep.

'Richard?' she called as she opened the door, but only silence greeted her. Going through the sitting room and into the kitchen, she paused to place the apples on the kitchen counter, then opened the back door for Pud. He flew in and wound himself around her heels until she produced a saucer of salmon. Barnaby trotted out into the garden and set about gnawing the bone as Miss Busby fetched in her sheets.

Voices and laughter drifted over from Rowena's garden, and Miss Busby's ears pricked as she heard a young man's voice she recognised. Barnaby caught it too, and began a circuit of the garden, barking madly.

She put the folded sheets on the stairs to take up later, and had just filled the kettle when a knock sounded at the door and Richard called, 'Isabelle? May I come in?'

'I'd almost forgotten what you looked like,' she said, taking in the sight of him. Smartly dressed in blue trousers, a pale blue shirt, sans tie, but with a linen jacket in deference to the waning day, his handsome face was lined but free of the furrows of pain. With his silver white hair brushed back from his forehead, he looked comfortable and relaxed, his colour better than she'd seen in some time. The silver-topped malacca cane at his side was the only indication of any ailment.

'I did telephone, several times today in fact,' he said. 'Montague mentioned you'd called.'

'Your new valet?'

Richard nodded. 'Decent sort. Needs breaking in a bit. When you didn't answer I thought I'd pop over and wait for you. Anthony drove me. Your new neighbour and her friends spotted him and insisted on dragging us in for drinks.'

'I thought I heard him. She snagged you too.'

'Yes. She's terribly attractive. I'm afraid I was rather easy prey.'

A spark of annoyance flared. 'I'm sure she is.'

'Vacuous, though,' he added, suppressing a smile. 'I made my escape as soon as I heard Barnaby barking. Anthony's still there. She writes gossip columns, would you believe?'

'Does she really? Well, then yes, I would believe it,' Miss Busby said.

'Her friends have just bought her a new Royal typewriter as a housewarming gift. I can't imagine what she'll find to gossip about here, but Anthony's talking to her about the publications she writes for. I fear he's got it into his head we could run a column in the *Oxford News*.'

Miss Busby wasn't at all sure that would suit, but it occurred to her that Richard's dashing son might be a rival to the inspector.

'Come and sit down,' she said, ushering him to the sofa. 'I'm making supper, and I have some fruit cake in the pantry. You look very well,' she continued, nodding at him in approval. 'Are you feeling better?'

'Much!' he replied, the smile escaping. He took her hand and kissed it gallantly. 'I am getting used to the treatment, and the pain isn't as severe now. Lucy has managed to find a specialist in Oxford, so there will be no need to travel to London any longer.'

'Oh, that's wonderful,' Miss Busby said with a sigh. 'It will be lovely to have you home more often.'

'I have missed spending time with you,' he replied, his green eyes dancing. 'What have you been up to?'

'That's a tale perhaps best told over tea and sandwiches. I'll arrange some.'

Miss Busby found herself both calmed and energised by Richard's company. They enjoyed a simple, informal supper by the fire, topped off with some of the fruitcake. Anthony ducked in to see if they needed anything, then rapidly returned to Rowena's cottage on being told politely, 'no thank you'.

'He looks like the cat that got the cream,' Richard remarked.

'Good,' said Miss Busby.

Richard laughed.

The familiar, considerate way he sat and let her explain all that had gone on in Cold Compton, Barton, and Stow helped her put her thoughts in order. It was just like when they'd wrestled their favourite crossword puzzles together: everything seemed simpler, and rather more fun, in his company.

'Shall I fetch your notebook?' he asked, reaching for his cane.

'I'll get it.' Miss Busby rose more easily to her feet.

'Any chance of another piece of that cake while you're up?' he asked with a hopeful smile.

'With a glass of sherry?'

'That sounds just the ticket!'

Supplies refreshed, Miss Busby settled deeper into her favourite armchair and rested the notebook on her lap. 'I should think the inspector has had to let Theodore go by now,' she said, looking at the notes she had already written.

'Yes, I've heard of Maurice Medley. He's known to be rather ferocious. I wonder why the boy didn't unleash him when the beekeeper was taken in.'

'He may well have threatened to do so,' Miss Busby considered. 'Although I expect he has to be careful. They're from rather different worlds, after all.'

'Actually, considering what you just told me…' Richard mused.

Miss Busby blinked, then smiled. 'Yes, I suppose they aren't so very different after all. But appearances still need to be maintained.'

'Any thoughts on how you'll help the lad without revealing his secret?' Richard asked.

'I'm really not at all sure.'

'Why not wait to speak to Theodore first?'

'Assuming he's released then yes,' Miss Busby mused. 'But I still can't help wondering about one or two things that don't seem to make sense. The body, for instance.'

Richard raised a brow. 'What about it?'

'Why it was moved,' Miss Busby said. 'She was shot from the woods, but it was made to look like it was from the house. Moving her meant the killer was trying to implicate someone in the house, and neither Kaleb nor Theo would do that.'

'Would the killer have known where Theo was? He's the most likely suspect, perhaps they thought he was in the house?'

Miss Busby considered that. 'They must have been watching the house, and known where the staff would be when they shot her. They'd have never dared cross the lawn to move the body otherwise.'

'So it's someone who's familiar with the movements of the household,' Richard said. 'Like Jimmy.'

She glanced at him. 'I do hope not.' She made a note of this nevertheless. 'And someone frequently shoots from the woods…' she explained about the old cartridges in the brook.

'How old were they?'

'I'd say very old to possibly more recent,' she replied.

'The sort of spot the young Lord might shoot from?' he mooted.

'Probably,' she admitted. 'I didn't like to ask the staff directly, I thought it might cause them to close ranks.'

'Hum…By moving the body,' Richard spoke slowly

as he thought things through. 'The suspicion would fall less on Theo, and more on the staff.'

'Yes, who all gave each other firm alibis,' she said quietly. 'And they didn't alert the police until quite a long time after they found the body just after three o'clock.'

'So perhaps this was their way of protecting Theo?'

'It could be. I've been wondering if they were all in it together.' She looked at him, weighing the people she'd spoken to, their words, their reactions. A lifetime spent teaching, observing, had given her a deep understanding of human nature. 'But I think they spoke honestly and truthfully.'

'What about the beekeeper and Jimmy's alibis?' He raised a sceptical brow.

She smiled. 'That sounded made up to me, but I really don't think they are murderers.'

'But one of them could have moved the body,' he said.

She nodded, but didn't agree. 'The estate manager, Mr Walton, was very protective of Theo when we met him in the lane.'

'Really? And is he a good chap?' Richard asked.

'Miss Townsend was very proud of him and she described him as being very considerate. I should have asked what time he returned from Stow with the awful Sykes, but we had rather overstayed our welcome as it was.' She smiled then asked, 'When did it last rain?'

'A few days ago, five, I think,' Richard replied. 'Why?'

'I'm not sure…' She shook her head, whatever thought had flickered in her mind had fled just as quickly. 'Theo had had an argument with his mother that morning and he'd left the house at eleven o'clock as a consequence. Then Sykes also argued with her before he and Walton went to Stow. No one said what either argument was about, but Sykes was agitated when we saw him and he accused the staff of talking to the police.'

'He sounds malicious to me,' Richard remarked.

'He is. He was Lady Compton's spy in the village. And an enforcer,' she added, recalling Kaleb's use of the term.

'An enforcer?' Richard laughed. 'How did he enforce anything?'

'Presumably by throwing villagers out of their cottages,' she replied soberly.

'Ah.' His laughter died away. 'Not a popular figure then.'

'No, and he told the butler that there was no one left in charge of the house now that Theo's taken. I fear he's ruling the roost entirely.' She sighed, then applied pen to paper. 'Let's go back through what we do know. Lady Compton argued with Theo before eleven, and then with Sykes in her parlour shortly after noon. Sykes then went to Stow with Walton and the staff worked in the house until their lunch downstairs in the kitchen at one o'clock. Then they remained downstairs until three o'clock, according to Emily's explanation. None of them heard the gunshot, but would have done if they'd been upstairs. So Lady Compton was shot between one and three,' she spoke as she wrote. 'I wonder why she went outside?'

'Someone came to the house and knew their way around well enough to find her?'

'Without ringing the bell, you mean?' She paused. 'Yes...because Chadwick would have gone to answer the door if they had. So it was someone she knew very well, and trusted.'

'Like her son?' he said softly.

'No, no. Surely not,' she replied. 'They wouldn't be so protective of him if they believed him capable of killing her.'

'Then who did it?'

She sighed. 'I truly have no idea.'

'Well, how about the evidence you've found?'

'We haven't found anything, other than the cricket ball Barnaby dug up in the wood... Oh!' she remembered. 'That's why I wondered about the rain. It was rather muddy. But who would bury a cricket ball?'

'I expect it had been there for years.'

'Adeline said it looked quite new. How did it get there? No one would play cricket in the woods.'

'It probably sailed over from the manor lawn. Someone hit a six,' Richard suggested.

Miss Busby thought it unlikely. She doubted Lady Compton would have tolerated games close to the house. And who there had the time for mere games? She wrote *Cricket?* and circled the word.

'Anything else?' Richard said and finished his sherry.

'Yes,' Miss Busby went on. 'I can't help wondering

who would have told the inspector Theo was close to Lara, when nobody seems to have told him about Kaleb.'

'Self-preservation,' Richard replied. 'If the boy isn't legitimate, he won't inherit. And if they all like him as much as they seem to, they'll want him to remain in charge.'

'Adeline and I thought of that, but he won't inherit if he's hanged for murder, and the relationship gives him a clear motive.'

'He has multiple motives,' Richard reminded her. 'But perhaps someone accidentally let his affection for Lara slip out under questioning. Just as Emily did when talking to you. Easily done, I should think. The issue of the boy's parentage seems a much more long-held secret. Harder to drill down to.'

Miss Busby looked at him with a smile. 'Yes, that could be it…and I know I don't need to mention this, but Kaleb and Theo's secret absolutely must not be repeated.'

'I quite understand,' he said, his eyes meeting hers. 'For one thing, it could be construed as withholding evidence from the investigation,' he said and smiled as she raised a hand to her cheek.

'Oh my goodness! Yes, of course. We were so taken up with the story it didn't occur to us.' She looked down at her notebook as though it were somehow incriminating.

'Don't worry,' Richard said. 'Everyone else seems to be keeping secrets too. It's the inspector's job to uncover the facts, not yours.'

'But—'

'No,' he said firmly. 'Neither of us will tell a soul, and neither of us will worry about it,' he lectured, then reached for her hand once more. 'Now, you have had a long day, and I ought to extract Anthony before he gets himself into any trouble with that firecracker two doors down.'

'Yes, speaking of which…' Miss Busby felt she ought to mention it, although wasn't quite sure how best to phrase it. 'Rowena is an old friend of Inspector McKay's and…'

'I know.' Richard grimaced. 'Lucy heard about the party. That's why she sent Anthony to drive me instead of asking Fletcher.'

Miss Busby laughed. 'She sent the poor boy as a diversion?'

'Less of the poor,' Sir Richard said, 'I haven't seen him look so cheerful in years!'

With their goodbyes said, and promises made to see more of each other now Sir Richard's arduous medical trips to London were to be a thing of the past, Miss Busby collected Barnaby from the garden, deposited Pud into it, shut the back door and headed wearily to bed.

## CHAPTER 17

Tuesday morning dawned cool and cloudy. Miss Busby erred on the side of caution and took her tweed jacket from the stand in the hall as she called Barnaby for his morning constitutional.

Despite her worries, she had slept well and after a light breakfast was feeling much more herself. The prospect of more time to be spent with Richard lifted her spirits, and she found herself humming beneath the grey sky as Barnaby trotted around the village green beside her.

The rumble of an approaching engine made them both look up as Dennis' post van trundled along the road towards them.

'Mornin' Miss!' he called cheerfully as he pulled to a halt and jumped out. 'Nothing for you today. Did you get yer apples alright? Miss Rowena liked hers. Said I oughta get her some blackberries too and then she might learn how ter make a pie! She said as far as she can see, that's what folk around here do all day, make cakes an' pies!' He beamed. 'She's lovely, isn't she?'

'Hmm,' said Miss Busby.

He was in such a good mood that he bent to ruffle Barnaby's ears. The little dog growled. He'd never quite warmed to Dennis, or postmen of any stripe.

'I'd best be off, Miss. She's got eight letters today. Eight! She's ever so popular!'

As he turned towards the cottages, Miss Busby suddenly remembered, and called, 'Dennis, do you know a postman by the name of Ernest?'

He turned. 'Old Ernie? From Cold Compton?'

She nodded.

'I know *of* him, Miss. He's too old and ever so grumpy. The postmaster says he oughtn't be doing the job, really, 'cos there's all sorts goes missing out that way.'

'Goes missing? Surely you don't think he's stealing?' Miss Busby asked, surprised.

'*I* don't Miss, no. I've never met him. But some of 'em do. I 'spect he's just old and confused and he probably forgets half of it. That happens when you get old, doesn't it, Miss?'

She narrowed her eyes.

'I mean…because I know you've got friends at Spring Meadows where all the… erm…' He scratched his thick curls, before giving up and saying, 'I'd best be off, then, Miss! Bye.'

'Goodbye, Dennis,' she replied archly, before adding, 'and thank you for the apples,' in a slightly mellower tone.

Having circled the green twice, she and Barnaby were heading home when the much softer purr of an engine in the distance drew nearer. Miss Busby turned, half expecting to see an impatient Adeline approaching. Instead, the bright red Sunbeam belonging to Lucy Lannister came into view.

Calling Barnaby to heel beside her, Miss Busby waved and smiled as Lucy pulled up beside them.

The young woman's dark hair, usually sleek and tied neatly back, was rather hastily pushed behind her ears, and Miss Busby noted that the collar of her blouse was askew beneath her tartan jacket.

'How lovely to see you, Lucy,' she said with a smile. 'No more long treks to London on the cards, I hear.'

'No, thank goodness.' Lucy's answering smile was rather half-hearted. 'Anthony's taking Daddy to the doctor in Oxford later today for his first consultation, so I'm free to pop over to Stow to deal with... something,' she said. 'I wondered if you might like to come along?'

'Stow?' Miss Busby's eyebrows rose. 'Are you going to see Inspector McKay?'

'Yes. Anthony and I were both called into the newspaper office early this morning. He told me you've been investigating the murder of Lady Compton. Do you want to hop in? We can talk on the way.'

Miss Busby felt a shiver of nervous anticipation. *Whatever has happened?* 'Might we wait a moment while I telephone Adeline?' she asked. 'She's expecting my call; she'll worry otherwise.'

Lucy nodded. 'Of course. Why don't you ask her to

meet us in Stow for lunch later? The Royalist serves fabulous food.'

Leaving Barnaby with Lucy, Miss Busby swiftly returned to her cottage to make the call. Adeline was as intrigued as she was, and quickly agreed to join them later.

Taking a moment to fetch her bag, and pop her notebook inside, Miss Busby left the kitchen window open for Pud, and picked up a handful of biscuits for Barnaby before rushing back to the car.

'The news missed the morning paper,' Lucy said, driving them out of the village. 'But there was another murder at Cold Compton last night.'

Miss Busby turned to her in utter astonishment. 'Another murder? Who?'

'Norman Sykes, the chauffeur.'

Miss Busby's jaw was in danger of dropping. 'Sykes? But why?'

'I was rather hoping you may have some idea,' Lucy said. 'Daddy mentioned you were at Cold Compton yesterday.'

'I'm afraid I don't…' Her mind was racing although she still couldn't make any sense of it. 'I thought you didn't deal with crime any more?' she said, remembering Lucy had been promoted to Arts & Culture soon after they first met.

'I don't, but when Anthony told me what had happened, I thought I ought to…step in.'

'In what way?' Miss Busby felt a tiny icicle of dread form in her stomach. 'Lucy, what's happened?'

'Well, there's a young reporter, Daisy Fellows, who wrote the article about the initial murder—'

'Rather well, if I recall,' Miss Busby interjected, remembering the level of detail she'd included.

'Yes, she's very promising,' Lucy said, smoothly steering them through the narrow lanes and up towards the main road. 'She's currently operating as an independent, hoping to find a full-time post. Anthony's impressed and thinking of taking her on the staff. But the copy she offered to us for this morning's edition is…well…it might be easier if you read it yourself.'

Lucy reached back and passed over a typewritten sheet. Miss Busby took it with no small amount of trepidation.

COLD COMPTON KILLER STRIKES AGAIN

*Police are no closer to catching the culprit as plucky local septuagenarian is forced to do their job for them.*

'Oh dear,' Miss Busby muttered.

'It gets worse, I'm afraid. But don't worry,' Lucy added hurriedly. 'We aren't going to release it until we've had a chance to verify the facts and edit it. That's what I need to speak to Alastair about.'

Miss Busby, intrigued despite herself, read on:

*Following the murder of his employer - the late Lady Sylvia Compton - Mr Norman Sykes, chauffeur to the deceased, was found dead in the brook bordering Cold Compton Manor just before 8pm on Monday evening. Early indications are that he was shot, possibly with the same weapon as her ladyship.*

'Well,' she said, shocked. 'I don't know what to say. Adeline and I were there all day yesterday, we even spoke to Sykes. Although to be more accurate, we were actually shouted at by him,' she added. 'Who found him? And how did Daisy manage to discover all this?'

'I believe it was the butler who found the body and one of the household called the police. And it was probably the telephone operator who informed Daisy,' Lucy admitted. 'It does happen. Journalists give out "rewards" for leads like that.'

'It wasn't our local operator was it?' Miss Busby frowned.

'No, it would have been someone working in Stow.' Lucy revved the car up a steep hill.

'So Daisy went to Cold Compton and interviewed people in the village. It must have been almost dark.'

Lucy glanced over at her. 'Not everyone goes to bed at nightfall,' she said with a disarming smile.

Miss Busby acknowledged that with a nod. 'What else did she discover?'

'No one seemed to actually know very much, or be particularly upset about his death. He was described as an unpleasant sort. Trouble is, no one seemed terribly keen on helping Alastair, either.' She sighed. 'Detaining two of their most loved residents in one day will do that, I suppose. As well as the fact that, three days after the event, he doesn't seem any closer to finding the killer. All of which meant there were plenty of people keen to gripe about him. Daisy went back to the office late last night, and did some digging around in the archives for Alastair's earlier cases and…' Lucy gestured to the paper once more, before checking over her shoulder and making a careful left turn, picking up speed as the road opened before them.

Miss Busby read on:

*The officer in charge of the investigation, Inspector Alastair McKay of Oxford Station, has already detained two innocent suspects for questioning from the village of Cold Compton. Having wasted valuable time in this manner, he is seemingly no closer to identifying the true culprit.*

*Did McKay's incompetence lead to the death of the second victim, Mr Sykes? Further investigation revealed a similar pattern in the inspector's previous murder cases.*

'Well, that's hardly fair,' Miss Busby objected. 'I'd like to see this young Daisy catch a killer. It's far harder than sitting behind a desk writing about it.'

'I know.' Lucy sighed. 'Anthony's had a word with her; imagine if it had gone to print like that. And with your name in the article, too.'

Realising she had worse to come, Miss Busby glanced back down.

*One Cold Compton resident, who didn't wish to be named, spoke of a Cotswolds lady, Miss Isabelle Busby, who has helped the hapless inspector on previous cases. She has been spotted at Cold Compton Manor, near to Grange Farm, and in the village of Cold Compton itself, and is believed to be taking a keen interest in the case.*

Miss Busby set the paper down, feeling she'd seen enough. *Thank goodness no one saw us at Barton*, she thought. 'The inspector will be livid. Couldn't you deal with this without getting him involved?' she asked. 'You could just have the article rewritten.'

'I could, but we need to see if there's anything he can give us for tomorrow's edition, because news of this murder is already spreading.'

Miss Busby thought for a moment. 'Much as I dislike the way this is presented, Daisy doesn't seem to have actually reported anything factually incorrect.'

Lucy looked at her, appearing momentarily hurt. 'Surely you wouldn't want details of where you've been over the last few days landing on people's breakfast tables?'

'No, of course not,' Miss Busby conceded. 'And thank you for stopping the article,' she added. She glanced out of the window as the open fields flew by, her mind troubled. She and the inspector had fostered a friendship of sorts, and respect for each other, over their two previous cases. This could be destroyed in just a few paragraphs, and Lucy had even more to lose from any falling out. And then there was the secret she was harbouring. She was pleased Lucy knew nothing about that or it would put her in an intolerable situation. 'How are you and the inspector getting on?' she asked.

'Oh, we've seen quite a bit of each other over the summer,' Lucy said, a flush warming her cheeks. 'I thought it was going rather well until he slunk off to that party at Holly Cottage.'

'Yes.' Miss Busby tutted her disapproval. 'Adeline gave him quite the piece of her mind.'

Lucy smiled. 'Bless her. I don't mind him going out, of course, and everyone has old friends, but he didn't tell me about it. *That's* what made me cross. I had to hear it from Daisy.'

'The reporter? She was there too?' Miss Busby turned in surprise.

'Yes, she's friends with Rowena.' Lucy slowed the car as they made their way along Stow high street. 'They went on a couple of writing courses together a few years ago and kept in touch afterwards. Daisy says women need to stick together when it comes to finding work. The men tend to dominate everything.'

Miss Busby wondered if this new reporter's friendship with Rowena had anything to do with the venom in her article. If the inspector had rejected Rowena's advances… Or even Daisy's… *Goodness, I'm thinking like Adeline*, she realised, giving her head a little shake. 'Perhaps Daisy might be more suited to the gossip columns, alongside Rowena,' she couldn't refrain from suggesting.

Lucy laughed. 'I wondered the same. Although, as you observed, she *did* stick to the facts.'

Stow was much quieter than it had been the previous afternoon, and there was plenty of room to park outside the police station. Lucy pulled up and turned off the engine.

Miss Busby climbed out and clipped on Barnaby's leash. She looked up at the door to the station, still feeling rather wary. 'He must be terribly busy,' she said, 'if he's dealing with Sykes' murder too. And Bobby said he was in a foul mood yesterday afternoon,' she remembered.

'Yes, but I expect he'll appreciate a friendly face,' Lucy said, smoothing down her black skirt and straightening her blouse. 'And possibly a bit of help, too?' She shot Miss Busby a hopeful smile before reaching into the cavernous bag she'd brought with her and pulling out a package wrapped in greaseproof paper. 'And I brought him his favourite sandwiches for later, in case he can't get out for lunch. It might cheer him up.'

Scooping Barnaby up under her arm as a gentleman walking a German shepherd approached, Miss Busby decided against leaving him outside, and all three of them entered the station. She'd expected to see Bobby Miller, but a smartly uniformed young constable stood attentively behind the counter.

'Good morning,' Lucy said. 'I wonder if you could tell Inspector McKay that Lucy Lannister and Miss Busby are here to see him? It's rather urgent.'

'Won't be a minute, Miss,' the constable said and went through a door behind him.

At the same moment a man emerged from a side door. Miss Busby recognised him. It was Charles Walton, the estate manager.

Barnaby suddenly remembered his dislike of men and lunged at him. He had to quickly side step to avoid the little dog's teeth.

'Oh!' she exclaimed. 'I am sorry.'

'Control that animal, would you, madam?'

She turned aside to keep the dog's teeth at bay. 'He was just taken by surprise.'

Walton frowned, then took a closer look at her. 'We've met, haven't we?'

'We have, it was in Cold Compton.'

'Ah, yes, you were with Lara.' His aquiline features relaxed a little. 'You and your friend are acquaintances of Miss Townsend?'

'We are. I am Miss Busby.'

'Miss Busby…yes…I…' He appeared puzzled, as though not sure what to make of things. 'And you were at the manor yesterday, I believe? Emily, our housekeeper, mentioned it.'

'Yes, we were out rambling and we… erm…lost my dog,' she indicated Barnaby.

Walton was dressed smartly in the same tweed suit and waistcoat, although his sandy hair was slightly dishevelled, as though he'd dashed out in a hurry. 'Rambling… really?' He looked more closely at her. 'Of course… Well, I must be going. Good day.' He gave a polite nod of the head, frowned again at Barnaby, then walked quickly out of the station.

'Who was that?' Lucy asked.

Miss Busby explained briefly. 'I suppose he must have been talking to the inspector.'

'He was.' The door behind the counter opened once more and a familiar, gruff Scottish voice rang out. 'And I assume you are here to do the same.'

# CHAPTER 18

Miss Busby, Barnaby, and Lucy followed the inspector into his bright and airy office. He read the article Lucy passed to him as they sat down, facing him across his polished oak desk.

'Well,' he said, with a rather determined and not quite convincing note of nonchalance, 'perhaps you ought to be sitting on this side of the desk, Miss Busby.' He passed the article back, green eyes narrowed beneath rust-coloured brows.

'You know perfectly well none of that came from me, Inspector,' she chided.

'Oh? Was it your "counterpart" in the village, perhaps?' he asked. 'The retired teacher, Miss Marjorie Townsend?'

Miss Busby thought it more likely to be Lara; Adeline had told the girl they knew the inspector and had cooperated with him before, and the young woman may have seen something of a kindred spirit in Daisy.

'I shouldn't think Miss Townsend would hold much truck with a young reporter,' she objected.

'No, well, I'm sorry to say she doesn't hold much truck with officers of the law, either,' he muttered. 'No one in Cold Compton appears to.'

Miss Busby hid a smile. 'Regardless, I didn't discuss anything of this sort,' she indicated the sheet of paper, 'with anyone there.'

'Well, somebody did,' he complained.

'Look, Alastair, what's done is done,' Lucy said. 'And we've caught it this time. The problem is, someone may do it again if we don't take control of the situation.'

He looked up. 'What do you mean?'

'Daisy's an independent reporter, she's not employed by us,' Lucy explained. 'There's nothing to stop her taking her article elsewhere if she wants to.'

'Elsewhere?' he scoffed. 'I shouldn't imagine any other news outlet is going to be interested in a backwater like Cold Compton.'

Miss Busby blinked in surprise. 'But of course they are. A member of the gentry has been murdered, and now her chauffeur. And an entire village has come together to provide each other with alibis. *Everyone* will be interested, Inspector.'

'But if you could give us something more positive,' Lucy added, before he could react, 'to show that you're on top of things, we can publish that in the *Oxford News* instead. That way,' she said, taking the article and putting it in her bag before pulling out her reporter's notebook and pencil in its place, 'if Daisy does go elsewhere with the article, she'll look a bit silly won't she? Besides,' she added, 'talking it through with us might help.'

The inspector was silent a moment, before rising to his feet and stating, 'I don't need any help, thank you. Now if that's all, I have more statements to verify this morning, as well as people to interview.'

*Men*, Miss Busby thought with a sigh and a slight stirring of anger. 'Lucy has not only stopped the press to spare your blushes, Inspector, but also driven all the way here to see you. So I should think the very least you can do is talk to her,' she chastised. 'And if you'd rather I wasn't present, I am perfectly happy to busy myself elsewhere in the meantime.'

He glanced at her with irritation. 'I think you've been busy enough,' he grumbled, before beginning to pace behind the desk. 'Why didn't you tell me you'd been speaking to people in the village?'

'I haven't!' Miss Busby objected. 'I have only discussed the matter with Marjorie Townsend, and I *did* tell you about that.'

Stopping to take a small notebook from his jacket pocket, he flipped back several pages. 'As well as Jimmy Hooper, Lara Brownlow, Alfred Brownlow, and Emily Shepherd,' he read.

'Well, yes… they all rather followed on. But I only spoke to them to set Nurse Delaney's mind at rest.'

'Ah, yes, Nurse Delaney…' He flicked back another couple of pages. 'The friend who wanted to talk to me regarding Lady Compton and a *delicate implication*. She hasn't been in touch,' he accused. 'Nor I have been able to contact her.'

'No. Well.' Miss Busby shifted in her chair, feeling rather flustered. 'She travels about seeing patients. I haven't seen her to talk to since, either. It's been a very busy few days,' she added sternly.

'As it has been for me,' he retorted. 'I have two murders to solve, if you haven't noticed.'

'Alastair, you're being horribly rude,' Lucy accused. 'Whatever has gotten into you?'

'I suspect Theodore Compton's lawyer may have had something to do with it,' Miss Busby said.

'How on earth–?' he blustered.

'People *talk,* Inspector. And I understand Maurice Medley is rather an aggressive lawyer,' she added, a note of sympathy breaking through her ire.

'Aye, he is,' he conceded, dropping into his chair and running a hand through his red hair.

'Are you still holding Theodore?' Miss Busby asked.

'No,' he admitted. 'We released him at seven o'clock last evening due to lack of evidence. Then as soon as we had a call to tell us Sykes had been shot dead we sought a warrant for his arrest, but discovered he had been with his lawyer all the time.'

'Oh, thank heavens,' Miss Busy said, feeling a huge weight lifting from her shoulders. The secret of Kaleb was now of far less importance…*unless he shot Sykes…* the thought slid into her mind. *No, he couldn't have. He was innocent, she was certain of it.*

'Do you still think Theodore Compton killed his mother?' Lucy asked, darting a worried glance at Miss Busby who had become silent and pensive.

Inspector McKay pinched the bridge of his nose and sighed. 'He has the most to gain and is the only one in the village without an alibi… But no, I'm not convinced he was responsible. I am, however, keeping an open mind.'

'Who *do* you suspect then?' Lucy continued.

The inspector didn't reply.

'Alastair,' Lucy pressed. 'The villagers are all annoyed that you detained the girl and then the young lord. They will be more inclined to cooperate if we can print a positive article about the investigation. '

'And I would like this killer behind bars,' he retorted. 'But they're all lying to me, and covering up for one another. Lara and the lord are obviously in love and may well have been in cahoots. Or her uncle may have been responsible, trying to clear the way for them to wed.'

That caused Miss Busby to sit up. 'Who told you about them being in love?'

'No one told me.' The inspector lifted his chin. 'Two youngsters in a village full of old folk - one pretty, one handsome? And I saw them together when they were here. I'm not as doaty as you may think.'

'It means daft,' Lucy explained, seeing Miss Busby's confusion. 'I'm learning all sorts of Scottish words.'

He looked at her with something like longing in his eyes, then hardened. 'I brought Lara in to question her, but also to scare Theodore. If he killed his mother to marry the girl she may know something, or he might confess if he thought Lara was in danger of hanging for his deeds.'

'And how did that work out?' Lucy asked wryly.

He looked away.

'And you thought that if it wasn't Theo, or Lara,' Miss Busby continued, 'then it may have been Alfred?'

'Yes. Why else would he have stayed in the village when both he and his niece have trades that would be welcomed anywhere?'

Miss Busby's heart sank to think of it, but she accepted that Alfred was a legitimate suspect. 'Yet you didn't arrest him,' she pointed out.

'No, it requires evidence, or a witness statement to do that,' the inspector said, scratching at his chin. He was dressed in his smart grey suit, but the slight stubble on his face was proof of the long night he had endured. 'It wouldn't have achieved anything. Not as long as they all close up against me. I have to find a way to break through their collusion.'

'Sykes might have done that for you,' Miss Busby said, then regretted it.

'Exactly.' McKay almost smiled. 'But he was conveniently killed last night.'

Lucy turned to Miss Busby. 'Didn't Sykes argue with Lady Compton the day she died?'

Miss Busby said nothing and Lucy turned back to McKay.

'He did,' he confirmed. 'Charles Walton has just made a statement.'

Lucy raised her brows. 'What was the argument about?'

'She wanted Sykes to evict Lara,' he replied. 'Even he could see it would be disastrous and said so in no uncertain terms.'

Miss Busby watched them both and suddenly felt a spark of something igniting deep in the recesses of her mind. 'What time did he and Sykes return from Stow the day Lady Compton was killed?'

'About seven o'clock, not long before Lord Compton called to inform us of his mother's murder. He and Sykes usually go to the pub for a drink after they've concluded their business in town.'

'Charles Walton seemed quite reasonable as we came in,' Lucy mused. 'Even when Barnaby objected to him.'

McKay nodded, indifferent to the minor drama.

'So,' Lucy continued. 'You've cleared Lara and Theodore, now if we can state this in the new article,' she went on, 'it might make you a bit more popular with the locals.'

'Which will make them more inclined to be honest with you,' Miss Busby added, knowing the Scot would object to the notion that he cared what they thought of him.

He drummed his fingers on the desktop. 'An article won't convince them to stop conniving together and it won't persuade them to give up their secrets either.'

Miss Busby thought again of Kaleb and felt her cheeks in danger of reddening. She picked at an imaginary spot of lint on her skirt.

'If the call came in shortly after 8 o'clock.' Lucy opened her notebook, returning to the reporter she was. 'What time was Sykes killed?'

'I'm waiting for the pathologist's report.'

'Roughly, Alastair,' Lucy pressed.

'He was still bleeding when we arrived there fifteen minutes later,' he said, then picked up a typed report from the desktop and read it out. 'Sykes and Walton had been eating in the dining room when the call came that Compton had been released. Walton returned to the dower house shortly afterwards to continue working. Sykes remained in the house for some time, then went to smoke on a bench by the brook. This was a nightly habit when the weather was clement. Lady Compton would not tolerate smoking in the house. The staff eat their supper at seven o'clock downstairs in the kitchen then clean up. They wouldn't usually have heard the shot go off, but around eight the boot boy was sent upstairs to retrieve a glass jug. He alerted the household to the gunshot and they all rushed outside to look. The butler spotted the body and recognised it as the chauffeur, Sykes. He went into the water to try to help him while the housekeeper made the call. The operator said she was barely coherent, and was breathless from running, and probably from shock, too.'

*How different to Lady Compton's death*, Miss Busby thought. The quick reaction, the panic. Was it because they knew Theodore was safe? Or because he would have had no motive to shoot the chauffeur? It certainly wouldn't have been because Sykes was any more liked than her ladyship. *Perhaps the previous murder has made them more nervous*, she thought, trying not to draw too many conclusions.

'And you think they were both shot with the same gun?' Lucy asked.

McKay nodded. 'Probably. Whoever it was removed the cartridge case.'

'Have you checked everyone's guns?' Lucy continued. 'To see who has what?'

'Of course we have.' The inspector tutted. 'But this is the countryside; they *all* have shotguns.'

'When you say *all*…' Miss Busby said, with a raised brow.

He sighed. 'Lord Theodore, Alfred Brownlow the blacksmith, Charles Walton, and Jimmy Hooper, the ex-gamekeeper. They all have 12-gauge shotguns capable of firing the type of shot used to kill both victims.'

'Not the postman?' Miss Busby asked.

'What would a postman want with a gun?'

'You could ask the same of a blacksmith,' she pointed out.

'Foxes, crows, pigeons, rabbits,' he reeled off. 'There's more than enough reasons.'

'Was Sykes shot from the woods?' Miss Busby asked, pleased to have returned to the meat of the matter.

'No, from the field behind the house. Although it

wasn't far from a spot near the brook where Compton frequently shoots,' he said. 'We'd already found old cartridge cases there last time we searched the area.'

Miss Busby decided against remarking on that. 'Did searching Lady Compton's rooms and effects not offer any clues?' she asked, in a rather poorly disguised attempt to change the subject.

'Nothing of note. The woman didn't seem to possess much in the way of valuables, for all her airs and graces. Certainly nothing worth killing over, aside from the estate itself.'

'No hidden bank accounts, or illicit love letters?' Miss Busby attempted to lighten the tone. The inspector looked tired, and a glance at the clock on the wall above his desk showed they'd taken rather a lot of his time. She felt a flicker of guilt.

'I'm afraid not,' he replied. 'There are monthly receipts from Hadley & Sage, the local solicitors' office. They're holding important estate documents, but they've been obstructive in allowing me access. Chief Inspector Long is driving over this morning for a meeting with them. He has the authority to demand they hand them over.'

'So *that's* what's been slowing you down,' Lucy said, her smile bright and lively now.

'Well, to an extent, but–'

'Wonderful!' Lucy rose to her feet. 'That's what we'll use in the article! It's perfect. And we can add that village attitudes haven't been helpful and have necessitated a robust approach. We'll turn it all around, Alastair.' She leant over the desk and kissed him lightly on the cheek, causing colour to rise in his cheeks. 'I'd best get straight to the office, but, oh - I brought you some sandwiches,' she said, handing them from her bag. She turned to Miss Busby. 'Will you be alright to wait at The Royalist for Adeline?'

'Very much so,' Miss Busby replied, thinking that a cup of coffee and a few moments alone to let her thoughts percolate would be just the thing.

# CHAPTER 19

As she passed by the front desk, she noted that Bobby was back at his post, and stopped to sooth the young sergeant's worried expression with a whispered, 'I think Lucy has cheered him considerably,' and walked out of the station to be greeted by bright sunshine. The grey clouds of earlier had dissipated to reveal a beautiful day, and the honey hues of the handsome Cotswold stone buildings lining the high street shone to their best advantage. Miss Busby strolled up towards the Royalist Inn, in no hurry, glancing into mullioned-glass shop windows as she passed. The bells of St. Edward's Church struck 11 just as a pretty lilac dress in one window caught her eye. Peering closely to see if she could make out a price tag, sudden reflected movement behind her caused her to turn; she saw the tall figure of Charles Walton exiting the Stow Provident Bank opposite. His head was down as he counted a thick sheaf of banknotes in his hand.

Pulling Barnaby in front of her and out of sight, she turned back to the window and watched as his reflection put the notes carefully into a leather shoulder bag and strode off up the street, whistling.

'How curious. Come along, Barnaby,' she said quietly, 'let's see where he's off to.' Keeping a good distance back, being in no way eager for a repeat encounter, she followed the estate manager. When he turned off onto Digbeth Street, she hung back, bending down and pretending to adjust Barnaby's leash as she peered cautiously around the corner. He disappeared into a gentlemen's outfitters.

That was one place she couldn't go without being noticed! Unsure how long he would be, Miss Busby eyed a little cafe at the far end of the street, and was about to make for it when the bell above the outfitter's door tinkled and Charles emerged with a large package under his arm. With a small gasp of alarm she ducked back around the corner, startling a woman pushing a pram towards the ice-cream cart up ahead. Gurgling happily, the baby pointed at Barnaby and grinned. Making swift apologies, Miss Busby hurried on to the yew hedge bordering the bowling green, ushering Barnaby behind her and using it for cover as she glanced discreetly out to see Walton emerge, walk on ahead, then turn in to the Newsagents. When he came out with his head buried in a copy of the *Oxford News*, she wished she'd thought to buy one; it made for excellent, and far more portable, cover. Turning the pages swiftly, she saw him smile before dropping it, almost pristine, into a nearby bin, then walk off, whistling again.

Miss Busby bent once again, this time under the pretence of tying her shoelace. He remained oblivious and strode to the end of the street, before turning left down Well Lane.

Barnaby, getting the hang of the game now, hurried beside her as they darted along in time to see him go into Chesterton's Estate Agent and Auctioneers.

After he had remained inside for some time, Miss Busby walked back towards the high street and bought herself an ice cream from the cart, thinking it both less suspicious than hiding in any more hedges and a pleasant way to cool down. When he finally resurfaced, he strolled up to the market square, where the green Morris Cowley she'd seen Sykes driving yesterday was parked.

Attempting a nonchalant lean on a convenient tree trunk, she watched the estate manager toss the parcel from the outfitter's into the back, before checking his shoulder bag was secure. He then slid into the driver's seat and motored smartly away.

Miss Busby stared after him for a few moments, deep in thought, and was about to tell Barnaby she was glad they couldn't follow him as her feet were beginning to ache, when a car horn sounded behind her and almost caused her to lose her balance.

'Isabelle! What on earth are you doing?' a loud voice boomed through the open window. Miss Busby realised she'd been so intent on her thoughts she hadn't registered the sound of the Rolls approaching from the opposite direction.

'Good morning, Adeline. I was keeping an eye on a suspect,' she explained. 'A moment sooner and you would have given me away! I wasn't expecting you yet.'

'I found I was rather bored,' she announced. 'And intrigued. Just wait there a minute,' she instructed. She wound the window up, reversed the car into a space, then dismounted. 'Now, what did Lucy want? Have you seen the inspector? And what suspect?' she asked in quick succession, looking around.

Miss Busby decided to attack the latter. 'The suspect is Charles Walton. I've just seen him acting very suspiciously.'

'The estate manager? Suspicious? In what way?'

'He was acting furtively,' she said, then realised he actually wasn't, not really.

'You think Charles Walton is a suspect? But how? He was in Stow when Lady Compton was shot.' Adeline furrowed her brow. 'And he is friends with Marjorie Townsend,' she continued. 'I can't see her being chums with a murderer and she said he was the only one who tried to talk sense into Lady Compton. So he can't be all bad. But why are we *here*, Isabelle?' she asked again.

'Oh! Of course,' Miss Busby remembered, 'you won't have heard! Sykes has been shot dead too!'

Had Adeline been wearing pearls with her bright, swirly-patterned summer dress she would doubtless have clutched them.

'Good Lord! When?'

'Come along, I'll explain while we go,' Miss Busby said.

As they walked along the high street Adeline listened raptly to the tale of the venomous news article and Lucy's heroic attempts to spare not only the inspector's blushes but also Miss Busby's privacy. They moved on to discuss Charles Walton's behaviour and McKay's progress with the investigation so far. Adeline was impressed that the Scot had spotted the young lord's romance. 'But of course, when one is in the throes of love oneself, it becomes rather easier to see in others,' she remarked.

Miss Busby smiled. 'Lucy does dote on him.'

Adeline lifted her chest proudly. 'I'm glad I intervened and made it clear to that young firecracker that he's spoken for.'

'Yes, I'm not sure he'll be *quite* so keen to attend any of Rowena's parties in future,' Miss Busby said, although she had Anthony in mind when she said it.

They stopped as the impressive sight of the Royalist Inn came into view. Large and welcoming, it was the smartest and most well regarded public house in the town. Ivy covered the stone walls of the porch, but had been trimmed neatly, and pruned back from the rest of the building. Wooden tables were set outside, and wooden barrels filled with colourful blooms stood sentry on each side of the heavy wooden door.

'Wonderful idea of Lucy's to come here. She has excellent taste. Just like her father,' Adeline added with a mischievous glance to Miss Busby. 'I'm sorry to have missed her. Let's sit inside,' she went on. 'It'll be cooler.'

Miss Busby glanced down at Barnaby.

'He'll be perfectly fine, he's only small and behaves rather well when he wants to,' Adeline said, dismissing her concern as she opened the door. 'I haven't been here since Jemima's boys played in the school cricket tournament last summer,' she called over her shoulder, looking around and nodding in approval at the decor. Heavy oak beams supported the low ceilings, and thick, darkly patterned wallpaper gave the large dining room a warm, cosy feel. The floorboards were rather worn, but soft, brightly coloured rugs were strewn about, and the leather-upholstered chairs and stools surrounding polished wooden tables spoke of both luxury and comfort. Two deep sofas stood either side of a large fireplace, laid but not lit, and Adeline made straight for the larger of the two.

'We shan't be troubled here,' she said, plumping a maroon velvet cushion with a smile. 'Do you see the witch-marks above the fireplace?' She pointed to strange markings crudely etched into the stone. 'Jemima is quite the history fiend and explained them to me. They are apotropaic!' she said with a hint of pride.

Miss Busby nodded, looking at them curiously. 'From the Greek, meaning to ward off evil.'

'Exactly so. Any sort of draughty location was thought to be fair game for evil spirits,' Adeline went on. 'Windows, doorways, fireplaces and the like. Perhaps it is spirits, and not the chill, that sets my joints aflame in the winter,' she suggested. 'Although spirits in a glass do help to lift them again,' she laughed.

'I'm sure they do.' Miss Busby laughed with her. Sometimes she forgot how much she enjoyed her friend's company.

A young man in a smart white shirt and dark trousers approached them, looking dubiously at the terrier panting at Miss Busby's feet. 'Um, is he–?'

'Should we have a sherry, do you think?' Adeline asked, ignoring him.

'Just a coffee for me, please,' Miss Busby said.

'Two coffees, with cream and sugar,' Adeline ordered. 'And a small sherry,' she added after a moment's pause.

'And may we have the lunch menu?' Miss Busby asked.

'And a bowl of water for the dog, please,' Adeline added.

The waiter frowned at Barnaby, then back to Adeline's determined expression before hurrying off.

'I went to Spring Meadows first, to see if Enid wanted to join us,' Adeline said, settling deeper into the sofa with a contented sigh. 'But Mr Waterhouse is under the weather this morning, and she was reluctant to leave him.'

'I do hope it's nothing serious,' Miss Busby said, knowing Enid was far fonder of the man than she let on.

'Sick to the stomach at losing at bridge yesterday evening, if you ask me,' Adeline said. 'I'm sure he'll recover.'

'Did his old valet know anything of cricket at Cold Compton?'

'He hasn't had a reply to his letter yet.'

'Oh, that's a shame. What did Enid make of Kaleb's tale?' Miss Busby asked, checking around to make sure they were still the only occupants and couldn't be overheard. Fortunately, it was too early for the lunch crowd.

'She was delighted by him. Said it would do me good not to always think the worst of people, if you can believe that.'

Miss Busby could.

'Hattie was there checking Mr Waterhouse over; she was smiling from ear to ear when I told her.'

'Adeline!' Miss Busby objected.

'What? Mr Waterhouse is hardly likely to be wandering around Cold Compton broadcasting to all and sundry. Don't *fuss*, Isabelle. Hattie was delighted that father and son are reunited, and thrilled there may be a happy ending on the horizon.'

'Hm,' said Miss Busby.

Adeline's eyes narrowed. 'What's the matter? I know it won't be easy for the boy, but having lost two parents, he's at least found another. There aren't many so fortunate.'

'It's just… have you considered…' Miss Busby held back, unsure.

'Out with it,' Adeline said, as the young man returned with a tray and placed their drinks on the low table beside the sofa. 'Thank you. We shall order lunch shortly,' she said, nodding at the menu he propped beside the sugar bowl.

'You don't suppose Kaleb could have shot Sykes, do you?'

Adeline blinked in surprise.

'He did seem to think Sykes was the most likely to give Theodore's secret away,' Miss Busby explained. 'If he discovered it.'

'Yes, but how likely is it that Sykes would have discovered it? He was universally loathed from what I can see, no-one would have told him.'

'Yes, I know. It's just the timing of it...'

Adeline took a sip of sherry and shook her head. 'You said Sykes was shot with the same weapon. Kaleb has a rifle, which is an entirely different matter.'

'But Theodore has a shotgun,' Miss Busby pointed out.

'Yes, and you said he was with his lawyer at the time and so hardly in a position to loan it out. Should we have cake, do you think? Or wait until after lunch?' She directed her attention fully to the menu.

'After,' Miss Busby said firmly. 'What if Kaleb shot him precisely *because* Theo had an alibi, to divert suspicion?' she suggested.

'Shot him with *what*?' Adeline arched an impatient brow. 'If Sykes had been killed with, say, a pocket knife, I might share your concern. As it is, I should dismiss it entirely. Also how would Kaleb know Theo had an alibi at the time? He doesn't have a telephone.'

'Well, perhaps he thought him still safely held at the station,' Miss Busby replied. She could have added that it would be easy for Theo to have simply given Kaleb the gun beforehand, but refrained from saying so.

Adeline finished her sherry and sighed. 'I suppose we

could pay Kaleb another visit to ascertain his whereabouts last night, if it will set your mind at ease.'

Miss Busby nodded, sipping her coffee thoughtfully.

'What about the estate manager, did he really seem shifty,' Adeline said, dropping two sugars into her own coffee and stirring vigorously.

'I can't explain it.' She looked at her friend. 'Something triggered my suspicions, but when I think of it, he was acting quite naturally. Except for the money, but there may be a reason for that too.'

'Marjorie Townsend holds him in high esteem,' Adeline mused. 'And we both saw how protective he was of Lord Theo when he stopped us in the car. You said he returned from Stow with Sykes just before Theo called the police. In which case, he could be the person who turned the body to exonerate Theo.'

'Possibly,' Miss Busby agreed, trying to use logic to quash her prickling instincts. 'But he was apparently in the habit of going to the pub with Sykes after their Friday visits to Stow.'

'Was he now,' Adeline sat up at that. 'Well that changes my view of him entirely. How could any decent chap voluntarily spend time with a snake like Sykes?'

'Quite,' Miss Busby's mind was beginning to churn. 'And he can drive. I saw him. He could simply have driven himself back to Cold Compton that afternoon and joined Sykes in the pub later.'

Adeline's eyes suddenly lit up. 'Yes, and now Sykes is dead, no-one can confirm what his movements were.'

'And he knows the workings of the staff very well.'

'What would his motive be, though?' Adeline's brow creased. 'The inspector always insists that's the primary consideration in these situations. Motive, means, and opportunity.'

'Well, he will have a shotgun or access to one, which is means. He lives on the estate, so he has opportunity,' Miss Busby ticked off on her fingers. 'As for motive, it could be anything. Frustration at the woman's refusal to accept his advice on running the place, for instance.' She took a sip of coffee, then placed the cup down suddenly. 'Perhaps we ought to look at Chesterton's! What if he took something valuable to the auctioneers? Something of hers?'

Adeline set her own cup down in surprise. 'Now this is more like it, Isabelle!'

'Yes... I'd assumed he was looking at houses for sale,' she said. 'But now...'

'Why would he be looking at houses for sale?' Adeline looked equally surprised. 'He has a house.'

'The dower house will be part of his job, it won't be his,' Miss Busby reminded her. 'And he'd just taken all that money out of the bank, so—'

'He might want to retire and move away entirely,' Adeline cut in. 'Far from the scene of the crime. I'll bet that was why he was flicking through the paper; no headlines, yet, which means he can still make a clean getaway. And the reason he emptied his bank account!'

'He's hardly of retirement age,' Miss Busby cautioned.

Then something else occurred to her. 'I wonder why *he* stayed in the village. We never thought about that. He's still reasonably young, no older than Alfred, anyway.' The inspector's observations about Theo and Lara echoed in her mind. 'We know Lara stays for love. And so does Alfred, albeit love for his niece. Love seems to be the only factor that overrides the misery of the place, Adeline. And duty, in Theodore's case. But why does Charles Walton stay?'

'Well, of course we didn't think about it, we assumed he was in Stow,' Adeline pointed out. 'But let's think. He has a good job, and a house to live in. And unlike the others, who all seemed to think Lady Compton so unpleasant, he seems to be the only one to have had her ear, even if… Oh! Isabelle! You don't think…'

'What?' Miss Busby asked.

'You don't think he was *in love* with Lady Compton?'

## CHAPTER 20

Adeline patted her stomach in a gesture of part satisfaction, and part regret, as they left the inn. She'd chosen the roast pork, which had been delicious but rather heavy. Combined with the sun, she'd proclaimed herself in grave danger of needing a nap, and had had to forgo cake afterwards in favour of two extra coffees as a precautionary measure.

Miss Busby had made the far more sensible choice of a light chicken salad, but had also forgone cake in a gesture of solidarity.

As the pub had grown busy with the lunchtime crowd, the background noise buzzing around them had given them plenty of cover to discuss Cold Compton, and why the estate manager remained when so many others had left.

'There were an awful lot of banknotes in his hand,' Miss Busby had remarked. 'Much more than you'd expect someone in his position to have access to. Unless, of course, he's been incredibly thrifty for some considerable time.'

'And he wouldn't have been flashing them about if he were used to handling that amount,' Adeline had pointed out. 'It's crass.'

'He was quick to put them away,' Miss Busby had objected. 'I think he'd only been counting them again to make sure.'

'Another sign he's not used to large amounts,' Adeline had insisted. 'The bank is hardly likely to have short changed him.'

'And although we never saw Lady Compton,' Miss Busby continued, 'we know she was older than him. I hardly think love would have come into it.'

'Well,' Adeline had huffed, having been initially rather taken with the idea, 'we oughtn't rule it out. Older ladies can still remain striking, and we know she liked to look after her figure, Emily said she didn't eat lunch. Come along, Isabelle, we may well have answers soon, and *that* will serve the inspector right!'

Caffeine-fuelled and raring to go, Adeline had insisted they head straight for Chesterton's.

'But they're hardly likely to tell us what he was up to,' Miss Busby objected.

'It's all down to how we ask,' Adeline declared. 'We simply just need a decent excuse…'

Miss Busby sighed, thinking about Adeline's recent excuses of 'hiking' and 'lost dogs'. 'What reason could we possibly have to ask about his private business?'

'I'm sure I shall think of something,' Adeline muttered determinedly, striding towards Well Lane.

'Or we could simply pass on what we know to the inspector,' Miss Busby objected, hurrying to catch up.

'There's a fresh murder to deal with. He'll be off detecting,' Adeline threw over her shoulder. 'And we're right here!'

The bell jingled over the smart black and silver door to Chesterton's, and Adeline walked in as if she had every reason to be there. Miss Busby hesitated outside with Barnaby a moment, glancing over the notices listed on the board outside, before Adeline shot her a look through the window. Looping Barnaby's leash around the base of said board, she duly followed her friend inside.

'Good afternoon.' A smartly dressed gentleman emerged from the rear of the shop and bowed obsequiously to the two women. 'May I be of help?'

'Yes,' Adeline said with determination. Then she floundered a moment, before adding, 'We should like to know if any new items have been listed for auction.'

The gentleman looked up with a quizzical brow. 'Several houses, and indeed horses, were listed just last weekend–'

'As in, new today,' Adeline interrupted. 'We are…hot on the heels of…certain items,' she added.

That raised his brow further, but he kept his voice politely neutral. 'Which items are you thinking of, madam?'

'Items relating to Cold Compton Manor,' she ploughed on.

Miss Busby gave an inward sigh. Whilst she couldn't fault her friend's enthusiasm or confidence, there was surely no way—

'Ahh, you mean Mr Walton's horse paintings.'

It was hard to tell who looked the more surprised, Adeline or Miss Busby.

Adeline was quicker to recover.

'Yes. Exactly so. When are they being sold?'

'On Thursday, madam. They have yet to be listed, but my associate will be examining the artwork in Cold Compton later this afternoon in order to estimate a sale price. If you would like to come back tomorrow for details?'

'Yes, I would. I mean, I will.' Adeline nodded. 'Thank you.'

As the gentleman bowed once more, putting what Miss Busby considered to be a very brave, if rather ill-advised hairpiece at considerable risk, the pair left the shop and Adeline assumed an air of triumph.

'You see?' She smiled. 'Seek, and ye shall find; knock, and it shall be opened unto you. I wonder if we ought to have a go at Hadley & Sage next?'

'Whatever for?'

'You said they are holding papers belonging to the Cold Compton estate.' Adeline stopped in her tracks on the pavement.

'Chief Inspector Long from Oxford is coming here for precisely that reason. I think we should steer clear,' Miss Busby said with a wry smile. 'But very well done,' she conceded. 'I wonder why he's selling paintings?'

'Because he is planning his escape,' Adeline decided, and headed for the market square. 'But now we know it won't be before Thursday, as he will want the funds from the auction. I think Theodore must be our next port of call. He may hold the answer to it all!' she exclaimed. An excited Adeline was an even swifter driver than usual, and Miss Busby barely had time to think as they swept around the tight country lanes.

'Should we call in at Midwinter Cottage first?' she suggested, clutching the dash as they squeezed past an omnibus approaching from the opposite direction. 'Marjorie could tell us more about Charles Walton.' She was still worried they were getting rather carried away. Although there was definitely something going on…

'No, we have danced around the matter for too long, Isabelle,' Adeline declared. 'It is time we spoke to his lordship.'

'Emily said he rode the estate in the afternoons,' Miss Busby reminded her.

'I shouldn't think he will today, not after what's happened,' Adeline said.

'What makes you so sure he'll speak to us?' Miss Busby asked.

'One word ought to do it,' Adeline said. 'Or one name, rather.'

'Adeline,' Miss Busby cautioned. 'The poor man put his trust in us, we mustn't use that name where anyone else might hear.'

'I know!' Adeline *tsked*. 'Discretion is my middle name.'

Miss Busby refrained from remarking on that. She

remained lost in thought until they arrived at the manor, the gravel on the driveway kicking up a swirl of dust as the Rolls crunched across it.

'Is Barnaby coming in?' Adeline asked, dismounting and straightening her dress.

'I think he'd better stay here.' Miss Busby peered at his sleeping form on the back seat. 'He had rather a large amount of your pork fat, as well as some of my chicken. We'll leave the windows open for him.'

'I'll turn around so he'll be in the shade,' Adeline said, gamely climbing back into the driver's seat.

Miss Busby couldn't watch. There was a rather ornate stone statue in range. As Adeline shot forward, then crunched the Rolls into reverse, the door opened and the elderly butler peered out.

Spotting the trajectory of the rear of the car, he leapt forward with unexpected sprightliness and flung himself in front of the statue, hands aloft.

'Madam!' he shouted, his rich voice deep and commanding. 'Stop!'

'There is no need to shout!' Adeline shouted back, moving forwards again, correcting her angle, and then reversing at speed. 'You see?' she said, getting out and shutting the door. 'Although your drive really ought to be wider.'

'The drive was designed for carriages,' he replied, then added, 'ma'am.'

'Times have moved on.' Adeline was in a combative mood, the caffeine and excitement fuelling her forwards.

'Good afternoon, Mr Chadwick,' Miss Busby called to him.

'And a good afternoon to you, ma'am, and welcome back.' The butler bowed stiffly.

'We're here to see his lordship,' Adeline declared rather too loudly.

'Ah, *ahem*... Is he expecting you?' Chadwick drew himself up to his full, rather impressive, height.

'Yes,' Adeline said, at the exact same moment Miss Busby said, 'No.'

'But I think he'll want to talk to us,' Miss Busby went on. 'It's rather delicate, we met... a friend of his, yesterday.'

Chadwick looked wary. 'I...I'm not sure I know what you mean...'

'Miss Busby?' Emily appeared in the doorway. 'Is everything alright? You haven't lost your little dog again?'

'He is in the car. We've just come back from Stow,' Miss Busby said, holding the housekeeper's eye. 'And we'd like to talk to his lordship.'

'It's urgent,' Adeline added.

Emily looked at Chadwick, then back at them.

Miss Busby tried to think of a way to convince her without giving too much away. 'Is Jimmy here?' she asked.

'No,' Emily replied. 'He only comes up to drop off...'

'Pigeons,' Adeline tutted.

'I wanted to thank him,' Miss Busby said swiftly. 'He gave us directions to a delightful hamlet yesterday. Barton.'

She watched closely as Emily and Chadwick flushed at the name. *So they both know*, she thought. *But how much?*

Chadwick recovered quickly. 'Jimmy has not worked here for close to a decade, ma'am. You would likely have better luck in the village. If there's nothing else?'

'It's alright, Chadwick,' a male voice, rich with rounded vowels, called through an upstairs window.

All four looked up in surprise.

Miss Busby recognised the young man's features instantly. He was his father's son. Blue-eyed with blond hair swept back from his forehead, the same broad shoulders and handsome profile they'd glimpsed as he'd ridden across the village green.

'Show them into the drawing room, would you? I'll be down in a moment. And could we have some cold drinks, Emily?'

'Certainly m'Lord. I'll make bees knees,' Emily said decisively.

'I beg your pardon?' Adeline asked, looking concerned.

'It's a gin cocktail. A lovely pick-me-up made with honey. You'll see.'

'Oh.' Adeline smiled. 'That sounds rather interesting.'

'I think something without alcohol may be better advised.' Miss Busby glanced at Adeline, who already had plenty of 'pick-me-up' buzzing through her veins.

'Oh tosh, Isabelle,' Adeline said.

'If you'd like to follow me, ladies?' Chadwick turned and led them into the cool interior of the manor house. A large Persian rug covered most of the flagged stone floor of the spacious hall. Furniture was sparse but polished to gleaming, including a grandfather clock and heavy bureau opposite the staircase, which rose sedately to a balustraded upper floor. The butler turned to the left and they followed him into the drawing room.

Dark oak panelling and ranks of bookcases covered the walls, but the bright sunlight falling through the windows, coupled with the colourfully embroidered cushions on sofas and wingback chairs, made for a warm and comfortable contrast. An oak table stood in the far corner of the room, chairs tucked neatly beneath, and a large vase filled with fresh-cut flowers set in the middle. The carved stone fireplace was set but unlit, the mantel arranged with silver framed photos and miniatures.

Miss Busby was pleasantly surprised at how cosy, and homely, it all felt. She glanced at the photographs: several family shots of what was clearly a young Theodore with his 'parents'. The late Lord Compton had a pleasant smile and friendly eyes; Lady Compton, although an attractive woman, had a colder, more distant look to her. There was an older photo, clearly taken before Theo's arrival, in which she looked softer, happier, hinting, perhaps, that things had once been different…

'Oh!' She hadn't noticed the young beekeeper standing nervously a little way beyond the door. 'Lara, how lovely to see you again.' Miss Busby smiled warmly at the girl.

'But…I thought you'd be angry with me!' she said, her eyes widening in surprise.

'Why?' Miss Busby asked.

'Because I talked to that reporter, and I think I said too much. I'm truly sorry!' she added quickly. 'She was asking so many questions, and seemed to think the Oxford inspector was awful, and so did I—'

'Shall we sit down?' The young lord strode into the room, dressed in riding gear with a pristine white shirt, suede waistcoat and breeches. He offered a reassuring nod to Lara en route before confidently taking Miss Busby's hand. 'I'm Theodore. I assume you to be Miss Busby?'

'I am,' she said in surprise.

'And you must be Mrs Fanshawe.' He smiled at Adeline, then turned to the butler. 'Thank you, Chadwick.' He dismissed him with a nod, and waited until the door was closed behind him before adding, 'won't you please sit down? My father has told me all about you both.'

## CHAPTER 21

'Kaleb says you have the heart of a lion, Mrs Fanshawe,' Lara said, taking a seat on the sofa beside her.

Adeline flushed, and simpered, and grew rather flustered.

'She was magnificent when we were under attack,' Miss Busby said proudly. She had taken a seat in one of the wingback chairs once she'd recovered from her surprise. Plushly upholstered in Victorian velvet, it was soft and comfortable, and most welcome after their exploits in Stow.

'Kaleb…my father, would never have hurt you,' Theodore said. 'You do understand? He was only trying to protect me. It's been very difficult, knowing and not being able to tell anyone…'

'Apart from Lara?' Miss Busby asked. It was the young beekeeper's turn to flush, but she was spared by a knock on the door and the arrival of the housekeeper with a tray of elegant cocktail glasses clinking with ice.

'Here we are, these will cool you down.' Emily smiled

at each of them as she offered the tray around. 'Is there anything else, your Lordship?' she asked.

'Yes, stay a moment, would you, Emily?' he said. Miss Busby tilted her head quizzically at the familiarity. 'Lara isn't the only one who knows,' he said, looking at Miss Busby. 'Emily's always known about me, not that she ever let on.'

Emily's eyes grew round with alarm.

'It's alright, they've met Father,' he reassured her. 'And they've been discreet and understanding about the situation. I owe them a great debt, and a toast at the very least.' He raised his glass. 'Thank you, ladies.'

They duly smiled and did the same. Adeline took an appreciative drink of hers, Miss Busby took a sip, then put the glass resolutely down.

'Oh, I'd best fetch the jug in case you want any more,' Emily said and hurried from the room.

'Emily was the young maid who brought the nurse to you when you first arrived, wasn't she?' Miss Busby asked.

'And cared for me.' Theodore nodded. 'I thought you'd work it out. Lara said you were clever.'

'Isabelle is the clever one, and I'm the brave one,' Adeline declared, then lifted her glass for a longer drink.

Miss Busby noticed she was already halfway through it.

'Kaleb mentioned your friend, the nurse,' Lara said, tucking one long leg elegantly beneath her as she settled more comfortably. She looked as though a weight had been lifted from her, and every bit as if she belonged there in the manor house. She wore the same white blouse and long red skirt, but her copper coloured hair was loose and falling softly about her pretty face.

'Yes.' Theo seemed equally at ease. 'I wanted to thank you for not saying anything to your policeman friend.'

'He's not our friend,' Adeline objected.

'How do you know we haven't told him?' Miss Busby asked.

'I should think he'd already be here, if you had,' Theo replied lightly. 'With handcuffs and a warrant to arrest me. If not for the actual act, then at least for arranging it.'

She smiled, and nodded respectfully to him, thinking him not only articulate and well-mannered, but also astute.

'Daisy said the Inspector is quite awful,' Lara added.

Miss Busby's ears pricked. 'The young reporter?'

Lara nodded. 'She said her friend is in love with him and he rebuffed her without a thought.'

Adeline shot forward on the sofa. 'Rowena?' she asked.

'I'm not sure of her name. She said she was another journalist who's just moved from Scotland.'

'It is Rowena!' Adeline's tone was heavy with distaste. 'The nerve of the girl.'

'He is already involved with a rather wonderful young lady and has been for some time,' Miss Busby said softly. 'Of course he would rebuff Rowena, he would have been an absolute cad if he'd done otherwise.'

'Oh! But Isabelle, we thought he was encouraging her,' Adeline said.

'We did.' Miss Busby nodded. 'And it seems we were rather off the mark.'

Emily reappeared with the jug and refreshed everyone's glasses, except Miss Busby's, then left quietly.

Theodore thanked her as she went out.

'Do any of the other staff know?' Miss Busby asked.

'That I'm not a true Compton? Apparently Chadwick and his wife have always known, but none other, I think.'

'What about Sykes?' Miss Busby asked. 'Would he have brought you and Lady Compton back from Berkshire that day?'

Theodore shook his head. 'Sykes wasn't in our employ then. Emily told me Mother used one of her father's carriages. She must have thought she was covering her tracks, but really all it did was make things look even more suspicious.'

'Some of the older villagers either know or suspect,' Lara qualified. 'Miss Townsend certainly does, and Jimmy and Alfred.'

And Henry White, Miss Busby thought. And probably others.

Theodore nodded. 'I'm pleased they do, not being a Compton is rather wonderful.' He looked to Lara, who gazed back at him with love in her eyes. 'But the villagers have kept the secret, and they've suffered so much. If I could only give something back to them, it might all feel...' He struggled for a moment. 'Worth it, somehow. It might make up for everything Mother did.'

Miss Busby nodded. Kaleb had suggested as much, and the villagers appeared to feel the same. 'Who would inherit, if you do not?'

'Your mother's family. The Granvilles,' Adeline answered rather loudly.

He shook his head. 'They died years ago leaving nothing but debts. The estate was sold to a property developer. And I expect Cold Compton would go the same way,' he said quietly.

'Do you have any idea who killed Lady Compton?' Miss Busby asked, watching his reaction closely.

He sighed. 'I truly don't, although the inspector doesn't believe me. And I think if he were to find out about my real father...' He shook his head.

'That's what worries us,' Lara added. 'And it feels like it's only a matter of time before someone says something.'

'Unless we find the murderer first,' Adeline declared in a ringing tone.

Miss Busby refrained from rolling her eyes and turned to Theo. 'Do you know where Kaleb was last night?' She tried to keep her tone neutral, but there was really no kind way to disguise the insinuation.

'He told us he was alone in his cottage,' Theodore said.

'But he could easily have come here,' Adeline said.

'And not been seen by anyone?' Theo countered.

Adeline scoffed. 'No one seems to see anything here that doesn't suit them!'

'He would never have shot anyone,' Theodore instantly sprang to his defence.

'He raised a gun to us,' Adeline reminded him quite forcibly, then drained her glass.

'I know.' Theodore nodded. 'But there's a world of difference between raising a gun, and firing one.'

'And he did say it wasn't loaded,' Miss Busby reminded her. 'When did you last talk to him?' she asked the young pair.

'He came by at dawn this morning,' Lara answered. 'He wanted to see if Theo had been released. He was genuinely shocked when we told him about Sykes.'

Theo glanced at her, his refined face showing wavering concern, then turned back to Miss Busby. 'I understand you have doubts, but I'm not sure what else I can tell you other than I have come to know my father well. He wouldn't have shot my mother, or Sykes.'

'But he was concerned Sykes may be the one to spill your secret,' Miss Busby pointed out.

'I'm certain Sykes knew nothing about it, he'd have probably tried blackmail if he had,' Theodore returned.

'Sykes thought there was another spiller of secrets,' Adeline remembered.

'Oh, yes!' Miss Busby couldn't believe she'd forgotten. 'Charles Walton made a statement to the police this morning, it included information about the argument.'

'Charles did?' Theo said in surprise. 'Which argument was he referring to?'

'I think it was the one between Sykes and Lady Compton. Apparently she had decided to evict Lara,' Miss Busby said.

Lara gasped. 'But why?'

No one replied.

'Theo?' She turned to him, her eyes wide with shock.

'I'm sorry Lara, she was being vindictive. She'd said the same thing to me earlier in the day, I argued with her and stormed out. I was sick of the whole situation.'

'Did you ever confront her about your parentage?' Miss Busby asked, her head tilting to one side.

His gaze turned towards the window. 'I'd intended to… She was difficult…remote, not like my father, I mean Lord Compton.' He corrected himself with a sad shake of the head. 'It was just the way she was, I'd long since accustomed to it. When I reached twenty-one I should have taken over the estate, as it was mine by right – or should have been if…well, you understand I knew nothing of my true birth at the time. But she became histrionic when I suggested taking over, saying I had a lot more to learn and she and Charles were used to running it together. In the end, we agreed she could continue until I reached twenty-five.' He shrugged resignedly. 'But things just got worse, the estate was becoming more and more run down, tenants left, or were thrown out…I fought for every one of them, but she reminded me of our agreement, and I acquiesced. I regret it, but I didn't have any legal means of wresting control from her. All the bank accounts were in her name. She had the titles to the land and all the legal documents under lock and key at Hadley & Sage in Stow. It was just a mess.' He sighed. 'And then earlier this year – the year

I turn twenty-five – she started backtracking, saying I should think about a career in the city because there was nothing for me here.' He pushed fingers through his blond hair. 'It was then that I contacted Maurice Medley, he's a chum from boarding school and a lawyer now. I explained the situation, he wanted to help and offered to waive his fee. Taking the decision to fight my mother for control of the estate was very difficult, but I felt I had no choice.'

'And then Kaleb turned up,' Miss Busby said.

His face fell. 'Yes. It caused me to reconsider everything… I've discussed it endlessly with Lara.' He glanced at her and she gave him a tight smile. 'And with Kaleb of course. I still want to stay and turn the estate around, and Lara and Kaleb think that would be the best outcome, but given my true birth, I don't have any legal right to do so.'

Miss Busby's mind had been notching up the gears and suddenly revved on all cylinders. 'And now that Lady Compton is dead?'

'I really don't know what to do, and taken altogether, it looks utterly damning,' he ended on a low note.

'I assume you had told your mother you were going to fight for the estate,' Miss Busby continued.

'Yes, some months ago now,' he replied. 'She'd been nasty about it, but I thought she was finally coming around.'

Miss Busby thought it extraordinary Lady Compton hadn't told him the truth of his birth at that point, but perhaps she was ashamed of what she'd done...or maybe had even loved the boy and was afraid to lose him?

'And did Mr Walton tell the police all this, I wonder?' she mused.

'I don't know. He's always been very loyal, so I doubt it,' he replied.

'He frightens me a little,' Lara admitted.

'Why?' Theo's head swung round as he asked her.

'He's so stern,' she replied. 'Sykes sneaked about spying on people. Lady Compton was just nasty and malicious, but Mr Walton has always been cold and aloof. He didn't really seem to care very much about any of us.'

'Charles is a professional - that's the way he approaches the job, but he truly did try to guide my mother. I think things would have been far worse if it weren't for him, and she never made his life easy either. He was a great friend of Fath... Lord Compton's.' He gave his head a little shake. 'They often went hunting together, to get away from it all...the pressures of running the estate... and away from her, too,' he added.

'We called her the Vixen,' Lara said.

He looked at her and suddenly smiled. 'You never told me that.'

'Well, I thought she was your mother!' she exclaimed, smiling back at him.

'The truth is coming out now,' Adeline said a little fuzzily. Miss Busby resolved not to let her drink any more of the cocktail.

'And I'm glad of it,' Theo admitted. 'My only regret is

the deceit practised on Lord Compton. He was a gentle soul. I really loved him.'

'Everyone felt the same way,' Lara said to him.

'Yes, you couldn't not, really.' His smile softened. 'He was never anything but kind. He used to sit in the schoolroom with me and help with my lessons. That was before I was sent to Marlborough, of course… and he taught me to play cricket. So did Charles when he came to work here, he was on the village team, their star bowler!' His smile broadened at the memories. 'They'd share a whisky in the evenings and let me stay in the room sometimes, long past my bedtime, to listen to them. They said I'd need to know how to run things one day.'

'And how did Lady Compton feel about that?' Adeline asked, eyes bright with curiosity.

'Oh, she didn't like Charles much even then. She always said Lord Compton should manage things on his own, and Charles was an unnecessary expense.'

'Is he terribly expensive?' Miss Busby asked.

'I really wouldn't know, I've never had access to the accounts. He lives in the dower house, it's part of his remuneration…although she was talking of moving into the dower house herself.'

'But the matriarch only moves into the dower house when the heir marries,' Adeline said archly.

'Do you intend to marry?' Miss Busby looked at Theo.

He glanced at Lara, whose cheeks blushed pink.

'It's always a possibility,' he replied.

'And if you wed, and took over the estate, Charles

would be out of a house and probably a job...' Miss Busby mused. 'That could be catastrophic for him.'

Theodore gave an unexpected bark of laughter. 'I shouldn't think so, he's an awfully tough sort.' He suddenly turned serious again. 'Except for Lord Compton's last hunt,' he added thoughtfully.

'Charles Walton was there when the lord sustained his fatal injury?' Adeline asked, leaning forward eagerly. Miss Busby could almost hear the cogs turning.

'Yes, it was just the two of them. Father, I mean Lord Compton, had recently lost sight in his left eye, that's why he'd given up driving. He was moving closer to a hind when a stag charged from the undergrowth and caught him with its antlers. Neither he nor Charles saw it coming. I can still remember Charles bringing him home, my poor father unconscious and covered in blood. Charles had torn his own shirt and wrapped it around the wound. It was the first time I'd ever seen a man cry, he was devastated.' Theodore looked off into the distance. 'The doctor was called, he tried his best, but realised Father was bleeding internally... It was very quick, there was nothing anyone could do.' His voice trailed off in sorrow.

Miss Busby recalled Miss Townsend saying the doctor had missed the internal bleeding, but people's memories can be clouded by their attitudes, as she well knew.

'Does Mr Walton collect artwork?' Miss Busby suddenly asked.

Theodore looked surprised. 'Not as far as I know.'

# CHAPTER 22

'Well, at least Theodore has been brought up a gentleman. And attended Marlborough, no less,' Adeline said, as they collected Barnaby from the Rolls and set out on foot. They walked around the rear garden and found the track leading up the hill to the dower house, hidden away behind another stretch of woodland. Barnaby ran eagerly ahead of them, having slept off his lunch.

'Yes, I think he has the making of an excellent Lord of the Manor,' Miss Busby replied.

Adeline blinked in surprise. 'He cannot keep this charade up, Isabelle, no matter how much potential benefit it might be to the villagers.'

'That isn't our decision to make,' Miss Busby reminded her.

'*Hum*, the truth will out, one way or the other,' Adeline said, 'and I still think you ought to have let him come with us. He should be the one confronting the estate manager!'

'We are not confronting, we are gathering a little more

information before we return to Stow and present our case to the inspector,' Miss Busby reminded her. Theo had been bemused by their decision to go and talk to Walton. He'd offered to accompany them, but she'd said they were simply going to discuss a couple of minor issues and told him quite firmly it wasn't necessary. He'd acquiesced but remained puzzled.

'Yes, yes,' Adeline waved the notion aside, 'but it all comes down to the same thing. Why didn't you tell him Charles Walton is planning to sell these paintings? He would be far better equipped to question the man on the matter. Walton's in his employ, after all.'

'Precisely.'

Adeline turned to her, confused.

'People aren't always honest with their employer, Adeline,' Miss Busby pointed out.

'And you expect he will be with us?'

'We are two harmless old ladies, we'll catch him off guard. It will be far more effective than going in mob-handed and demanding answers,' Miss Busby said, recommencing her steps.

Adeline muttered, 'Less of the old, thank you,' as they continued along a small rise lined with oak trees. After a few moments, she added, 'But he'll recognise us, Isabelle. Won't that make him suspicious?'

'I have a plan,' Miss Busby said, continuing in the direction of the dower house, which could now be seen quite clearly. A rather stark building, of red-brick instead of the traditional Cotswold stone, it looked out of place standing lonely amidst a garden of overgrown roses. The green Morris Cowley was parked in front of it, next to a shiny black Ford.

'What is it?'

'I am thinking to use this morning's encounter to our advantage.' She lengthened her stride with fresh purpose.

'How?' Adeline called, hurrying after her.

'I'm still working out the details,' Miss Busby said.

'Oh! Look, Isabelle!' Adeline exclaimed and stopped in her tracks.

As they watched, the tall figure of the estate manager could be seen in the front doorway with a shorter, stouter man, looking uncomfortably hot in a dark suit. Charles ushered the smaller man inside, leaving the door open.

'Isabelle, do you believe these paintings he's selling could be stolen from the manor?'

'Yes,' she replied without hesitation.

'And he has all that money he took from the bank this morning. What does he need more for?'

'You may well ask,' muttered Miss Busby.

'Come on,' Adeline insisted, 'let's look in the car while they're busy. His leather bag might still be in there.'

'Adeline! You can't—'

But Adeline, it appeared, could, and was striding down towards the house before Miss Busby could object further.

Sighing, she scooped Barnaby up lest he follow.

Adeline ducked as low as she could manage, and using the car to shield her from the house, she peered cautiously through the windows on her side.

'I can't see,' she hissed. 'I'll try...' She slipped the nearest door open. 'I still can't...ah! Wait a minute,' she hissed, and leaned into the vehicle, then emerged triumphantly with an envelope.

'Duck down,' Miss Busby warned her.

'I am,' Adeline hissed then waved a handful of white banknotes. 'Look. There's masses of them!'

'Put them back,' Miss Busby whispered as loud as she dared.

She did, then rushed over to where Miss Busby waited behind a huge rambling rose. 'The bag is filled with such envelopes! If each one contains as many notes, he must be getting away with thousands of pounds! He can't have come by such a sum honestly. We have to stop him!'

'Let me do the talking,' Miss Busby said and walked forward with far more confidence than she felt.

Adeline followed, round-eyed, as she knocked determinedly on the door. A moment later Walton arrived, a frown between his brows.

'Good afternoon, Mr Walton,' she said politely.

'I... What do you want?' He stepped back looking perplexed.

'We have come to enquire about the artwork you're selling. I should like to buy a painting for my nephew.'

Adeline looked almost as surprised as the estate manager.

'What?' He was astounded, and sceptical, but the other man, presumably the valuer from the auctioneer's, arrived behind him, and Walton's attitude underwent an immediate change.

'I'm afraid the paintings are on their way to Chesterton's.' He indicated the short man, who appeared nonplussed.

'As we are quite aware,' Miss Busby declared. 'We too are patrons of Chesterton's, and I had asked them to inform me immediately should any suitable paintings be listed.'

'Yes,' Adeline added, catching on. 'And Miss Busby would prefer not to have to wait for auction day. It is her nephew's birthday tomorrow, as it happens. If you were to sell to us directly, he shall have an enjoyable birthday, and you will save yourself the auctioneers' fees.'

The two men looked at each other.

'I...I don't think this is...' the short man said. 'I mean, this is highly irregular. And the paintings will doubtless fetch a handsome price at auction.'

'We can afford it,' Adeline replied archly. 'I own a Rolls Royce, I'll have you know.'

Miss Busby turned to her with a look of admiration, then said, 'Shall we discuss prices indoors, Mr Walton? It's rather warm out here.' She fanned her face in what she hoped was an endearingly old-lady-like manner.

'Wait here a moment,' he said, before turning to the valuer, whose mouth was even now hanging open.

'I think that worked,' Adeline whispered as the men hustled back along the hallway.

'I'm not so sure,' Miss Busby whispered back, concerned. 'We can only hope...'

Adeline looked chagrined and hissed back, 'But you are convinced of the man's guilt?'

'Yes, I don't think there's any doubt he's been stealing. But I don't know if that is his only crime.'

'You mean…'

The men returned, Walton looking tight-lipped while the valuer tipped his hat.

'Ladies, I wish you good day,' the short man said politely and moved towards his car.

'Wait a moment.' Adeline darted off to follow him. She spoke quietly and animatedly for a minute and then returned, smiling gaily. 'Just a little business. I'm thinking perhaps of a new car in the future, and Chesterton's recently auctioned a rather handsome Bentley.'

Walton frowned and watched as the valuer drove the Ford off at some speed.

'Now then,' he said. 'Shall we go inside and discuss details?' He waved them indoors and entered the dingy hallway with Barnaby beside them, before closing the front door behind them and quietly turning the key. 'This way.' He smiled wolfishly and showed them into an untidy drawing room.

The furnishings were mismatched and uncared for. There were marks on the dusty walls where pictures had clearly hung, and a small bookshelf standing forlorn and empty in the corner. It looked as though he was moving out.

'Barnaby, leave it,' Miss Busby said, as the dog snuffled around a rusted coal scuttle, empty save for a coal shovel and an almost bald brush. The wicker log basket was full of empty whisky bottles, which made the dog's nose twitch. 'Sit,' she told him. He cast her a rueful glance before circling the tatty rug in front of the hearth and lying down.

'Might we have a bowl of water for the dog?' Miss Busby asked, perching on the edge of a hard-backed chair.

'No,' he said, his voice low and dangerous. 'What sort of game are you playing?'

'We might ask the same of you,' Adeline replied forcefully.

He advanced towards her.

Things had spiralled entirely beyond Miss Busby's expectations, but she wasn't going to back down now. She cleared her throat. 'You play cricket, don't you, Mr Walton?'

He swung on his heel. 'What?'

'We found the cricket ball.' She rose to her feet, it was all falling into place in her mind.

He glared at her, fury in his eyes.

'You hit her on the back of the head with the ball in your hand, didn't you,' she accused him to his face. 'Sykes was upstairs pretending to have an argument with her, but you had lured her behind the laurel hedge. You and Sykes were in it together. Why did you kill him? He would have blackmailed you, wouldn't he?'

'You interfering old bat–' He went to grab a large canvas bag on the floor behind the door.

'After you killed her with the ball, you hid her body in the woods and went with Sykes to Stow,' she continued. 'You returned later when you knew the staff would be in the kitchen and carried her to the lawn, then shot her in the back of the head from the woods.'

'Shut up,' he bellowed. He'd been rifling through the bag, stuffed with clothes, and now pulled a shotgun from it.

'Isabelle, look out!' Adeline shouted.

Barnaby started barking. Adeline stooped to pick him up.

'We were going to be kicked out. Both of us. Disposed of, like trash. That's all she thought we were, just lackeys to be thrown out when we were no longer useful.' His face had turned red with rage. 'The bloody little lordling had his fancy lawyer and she said there's nothing she could do about it. All these years I've waited, she said I'd get it one day; her precious boy wouldn't want to stay in a miserable hole like this.' He fumbled to load cartridges into the breach. 'She said he'd be away to the city when he was old enough. Then I could take it over, make it pay, sell off the cottages and farms. We could live here together. I worked for years for nothing, dancing around her, keeping her happy, not that she was ever happy.' He snapped the breach closed.

'You stole from her.' Miss Busby had noticed movement outside, through the windows. She edged towards them.

'I earned that money,' he growled. 'She gave me those paintings to hang in here for her, she was going to move in after I was kicked out.'

'You were her lover,' Adeline accused him.

'Ha.' His lips curled back in contempt.

'You killed the old lord,' Miss Busby said, giving voice to her growing suspicion.

'For her. All for her,' he snarled, cocking the gun and raising it to his shoulder.

'And you killed Sykes,' Miss Busby kept moving backwards.

'And now I'm going to kill you.' His finger gripped the trigger.

'Lord Compton is here,' Miss Busby shouted.

Walton glanced toward the window. Theodore could be seen jumping off his chestnut horse. He'd galloped up, bareback.

Barnaby began to bark more loudly, distressed by the shouting.

'Well, he's too late. I've got nothing left to lose thanks to you.' He levelled the gun at Miss Busby; her face drained white with terror.

Theodore must have tried the door and found it locked. His frantic shouting and hammering thundered through the house, then stopped to give way to the sound of feet racing away, towards the back.

'Stop it,' Adeline commanded. 'Put the gun down.'

'You're next,' Walton bellowed, consumed with rage. 'You damned women are all the same.'

Barnaby's barking rose to a frenzy, he wriggled out from Adeline's arms to jump to the floor. Teeth bared, the little dog ran circles around the man, diving for his ankles. Walton yelled in pain, twisting and turning to get him off.

Adeline took her chance and moved like lightning: she lunged for the coal shovel, and with one hefty backswing, bellowed, 'Take that!' and cracked it against the back of Walton's skull. He instantly crumpled to the floor.

The room fell silent.

'Adeline...' Miss Busby breathed.

Adeline's hands began to tremble, and she dropped the shovel. 'I had to, Isabelle,' she said quietly, her voice shaking. 'I thought he was going to kill you.'

'So did I.' Miss Busby raised her hand to her chest, her heart beating too fast.

A fresh commotion sounded outside the window, and both women looked out to see the startled face of Sergeant Bobby Miller looking in with horror.

'Inspector! They're in there,' he called frantically over his shoulder as the stern figure of the fiery-haired Scot appeared at a run and raced to the front door.

'It's locked,' came the shout, then more running feet.

'Hold on, Miss!' Bobby yelled, before disappearing.

The crash of splintering wood rang out from the back of the house, followed by the thud of a door being thrust aside. Theo ran into the room.

'What happened?' He came to a halt as he saw Walton slumped on the floor, the shotgun still in his hand. He strode to pick it up.

'Adeline...' Miss Busby looked at her, ashen faced and trembling.

'Thank God you are alright,' he said, breaking the gun open. 'I'm sorry I took so long. Chadwick thought Chesterton's man was a reporter and wouldn't let him in. Then he said the lady in the floral frock had sent him and called out for me.'

Miss Busby laughed, nerves, tension, and excitement all getting the better of her. 'I am just so glad you did come. Otherwise I fear Mr Walton may have added two more murders to his list.'

'Isabelle!' Adeline cried. 'Not even in jest.'

Bobby Miller and Inspector McKay ran into the room.

'How did you get here so quickly?' she asked them.

'We'd just arrived at the manor to interview Lord Compton.' McKay went straight to the figure on the ground. 'We received the estate papers from the local solicitor's.'

'What do they say?' Adeline asked.

McKay wasn't listening. 'Who hit this man?'

'I did,' Adeline said.

'She had to.' Miss Busby moved closer. 'He was going to shoot me.'

McKay looked up at that.

'Here.' Theo held the gun out to him. 'It's true, he was about to shoot Miss Busby. I saw him through the window.'

'Miller, handcuff Walton,' McKay ordered as he took the proffered gun from Theo.

'Chesterton's man said it was urgent, so we all came straight here,' Theo explained as they watched Bobby

Miller handcuff the comatose man. 'I can hardly believe Charles raised a gun to you.'

'It's barely been a day since we were threatened in the same manner,' Adeline reminded him.

'Not quite the same,' Miss Busby corrected her.

'Indeed,' Adeline said, with a shudder. 'Whatever were you thinking, Isabelle?' she asked crossly. 'If I hadn't played so much tennis in my youth, I should never have been able to hit the man so hard.'

'The sound, Adeline,' Miss Busby said, her face haunted, before an unexpected giggle escaped her lips. 'It was like someone ringing the dinner gong!'

Adeline looked horrified, before a smile slowly crept across her face in turn. 'It did, rather,' she agreed. 'And thank heavens for Barnaby, snapping at his ankles like that.' She bent to stroke him. He'd sat down, now that the shouting had stopped, and was watching Walton, his ears pricked as though ready to dash back in should the need arise.

McKay had removed the cartridges from the breach and was examining the gun, but paused to frown at Miss Busby. 'You could have been killed.'

'But he confessed to the murders,' she said.

He let out a sigh, then turned to Bobby. 'Miller, go and call the station, tell them to send a secured vehicle, and an ambulance, just in case.'

'Aye sir.' Miller saluted and raced off toward the manor house.

The easing of tension somehow enabled Miss Busby

to gather her thoughts, and she took a breath to explain all Walton had said, or rather bellowed, at them.

They asked any number of questions. McKay took notes with quick short strokes. Theo could hardly believe it and made her repeat what Walton had said about killing the late Lord Compton, and the machinations of Lady Compton.

'He must have used an old antler to stab him with…' Theo was shocked as he realised the full extent of Walton's crimes.

'What put you on to him?' McKay asked when she'd finished.

'Cricket,' Adeline said.

'Ah, yes.' Miss Busby's cheeks turned from pale to pink. 'Perhaps we should have given the ball to you.'

Adeline wasn't so apologetic and proceeded to tell all to the inspector while his fiery brows grew closer and closer together.

'Walton was supposed to put those paintings in here. And I know Lady Compton sometimes gave him things to sell, but God knows what he actually did with them,' Theo said to McKay, trying to divert his wrath once Adeline had finished. 'And I think we need to bring my lawyer in to find out if anything more has been stolen.'

'Aye, I suppose that'll be something useful for your man to do,' McKay said wryly. They began a muted debate about the estate and what Walton had been responsible for.

Miss Busby took Adeline's arm, called Barnaby and led them outside into the sunshine. 'I'm so sorry. I didn't mean to put us in danger like that.'

'Well.' Adeline drew herself upright. 'It was really rather unwise, Isabelle…but so very satisfying!' she said, and although pale and somewhat shaky still, they both began to laugh and found they couldn't stop for some considerable time.

# CHAPTER 23

Miss Busby slept luxuriously late on Wednesday morning. Hattie had popped around to check on both her and Adeline after they returned from giving their statements at Stow station. McKay had insisted — he'd been almost as concerned as he was angry. The nurse had proclaimed them both remarkably well, considering their ordeal, and prescribed rest and a complete avoidance of stressful situations for the next few days.

Having given the animals their breakfast and enjoyed her own cup of tea and slice of toast in the back garden, she was in the kitchen putting the final touches to two apple pies when a knock sounded at the door. Barnaby, who'd been dozing in the garden while recovering from his own heroics, flew through to the front and let forth a volley of excited barking at the window.

'That will do, thank you,' Miss Busby told him, as she opened the door to find Inspector McKay standing on the step. His grey suit was uncommonly rumpled, his tie slightly askew, and his red hair looking in need of a comb.

'How are you feeling?' he asked, fatigue etched in his features.

'Surprisingly well,' she said, suspecting he couldn't quite say the same. 'I thought I might have nightmares, but I slept like a log.' She imagined the comforting presence of the stalwart little terrier beside her on the quilt may have had something to do with it. 'But do come in. Tea?' she asked, ushering him through to the sofa in the sitting room.

'I don't suppose you have any coffee?'

'Of course. Have you eaten?' she pressed, peering at him with concern of her own.

He seemed to have to think about the question. 'No. I was interviewing Walton until late last night, and again first thing this morning. It wasn't easy, he refused to talk for hours, but we finally obtained a full confession.'

'To all three murders?' Miss Busby called over her shoulder in surprise, as she put two slices of bread on the griddle and filled the kettle.

'Two of the three.' A suppressed yawn sounded in his reply. 'We had both your and Mrs Fanshawe's statements regarding Lady Compton and the chauffeur, as well as Theodore Compton having seen him raise his gun to you both, and there was nothing he could say to get round that. With Lord Compton's death having been so long ago, however, I'm afraid it's rather more complicated.'

'Will he hang?' Miss Busby asked. She came back into the sitting room to find Pud perched and purring on the inspector's lap.

'Probably,' he said, a note of resignation in his tone as he scratched behind the ginger tom's ear. 'But he can appeal.'

'On what grounds?' She took a seat in the armchair across from him. Barnaby sat between her feet, keeping an eye on the inspector.

'That he was protecting others from great cruelty and abuse, in both the recent cases. He opened up when he realised there was no escape, but tried to pretend that Lady Compton and Sykes had caused so much misery that he acted out of desperation. I don't imagine it will work. The murders were premeditated, and we now know he had much to gain from them.'

'I can see Lady Compton's was, but Sykes?' Miss Busby mused. 'If he'd planned it, I'd have thought he'd have set the murder up to make it appear as if Theo was the culprit.'

'I think that was his intention when he heard Theo had been released. He wouldn't have realised he'd decided to delay his return to talk to the lawyer. And it seems Walton was a heavy drinker. I should imagine he and Sykes fell out over the finances of their collusion; they both seemed to be greedy individuals, and it doesn't take much imagination to envision Walton reacting violently.'

'Just as he did with us…' she replied with a slight shudder. 'And how was Lady Compton cruel to him? He seemed to fare better than most.'

'Until the end, aye, when she reneged on their agreement - if what he told you is true. In custody, he claimed she cut his salary by three quarters when the old lord died, saying he'd had a good run up until then, and that he could either accept the new terms, or leave.'

'But he was her lover, wasn't he?' Miss Busby's brow creased in confusion. 'He said he worked for nothing. And I'm convinced he killed the old Lord Compton - *for her*, he said.'

'He wouldn't admit to either, and we have no means of proving it now. He was in charge of the accounts, remember, and would have been well able to falsify salary records to his advantage. He purported he was the only one in any sort of position to lessen the effects of the woman's spiteful decisions on the villagers.'

'That sounds uncommonly altruistic for a man capable of multiple murders,' Miss Busby noted.

The inspector nodded. 'Indeed. And this supposedly altruistic man began to steal from the family.'

'What did he say he needed the extra money for?'

'His retirement and to make up for the loss of his earnings.'

'But he claimed he wasn't receiving any earnings!'

The inspector sighed. 'He blames everything on Lady Compton. Part of me wonders if the man has got lost in his own lies over time, so entangled were they with her own for so many years.'

'Imagine being raised by such a woman. Poor Theodore,' Miss Busby sighed in turn. 'And poor Lord Compton. His murder will go unpunished, I take it?'

'I'm afraid so. Walton has denied it, and, again, the

burden of proof in a case of murder is heavy. Speaking of which, I will need that cricket ball.'

'Ah, yes, Adeline has it. I will remind her,' she promised.

He narrowed his eyes. 'And you are aware, I'm quite sure, of the rumours surrounding the boy's parentage.'

Miss Busby cleared her throat. 'Um, yes, we had heard something along those lines.'

'And you didn't think to mention anything to me?'

'Well,' she hedged, 'we weren't sure it was pertinent.'

'Nor the cricket ball.' He gave her a long look, punctuated by a *tut*. She felt herself suitably chastened.

'I'll just bring the coffee,' she declared and scooted into the kitchen to pour coffee and butter the toast. She arranged plate, cup, and napkin onto a tray and brought it to place on the low table in front of him.

He smiled and thanked her. Barnaby swiftly changed allegiance, hopping up onto the sofa beside him and casting hopeful glances with bright eyes. The inspector broke off two small crusts of toast and gave one each to Pud and Barnaby. *He really is mellowing*, Miss Busby thought with a smile. For a second, she imagined him with two young children and felt a rush of warmth.

'We saw Lord Compton's will, along with all the other estate paperwork held at Hadley & Sage in Stow yesterday morning.'

'Really?' Miss Busby sat up.

'The old Lord Compton knew that the boy wasn't his own, and made moral provision accordingly in his will.'

Miss Busby froze in her seat, captivated. 'Good heavens. In what possible manner?' she asked, a tremor of hope in her voice.

'He stated in the document that he had always loved the boy as *if* he were their own, and as such wanted the estate *in its entirety* to pass to him upon his coming of age.'

'Oh!' Miss Busby's heart leapt. 'But that's wonderful!'

He didn't appear to share the sentiment. 'Actually, once we'd read that and realised the import, we raced to Cold Compton intending to arrest Theodore yesterday. He had every possible motive to murder Lady Compton. If you hadn't cornered Walton, it would have gone very hard on him.'

She nodded. 'We were fearful that would be the case. But now the young man will keep his home, and the villagers will have someone managing the estate who cares about their welfare.'

'He won't keep the title,' McKay said.

'No, but I shouldn't think he'll lose a moment's sleep over that,' Miss Busby agreed, thinking how it would free Theodore just as much as the villagers. He could marry Lara. Kaleb could live with them and tend the horses; the possibilities were glorious and endless. 'I wonder if she truly did love him? Walton referred to him as "her precious boy".'

'Perhaps. She certainly went to drastic lengths to obtain him. Or perhaps it was merely a pretence and all she really wanted was to hold on to the estate,' he countered.

'It's possible,' Miss Busby agreed, but thought that even someone as selfish as Lady Compton must have developed some feelings for a child she'd raised from a baby. 'She knew she had to let it go to Theodore on his next birthday, though. He had already spoken to Maurice Medley about taking legal control.'

'Yes, and Medley wrote to Hadley & Sage some time ago. They must have known some of the contents, and that her ladyship had been suppressing the facts since the late lord died.'

She thought about that. If Medley read the will, the truth of Theo's birth would be exposed. She'd fought to hide it all those years, then finally agreed to cede control to him rather than let the secret escape. 'Will they face consequences for doing that?'

'They will,' he said sternly.

'And so they should.' Her face darkened.

'They were charging extortionate fees for "safeguarding her documents".'

'Ah, another financial weight on her shoulders,' she said quietly.

'Yes, although they were also bound by client confidentiality,' he said. 'Walton was at pains to tell us she was about to dismiss him and Sykes. He was incensed about it, but he didn't know the full extent of her deceit.'

'No, if they'd found out about Theo's real parentage he and Sykes would probably have blackmailed her… although I do wonder if she'd picked up some inkling of this?' Miss Busby thought of Jimmy, or even Miss

Townsend, and the rumours flowing about the village. 'All the more reason for her to be rid of them.'

'And the reason why matters had come to a head.' He finished his coffee and set the cup down, resting one hand on the little dog's head, one on the cat's.

'Did Walton move the body?'

'No, I don't know who did that, nor did he. He seemed aggrieved by it.'

Miss Busby thought she could guess. Emily was protective of Theo, Jimmy was protective of Emily. Jimmy was a gamekeeper, he wouldn't be put off by blood and death. Did Emily persuade him to move the body? The household may well have spent that afternoon discussing what best to do. She would not voice such suspicions though.

'A maze of secrets and lies,' the inspector continued, pushing Pud gently off his knee and shifting forward on the sofa.

'Would you like some more coffee?' Miss Busby asked a little too brightly.

'I ought to get back to the station,' he said, somewhat regretfully. 'There's no end of paperwork awaiting me. But thank you.'

She nodded. 'One more question, Inspector, if I may?' she asked.

He smiled. 'I suppose you've earned it, in this instance. Although I don't condone you putting yourself in danger the way that you did.'

She shook her head, chastened. 'Nor do I, I assure

you. But what will happen to the money Charles had in his leather satchel?'

The inspector rose to his feet and brushed ginger fur from his trousers, it being moulting season. 'It's confiscated for now, but Chesterton's will compile a full list of what they sold on Walton's behalf. If the items were from Cold Compton Manor, the money will go to Theodore.' He paused and looked down at her. 'If you hadn't seen him go into Chesterton's, Miss Busby, he might just have gotten away with it. In fact, I'm sure he would have done.'

'Oh,' Miss Busby said, her cheeks colouring. 'But that was also down to Adeline! She was the one who went in and found out what he was selling.'

'Well, you make quite the team,' he conceded gracefully, not being, she knew, Adeline's biggest fan. 'And I am very grateful to both of you. Thank you,' he said sincerely, his green eyes holding her own. 'But please, will you come to me directly next time? If there ever *is* a next time? Don't put yourself, your friend, or this little fellow,' he bent to give Barnaby a goodbye pat on the head, 'in danger like that again.'

She nodded, and smiled, wishing him a good day before closing the door and resting her back against it for a moment, thinking of how very fortunate she'd been.

## CHAPTER 24

Miss Busby took a moment to stand in the kitchen and look out at all of her friends gathered in the garden of Lavender Cottage. The large tray of sandwiches and nibbles she'd spent the afternoon preparing was almost depleted, and there was only the second apple pie left. She was waiting for it to cool by the window before taking it out for them to share.

'Penny for them?' Sir Richard Lannister asked, coming in to stand beside her.

'I was just thinking how lucky I am, to have such wonderful friends,' she said.

He smiled, looking into her eyes and taking both her hands in his. 'I often think the same. You are a marvel, Isabelle. Solving crimes *and* making delicious pies. *Be still my beating heart.*'

She could never help but blush when a handsome man paid her a compliment, and well he knew it. He was dressed extremely nattily that evening in a jacket and tie he'd bought in Oxford the day before, and Anthony had taken him to a new barber. The haircut, combined with the pain relief the Oxford doctor had prescribed, had taken years off him.

'Don't be silly.' She swatted his hands away, but smiled. 'Why don't you make yourself useful and freshen the pot?' she asked, as she fetched bowls from the cupboard.

'Is there custard?' Adeline asked, ducking her head through the window.

'Of course there is!' Miss Busby laughed. 'I'll bring it out in a moment. It's a shame Lucy couldn't be here,' she said, turning back to Richard.

'She's off out somewhere with Alastair,' Richard said, struggling to get the tea-cosy on the pot. 'Spent hours getting ready. Kept asking me what I thought of her hair.'

'Let me.' Miss Busby offered. She knew the rheumatism was a hindrance, and worried about him.

'I can manage,' he said determinedly. 'I have to keep moving, that's what the doctor said. Nothing strenuous, or taxing. I think our gadding about to the opera and so forth might be off the table, but if there ever comes a point when a man can't make a pot of tea, he's truly in trouble.'

'I won't really miss the opera,' Miss Busby told him. 'We can listen to it on the wireless instead. And as long as we can sit in the garden in the summer, or by the fire in the winter, and solve crossword puzzles, I shan't have any complaints.'

'Me neither. There!' He presented the pot.

'Perfect. Let's feed the hordes.'

Sitting around the wooden table under the tree were Nurse Hattie Delaney, Enid Montgomery, Anthony Lannister, Adeline Fanshawe, and the one surprise in the pack, Rowena from two doors down. She was currently engaged in close conversation with Anthony.

'Are you quite sure you ought to encourage him?' Miss Busby whispered to Richard, flicking her eyes towards the latter as they took the two trays outside.

'Best to let him make his own mistakes,' he whispered back. 'Besides, she's not *all* bad.'

Miss Busby, although she had her reservations, had felt far kinder towards the girl after realising the inspector wasn't in love with her, and was in fact dedicated to Lucy. And unlike her reporter friend, Daisy, Rowena didn't seem to hold a grudge over the matter. 'I missed my chance with Alastair,' she'd said when Enid had insisted on inviting her this evening, and immediately asked her about it. 'But there are plenty of other fish in the sea!'

'Here we are,' Miss Busby said, placing the tray on the table and instructing everyone to help themselves to a slice.

She perched on the garden wall with her own bowl, enjoying the sweetness of the apples from her orchard, and feeling an immense sense of relief that the man responsible for two murders, or indeed three, as she believed, was safely behind bars.

'You were awfully brave,' Rowena's voice preceded her. 'Anthony told me all about it.' She perched next to

Miss Busby without asking. 'I could write about you in the *Henley Herald*, if you'd like. Or the *Berkshire Beagle*. Absolutely everyone loves a plucky pensioner!'

'Thank you, but no,' Miss Busby replied tartly.

Rowena laughed. 'Didn't think so, but the offer's there if you change your mind!' She wandered off towards the orchard, Anthony following her like a lost dog.

Miss Busby went to sit at the table now there was room.

'You have done it again, Isabelle,' Enid said. 'And with no help from me this time. I feel rather left out.'

Miss Busby laughed. 'It was you who set the wheels in motion, telling us to go back and talk to Lara. If we hadn't done that, we wouldn't have discovered the half of it.'

'And if Hattie hadn't been called out that day nearly twenty-five years ago…' Enid added.

'Oh, the inspector would have got there eventually,' Miss Busby said. 'He always does.'

Adeline raised a sceptical brow.

'Well, he did rather better this time. He worked out that Theodore was in love with Lara all by himself!'

'She's a lovely girl,' Enid said, pouring tea into cups for each of them. 'She popped into Spring Meadows this afternoon to talk to Matron about the bees.'

'Did Theodore drive her?' Miss Busby asked.

'Yes. He's rather dashing isn't he? I'm afraid all the old ladies descended on him like a pack of wolves!'

Miss Busby laughed, not least at the fact Enid would

never consider herself one of them. *But then, nor would I*, she thought. 'I suppose he'll have a lot of changes to get used to.'

'And all of them good, by the sounds of it. There's far more to being a gentleman than a title, or one's parents, and it seems to me that the young man is the perfect example of a gentleman just the way he is.'

'You ought to ask Lara to make some honey syrup for that cocktail,' Adeline said, rather out of the blue. 'What was it called, Isabelle?'

'The bees knees, I believe.'

'Speaking of which…' Enid looked down at her cup. 'Do we have anything stronger?'

'I'll go,' Adeline offered, rising and heading for the kitchen.

'I've often thought of that little blue-eyed baby over the years,' Hattie said into the contented silence that followed. 'I'm glad he knows the truth at last. I only wish his mother could have survived to see it.'

'It can't be helped, Hattie,' Enid said softly. '*Oh what a tangled web* the gentry *weave, when first* they *practise to deceive.*'

'Not all gentry,' Richard added, a little hurt.

'No. Not all gentry.' Miss Busby smiled across at him, before something over his shoulder distracted her.

'Oh, wonderful. Adeline has found the sherry.'

# EPILOGUE

*20th September 1923, Cold Compton Manor*

'They make such a lovely couple,' Marjorie Townsend said, watching from beneath what Miss Busby presumed to be her 'occasion' wig. Much less faded than her everyday hairpiece, it was rather more startling and took some getting used to.

Following the older woman's gaze, Miss Busby turned her attention to where the newlyweds, Theodore and Lara Brakspear - the young man having now taken his true father's surname - danced in the drawing room. They looked utterly content, and very much in love. Lara in bridal white with her long copper curls flowing down her back, Theo in a smart tailcoat perfectly fitted across his broad shoulders.

The furniture had been pushed aside to clear a makeshift dance floor, and a gramophone played from a side table in the corner. Jimmy and Emily danced in slow steps and Chadwick moved sedately to the music with Cook, his very plump wife. The whole house was filled with well-wishers from the village who'd followed the happy couple back from the church. The sound of laughter and happy chatter filled the rooms.

'It was a beautiful service,' Miss Busby said. She was seated on the cushioned bench under the window beside Marjorie. 'Didn't Alfred look handsome in his suit, giving her away?'

'Alfred?' Marjorie turned to her. 'Now, I thought you were spoken for…' she teased with a mischievous smile.

'What's this?' Sir Richard Lannister appeared as if summoned, and both ladies looked at one another and laughed. 'Ah, like that, is it?' he said. 'Shall I fetch more drinks?'

'Not for me, thank you,' Miss Busby said.

'I'll have a cider,' Marjorie said.

He gave a stiff bow and went to oblige.

'He does make for a handsome man, too,' Marjorie pointed out. 'And a gallant knight of the realm, to boot. Do you never think of snapping him up before someone else does?'

'Oh, we're just friends,' Miss Busby said. 'I'm awfully fond of Richard, but my heart will always belong to Randolf.'

'Hm,' Marjorie said. 'Well, I should never say never, if I were you. I might try and steal him from you myself.' She patted her ringlets.

Miss Busby looked at her in surprise, only to see her chuckling. 'How are you with crossword puzzles?' she asked, narrowing her eyes.

'Awful,' Marjorie confessed. 'I never could get the hang of them. Why?'

Miss Busby smiled. 'No reason,' she replied cryptically.

The scratchy crackle of the record reaching its end filled the room, and a round of applause ensued. Lara came skipping over, her cheeks flushed and her eyes alight with happiness. Her simple white dress suited her to perfection, with small pearl earrings and a classic gold wedding ring adding a hint of sparkle to her natural, unadorned beauty. Her hair was held back from her face with a bright, honey-coloured ribbon, and Theo had matched the colour in his tie and pocket square.

'I'm so glad you could come, Miss Busby,' she said, taking the older woman's hand. 'It means so much to us both.'

'I wouldn't have missed it for the world,' Miss Busby told her earnestly. 'How have the pair of you been managing?'

'It's been quite difficult for Theo,' she said, sitting down beside them and catching her breath. 'There really is no money at all left. Although when he told the staff this, they said it was no matter and they would stay on. It's their home, just as it is ours.'

'What about Jimmy?' Marjorie asked, watching as he spoke quietly to Emily in the corner.

'I think there could be wedding bells there shortly, too. Jimmy has his cottage back and he's been repairing it with Alfred and Kaleb's help. When it's finished, he may very well ask Emily to join him,' she confided, her lovely face almost glowing with happiness. 'The whole village has been busy fixing up their cottages. The money Walton stole was returned to Theo and he's shared it between everyone. He says we've all suffered equally, and must benefit equally. It's been quite marvellous, he had so many plans for the estate. He's even bought a tractor!'

'He's a good man.' Marjorie nodded. 'Head on straight. Practical sort.'

'The sort to *rise to responsibility*,' Miss Busby noted, remembering Marjorie's words when they'd first met. The older woman nodded.

'I'm so lucky,' Lara said, watching him with a loving smile as he talked to an old man in the corner.

'Goodness me, is that…Ernest?' Miss Busby asked, looking closer. 'I hardly recognised him!'

The elderly postman was wearing a suit two sizes too large for him, and had oiled his hair back and put a rather unusual flower in his buttonhole.

'It's the smile,' Marjorie said. 'It's joyous to see him smiling again. Theo has spoken to the postmaster, and Ernest is being retired on a full pension. I think they're both as pleased as one another, as Ernest had a habit of misplacing the mail which must have caused no end of consternation for his superiors. And his buttonhole is willow-herb,' she said, noting the direction of Miss Busby's gaze. 'It's his favourite, no matter how many times you tell him it's a weed.'

'The bees love it,' Lara said, laughing.

'Will you be keeping your hives?' Miss Busby asked.

She nodded. 'I'm able to sell the honey to other villages, now, and shops. Her ladyship never permitted it before. I can help bring more money in,' she added proudly.

'So very modern,' Adeline said, arriving from the hallway. She'd been out in the field with Jemima and the boys, who'd been taking turns riding Theodore's chestnut mare. 'Just like you, Isabelle, when you lost Randolf and had to use your talents to support yourself,' Adeline continued, in an approving tone. Her long gold sequinned dress sparkled, and every eye turned her way as she walked. Miss Busby had initially suggested she might want to wear something simpler, so as not to outdo the bride, but Adeline had a tendency to naturally be the centre of attention whatever she wore. And she would never attend anything as important as a wedding without looking her very best. *Mrs Harrison made this for me specially for the occasion,* she'd objected. *I said it ought to be golden, like honey!* Her heart, as always, was in the right place.

'Mrs F!' Anthony Lannister said, striding through from the sitting room and catching sight of her. 'You look like a bright star fallen from the sky. May I have the pleasure of the next dance?' He looked across to where Rowena, at a nod, changed the record on the gramophone she'd brought along for the occasion, and lowered the needle.

'You may,' Adeline acquiesced with a graceful nod, raising her hand and letting herself be swept away.

'Miss Busby,' Lara said softly, 'would you pop to the library with me? Kaleb wants you to have something.'

Intrigued, but insisting there was nothing at all she needed, Miss Busby rose to follow the girl through. Kaleb was quietly talking to Hattie Delaney.

'Miss Busby,' he said, looking a little shy. 'I have something for you. It isn't much, but I wanted you to know how much I appreciate what you did for my boy and me.'

'Oh, it was nothing,' she said, trying to wave the matter aside.

'It was everything,' he insisted. 'You listened, and you put your trust in me, and that isn't something I'll never forget. And if there's ever anything I can do for you in return, you've only to ask.' So saying, he presented the hand-whittled beehive Miss Busby had first seen, incomplete, on his mantel in the tumbledown cottage in Barton.

She took it with a delighted smile. 'Oh, you finished it! It's beautiful! So clever! Are you quite sure?'

Kaleb nodded, adding, 'Open it.'

A small brass hinge was fitted to the back of the hive and a catch on the front. She opened it to reveal a perfect little brooch in the shape of a bee, delicately fabricated from gold and silver wire. 'Oh,' she gasped in delight.

'I wish it was more,' Kaleb said, 'but–'

'It's absolutely wonderful,' Miss Busby told him and tried to pin it to her dress. Lara moved to help her. 'Thank you so much, Kaleb. I shall treasure it, truly.'

'There you are!' Richard said, popping his head

through the door. 'I thought you might have gone to watch the cricket - there's a game in full swing on the back lawn. Your dog is playing at mid-wicket and causing quite a stir.'

'Oh dear, is he?' Miss Busby's eyebrows rose. 'I'd really rather he didn't lose his teeth on the ball.' She felt a moment's queasiness thinking of their last encounter with a cricket ball, before remembering that the one in question was safely in the possession of the authorities.

'I think the ball's in more peril than the dog,' Richard said. No one can get it away from him when he fields it. Adeline's young grandsons brought it with them, and Chadwick found a bat, and– oh, sorry, am I interrupting?'

'Not at all,' Lara said, looking at Miss Busby and then back to him, eyes shining. 'Have you come to steal our super sleuth for a dance?'

'I thought I'd try, yes! What do you say, Isabelle? Shall we?'

She could hardly resist.

As they made their way back to the drawing room, they saw Lucy and the inspector dancing closely together.

'They seem to be getting on better than ever,' she said to Richard.

'Yes. He's taking her up to Scotland next week. She's being rather coy about it, but I can tell she's thrilled. And as for Anthony, I haven't seen him so happy in years.'

Miss Busby looked over his shoulder to see Anthony laughing with Rowena.

'Hm,' she said, trying to reserve judgement.

'And, I have to say, Isabelle, I'm rather happy too,' he continued.

She looked back at him and smiled. 'Yes, it's been a lovely day.'

'Then let's make the most of it, shall we?'

'I rather think we should,' she laughed as he took her hand and led her onto the dance floor.

I do hope you have enjoyed this book and if you'd like to leave a review, I will be eternally grateful!

Would you like to take a look at the Heathcliff Lennox website? As a member of the Readers Club, you'll receive the FREE audio short story, including the ebook itself, 'Heathcliff Lennox – France 1918' and access to the 'World of Lennox' page, where you can view portraits of Lennox, Swift, Greggs, Foggy, Tubbs, Persi and Tommy Jenkins. There are also 'inspirations' for the books, plus occasional newsletters with updates and free giveaways.

You can find the Heathcliff Lennox Readers Club, and more, at karenmenuhin.com

You can also follow me on Amazon for immediate updates on new releases, plus special deals, sales and free giveaways.

\* \* \*

Here's the full Heathcliff Lennox series list. All the ebooks are on Amazon. Print books can be found on Amazon and online through your favourite book stores.

Book 1: Murder at Melrose Court
Book 2: The Black Cat Murders
Book 3: The Curse of Braeburn Castle
Book 4: Death in Damascus

Book 5: The Monks Hood Murders
Book 6: The Tomb of the Chatelaine
Book 7: The Mystery of Montague Morgan
Book 8: The Birdcage Murders
Book 9: A Wreath of Red Roses
Book 10: Murder at Ashton Steeple
Book 11: The Belvedere Murders
Book 12: The Twelve Saints of Christmas
Book 13: Saint Valentine's Day Murder

There are Audio versions of the Heathcliff Lennox series read by Sam Dewhurst-Phillips, who is superb. He 'acts' all the voices – it's just as if listening to a radio play.

The audio versions of Miss Busby Investigates are narrated by the amazing Corrie James and extremely popular.

These can be found on Amazon, Audible and Apple Books.
Here's the list so far of the Miss Busby series.

Book 1: Murder at Little Minton
Book 2: Death of a Penniless Poet
Book 3: The Lord of Cold Compton
Book 4:  A Very Elegant Murder

## A little about Karen Baugh Menuhin

1920s, Cozy crime, Traditional Detectives, Downton Abbey – I love them! Along with my family, my dog and my cat.

At 60 I decided to write, I don't know why but suddenly the stories came pouring out, along with the characters. Eccentric Uncles, stalwart butlers, idiosyncratic servants, machinating Countesses, and the hapless Major Heathcliff Lennox. A whole world built itself upon the page and I just followed along.

Now, some years later I have reached number 1 in USA and sold over a million books. It's been a huge surprise, and goes to show that it's never too late to try something new.

I grew up in the military, often on RAF bases but preferring to be in the countryside when we could. I adore whodunnits, art and history of any description.

I have two amazing sons – Jonathan and Sam Baugh, and his wife, Wendy, and five grandchildren, Charlie, Joshua, Isabella-Rose, Scarlett and Hugo.

My wonderful husband is Krov Menuhin, a retired film maker, US special forces veteran and eldest son of the violinist, Yehudi Menuhin. We live in the Cotswolds.

For more information you can
contact me via my email address,
karenmenuhinauthor@littledogpublishing.com

Karen Baugh Menuhin is a member of The Crime Writers Association, The Author's Guild, The Alliance of Independent Authors and The Society of Authors.

\* \* \*

## ABOUT CO-AUTHOR ZOE MARKHAM

I'm an ex-teacher living in West Oxfordshire with my teenage son and our Jack Russell terrier. I'm fortunate enough to edit fiction for a living, and have had three Young Adult novels published. Miss Busby is my first foray into both adult fiction and the 1920s!